# BRITTA BOLT

# Deadly Secrets

**MULHOLLAND
BOOKS**

HODDER

First published as *Barmhartig* in the Netherlands in 2016 by De Arbeiderspers

First published in Great Britain in 2016 by Mulholland Books
An imprint of Hodder & Stoughton
An Hachette UK company

1

A CIP catalogue record for this title is available from the British Library

Trade Paperback ISBN 978 1 444 78733 7
eBook ISBN 978 1 444 78734 4

Typeset in Plantin by Hewer Text UK Ltd, Edinburgh
Printed and bound by Clays Ltd, St Ives plc

Hodder & Stoughton policy is to use papers that are
natural, renewable and recyclable products and made from wood grown in
sustainable forests. The logging and manufacturing processes are expected
to conform to the environmental regulations of the country of origin.

Hodder & Stoughton Ltd
Carmelite House
50 Victoria Embankment
London EC4Y 0DZ

www.hodder.co.uk

To the saintly Stroke Unit staff at OLVG Hospital

# AUTHORS' NOTE

The city of Amsterdam really does give 'Lonely Funerals' for anonymous corpses found within the city limits, with music, a poem especially written for the deceased, flowers and coffee. This book, however, is a work of fiction. Our characters bear no relation to the real-life incumbents of similar posts, and our Department of Emergencies and Internment, its structure and ways of working, are entirely fictional. Similarly, although the Hotel Krasnapolsky and the OLVG Hospital both exist, the staff, procedures and practices described in each case in this story are entirely fictional.

# TUESDAY

## 17 April

# I

Ben Olssen checked the wall clocks for a third time. TOKYO, NEW YORK, AMSTERDAM. After eight o'clock on that one. She wasn't coming. He reached for his phone, hesitated. He wouldn't text. Not again. He'd corner her at the conference. Ben put the phone back on the table, and grimaced at the last sip of bitter coffee. The cup rattled as he replaced it on the saucer. His eyes flicked around the room. High ceilings, burnished mahogany, potted palms, dimly lit. More like a movie set than a station café. You half expected an Edwardian touring party to come in through the door; a shiny black locomotive to be steaming alongside the platform, rather than the grimy yellow and blue Dutch Rail train he could see through the window, filling with stragglers from the evening rush hour. He would wait until that pulled out, and then he would leave.

A waiter – black tie, full apron – passed the table. Ben signalled for the bill. He flipped his laptop closed, rested his fingers on the lid for a moment, then re-opened it and shut the computer down completely. It was running slowly again. He didn't like that. Maybe that firm the concierge recommended would be able to find out what was up, better than the Helsinki IT guys could.

The train pulled out. Ben dropped a couple of coins on to the bill in the saucer, and got up to go. As he put on his coat, he caught a man in a grubby grey anorak, two tables away, watching him. But no, that was ridiculous, Ben thought.

Nothing wrong with that. People in cafés always glanced up as you came or went. He was getting paranoid: the feeling somebody had been watching him at the hotel, and now this. All the same . . . he was glad he'd been able to get out to the houseboat that afternoon, even if there hadn't really been time to talk things through.

Ben left the café, taking the escalator that ran down from the platform to the station arcade. At the foot of the escalator he turned right, towards the rear entrance. For a look at the old Shell building across the IJ, he told himself. For old times' sake. He knew, though, that he was waiting for a call or a text, that he might even double back and check out the café again, to see if she was there.

The back of the station was a mess, an obstacle course of holes, hoardings and scaffolding. Pedestrians and bicycles tangled with building works; ferries pushed up against each other at the piers. Across the water, the former Shell HQ thrust up, floodlit, covered in some sort of artsy cladding. It had been the scene of the start of his glittering career. Ben gave a little smile. And of many another conquest. Ben the Bedder, they'd called him. But there were still people who hadn't forgiven him for hopping from an internship at Greenpeace to a job with the enemy, people who didn't buy his 'I'd rather be inside the tent, and fight from behind the lines' argument. If they only knew . . . His phone chirruped an incoming message. He glanced at the screen. At last.

> Sorry sorry sorry. Problem this end.
> Only got away just now. Forgive me?
> Lunch tomorrow maybe?
> xoxo
> PS You still so gorgeous?

Ben replied with a single 'yes', in answer to all three questions, and pushed the vivid image of her that the text had sparked, the smell of her, to the back of his mind. Lunch would work, just. Yes, he could wait that long. He frowned, crossed a bicycle path without looking, nearly colliding with a cyclist, and walked along the waterfront, eyes still down on the pavement. He shrugged off his overcoat. Camelhair. Heavy. Too much with the sweater he was wearing. He hated travelling in shoulder seasons. April was always like this. The weather had been cold, blustery and raining when he set out earlier in the evening, but now the night seemed almost balmy. He felt uncomfortably hot. He decided to go straight back to the hotel, cutting through the subway that ran under the tracks a little further up, rather than doubling back to the station arcade. Ben let out an irritated curse at the 'No Pedestrians. Use Other Side' sign at the entrance to the subway. He was buggered if he was going to cross through the arches then over four lanes of traffic just to have to repeat the performance in reverse at the other end of the tunnel. The walkway here was quite wide enough, the sodium orange light that criss-crossed through the shadows of the arches more than ample. Besides, there was already someone coming towards him from the other end. And someone following him in.

It was only when he was halfway along that Ben began to feel uneasy.

The junkie slipped into an alley off the Warmoesstraat, on the edge of De Wallen. Behind him, the stream of tourists surged, clotted momentarily, flowed again. People out for a festive night in the red-light district. But the alley was quiet: a single, smart restaurant at the far end, the rest back doors and blank walls, leading to a waterfront dead-end. The junkie took a few unsteady steps down the deserted street. Stopped. Listened.

He swayed slightly, as if to music no one else could hear, stared a long while at a cigarette butt lying on the paving stones, moved on. He was wearing a T-shirt and a thin blue jersey, with a rip down one side; a black woollen hat. And a heavy camelhair overcoat. He'd had a stroke of luck earlier. And not only with the coat. There had been a thin leather fold-over with a credit card and some cash buttoned in a small inside pocket. Rich toffs often did that: hid away a little something to be safe. He'd traded the card, and a wad of the cash had gone straight away, too. On more than he'd been able to score in a long time. He'd already spiked. Pure. Like kissing the creator.

The junkie headed to the darkened alcove of a fire exit where he often took shelter, warmed by the kitchen on the other side of the door. He leaned against the doorpost, slid down to the ground, and began to fumble in his backpack for his gear.

The restaurant door opened and momentarily cast a pale, trapezoid shaft of light across the alley as a couple came out: blond, well-dressed, arm-in-arm. They glanced down at the junkie, lying inert in a doorway, then at each other. She arched her eyebrows slightly; he released one of those secret, comforted smiles upright onlookers in De Wallen give as they step by the fallen – in affirmation of their own self-control. The couple continued, joining the flow of the Warmoesstraat, and then turning left into the Nieuwebrugsteeg. They hesitated a little outside a café, looking in at the warm, wood-panelled interior. 'De Dolle Hond,' she read aloud, and cocked her head to the lit window, suggesting a nightcap. He bent towards her, whispered something, and pulled her in closer. She giggled, and they walked on.

At about the time the junkie in the alley around the corner was becoming the next case for the municipal Funeral Team, Pieter Posthumus was comfortably positioned on his customary stool at De Dolle Hond, where the bar met the wall, beneath a collection of old medals and badges. From the other side of the counter, Anna nodded towards his empty glass.

'Better not. School night,' said Posthumus.

'Go on,' said Anna. 'On the house. The place will be dismal if you go, too.'

The last of the regulars had left a few minutes earlier. De Dolle Hond was quiet, even for a Tuesday, with only a handful of other drinkers. A couple, arm-in-arm, paused in the street outside. For a moment it looked as if they were about to come in, but they turned and walked on. Anna dangled a bottle of Posthumus's favourite wine at him.

'All right, but just a drop,' he said, tapping his glass below the halfway mark.

Anna poured him some wine, then moved away to serve a customer at the other end of the bar. Posthumus watched her go. He didn't like that 'dismal'. Since the business with Paul, Anna had put up the barriers. She had made no contact with the man, no longer had musicians in the bar, and never spoke of him. That was her way: total, 100 per cent. After all these years – decades – Posthumus knew that, but he was used to being admitted to her side of the wall. Not this time. That hurt. It made him feel left out, powerless. He'd always been able to help before. He knew not to push it, though. He also knew how to respond to Anna's subtle signals. Like that 'dismal'.

Posthumus got up off his stool, and began to collect glasses around the café. A late night wouldn't hurt, his work for what people had come to call the Lonely Funerals Team – the municipal department that arranged burials for anonymous corpses found within the city limits, or for those who died without friends or family – was quiet at the moment. There had been only one funeral in the past few days: a woman who had died

7

alone, on the sofa, in front of the TV, surrounded by mounds of fag-ends and empty wine bottles. He neatened some scattered beer-mats back into a pile. The only outgoings on her bank statement were payments to the supermarket, tobacconist and off-licence: a sad succession that told a lonely tale. Cornelius, who from time to time now came with him on house-visits, had used that in his poem for the funeral. Posthumus put the empty glasses he had collected on the corner of the bar, and sat down again. The elegy had been one of the poet's best so far. Posthumus had been telling Anna about it.

'Thanks, PP.'

Anna moved the glasses he had gathered to the washing area, and picked up the conversation again.

'So, did anyone come?' she said. 'To her funeral.'

'Two ex-colleagues, from before she retired,' said Posthumus. 'More out of guilt than anything else, I suspect. But she had some beautiful embroidered pashminas in the apartment, and we draped one over the coffin, so there was at least some sort of personal touch.'

'I hope that didn't go up in smoke with the rest of her!' said Anna.

Posthumus smiled. That was more like the Anna he knew.

'And what is this, anyway?' Anna went on. 'A parable? You trying to tell me something? "Reclusive old woman dies alone, and gets eaten by her cats"?'

Posthumus shot her a quick glance to reassure himself she was joking. Perhaps this was the moment to attempt a step behind the wall, to get her to talk a little – but a cascade of laughter came from the small entrance area at the outside door. Anna looked over in immediate recognition.

'Gabi!' she said, even before Cornelius's wife had come through the inner door. 'I'd recognise that laugh anywhere,' she added as Gabi walked up to the bar.

Posthumus smiled and nodded a greeting. Gabrielle was with a sharply dressed woman, tanned, fit-looking, younger than she was.

'And it hasn't changed in *years*,' said the woman. 'Teachers used to say she was doing it on purpose, and threaten dark punishments.'

'I don't know if you've met Christina,' said Gabi. 'Christina Walraven?'

Posthumus shook his head, and Anna murmured something about not quite being able to place her. Gabi did the introductions.

'You were at school together?' said Posthumus to Christina.

'You needn't sound *quite* so disbelieving,' said Gabi, with just a ripple of that cascade again. 'She's not as young as she looks, there're only two years between us. And yes, we were. In London.'

'Daddy was posted to the embassy while Gabi's father was ambassador, and she had instructions to look after the new arrival,' said Christina. 'Slumming it with the daughter of a lowly attaché.'

'Oh, nonsense,' said Gabi, turning to Anna. 'She was always going on like that. Not *true*, don't believe her!'

'Either way, two years was a *big* age gap back then, to a sassy teenager with an innocent of fourteen in tow,' said Christina. 'Good Catholic girl that I was.'

'It wasn't like that for long,' said Gabi, with a grin. 'By the way, has anyone been asking for me, or left anything behind the bar? Tall young guy with glasses.'

'No one's given anything to me,' said Anna. 'You expecting someone?'

'My new assistant. He was supposed to be with us tonight, but the sweet kid's been working late to put together some material I need for tomorrow. Never mind, he'll probably be along in a tick. Meantime, drinks! Piet, come and join us.'

'Is Cornelius coming in?' said Posthumus. He moved over to a table near the fireplace, the one he knew Anna liked friends to sit at because it was within conversation distance of the bar.

'No, he's at home with Lukas,' said Gabi.

Posthumus nodded. Lukas was a serious little lad, and quite responsible, but probably not yet old enough to be left alone in the evening. The others joined him at the table, as Anna went about getting their order.

'Gabi told me about this place,' said Christina, looking around at the heads carved along the top of the wainscot, the old tiles in the fireplace and big Delft vases. 'I didn't know bars like this still existed so near De Wallen. This part of town's so *tacky* usually.'

She took out her phone, clicked a rapid succession of photographs, and dropped it back into her handbag. (A Hester van Eeghen, Posthumus noticed, and not only that but in a colour that proclaimed it didn't have to serve for every day, that there were more designer thoroughbreds awaiting outings in the home stable.)

Christina read his glance. 'Your shirt's not too bad, either,' she said. 'Zegna? It's an unusual shade.'

Posthumus coloured slightly. The shirt had been in a half-price sale but even he had winced as he bought it.

'*Touché*,' he said, and Christina laughed. Posthumus let the moment go, and lighted again on De Dolle Hond.

'The building is 1620s, probably,' he said. 'It's been in Anna's family a hundred years or so, hence all the stuff.' He waved a hand at the constellations of old prints, brasses and Toby jugs that rose above the wainscot.

'Anna's done wonders. You'd hardly know,' said Gabi *sotto voce* to Posthumus, as Anna came over with the drinks.

It was true. The damage caused by the fire a few months earlier had been seamlessly repaired. All that remained was a faint, lingering burned smell. That could stay for a year or so, the cleaners had said. Otherwise De Dolle Hond looked pretty much as it had before. Apart from no longer having a piano.

Anna placed the drinks on the table, and took a seat. 'It's a bit dead tonight, so I can join you for a while,' she said.

She turned to Christina, who had her phone out again, and was skimming through incoming emails. 'You live in Amsterdam?' she asked. 'I know your face, we've met somewhere with Gabrielle before, I think.'

'Greenpeace, maybe? I did a short stint there with Gabi in the nineties. But, no, I live in London. I stayed on for university after Daddy was posted to Brussels, and I've been there ever since,' said Christina. 'It's odd, I guess these days I feel more a Londoner than anything. It's home.'

Posthumus detected a slight creakiness in the way she spoke, an occasional hesitancy or lapse into English that indicated she didn't exercise her mother tongue very much. It was oddly alluring, a bit like a husky voice.

'I'm over for Earth 2050, you know, the big economics conference that starts tomorrow?' said Christina, still multitasking with her telephone.

'Know about it!' said Anna. 'Our finance minister has been trumpeting the "Summit for the Future" and "growth and sustainability" for weeks. Today's early registration, isn't it? The trams are packed already, and you can hardly move in town. Still, I can't complain. I've been taking in a bit of the overflow in the guest-house.'

She nodded back over her shoulder to four men sitting at a table in the corner, Earth 2050 tote bags hanging from chair backs, or propped against the wall beside them.

'I've just hung up my first ever "No Vacancies" sign next door!' she said.

'Cornelius said you'd taken over Marloes's old place,' said Gabi. 'He says you've done it up marvellously.'

'The "marvellously" bit is more PP's doing,' said Anna.

'Just a lick of paint, some new furniture, and a tactful retreat behind the screen of "Dutch minimalism",' said Posthumus.

Christina laughed.

'Haven't you got enough to do as it is, with this place?' said Gabi.

Posthumus shot her a quick glance. Giving Anna a focus, a project, after the whole to-do with Paul was part of the point.

'PP persuaded me to keep on the last of Marloes's found-lings to work as a sort of cleaner-cum-caretaker,' said Anna. 'You've probably seen her. She was around quite a bit during that whole . . . time.' It was just a beat. Within a second, the tough, tousle-haired, can-do Anna was back. 'Little Tina,' she said. 'Just the sort Marloes always took under her wing.'

'That skinny little thing, just out of her teens, who'd been on the game?' said Gabi. 'She looked like she was still a user.'

'Heavens, that's a risk,' said Christina. 'And you're OK with that? She's not turning the place into a drug den or a bordello or anything?'

'Tina is *blossoming*,' said Posthumus. And she was. Timid, damaged Tina seemed inches taller, moved with a new energy, and cared for the place with proprietorial pride.

'Well, we must be doing something right, we're already averaging four stars on TripAdvisor,' said Anna. 'So spread the word if you know anyone coming to town who needs a room for the night.'

As if on cue, three guests from the B&B came in for an after-dinner drink, and Anna got up to serve them.

'So, you're still involved with Greenpeace? Or do you work with Gabrielle in Green Alliance?' said Posthumus to

Christina, claiming a spot of undivided attention before she returned to her phone.

He knew from Cornelius that Gabrielle's organisation was swimming against the tide, but deeply involved in Earth 2050: part of a vociferous environmental lobby determined to make itself heard among the conservative economists and mainstream bigwigs who formed the majority of delegates.

'No, these days I'm tigers,' said Christina.

'Tigers?' Posthumus's brow furrowed. Perhaps it was an acronym. 'Real, live tigers?'

'They're arguably the world's most endangered species, after rhinos,' said Christina, 'so, yes, and the Amur in particular, which you'd probably know as the Siberian tiger.'

She tapped a few times on her phone.

'Here, they're beautiful creatures, have a look. There are probably only about 500 left in the wild, in the far east of Russia, near the Korean and Chinese borders. That's the problem. Medicine and body parts, you know, and the hides of course. At one time they were being poached at the rate of one a day, and the only reason that is dropping is that they're becoming harder to find. Well, not the only reason. We are having some effect, but what with poaching, and logging eating away at their habitat . . .'

'Don't get her started!' said Gabi.

'No, I'm intrigued,' said Posthumus, leaning over for a closer look at the picture on the phone: a female playing with her cubs, a magnificent, glossy animal glowing soft orange against a backdrop of black tree-trunks and snow. 'What a beautiful creature!'

'The world's largest cat,' said Christina. 'In the 1930s there were only forty or so left in the world. That was mainly because of hunting for the skins. Things improved a bit after they were made a protected species, but now there's this other onslaught, as people in China are getting richer and paying over the odds. It's the same with rhino horn.'

'And this is why you're here for the conference?' said Posthumus.

'It might seem peripheral to you, but we need to make our voice heard,' said Christina, with an edge of defensiveness. 'Issues like this shouldn't be allowed to disappear in the general discussion of economics and resources. Our profile has been much higher since we've had Leo onside—'

'DiCaprio,' said Gabi, for Posthumus's benefit.

'And we have other major players and payers, but we still have to work hard to make sure the issue remains part of the powwow. Not just the Amur tiger, but the Asian too, and rhinos and all sorts of other animals that are in danger of being drowned out in the clamour of all the other discussions. But for me, here, now, it's about networking, mainly. I mean *everyone's* here.'

'We've just been to this amazing riverside cocktail party out along the Vecht,' said Gabi. 'Christina's helping me land a celebrity for Green Alliance.'

There was a clatter of bicycle handlebars against the window. A tall young man wearing heavy-rimmed designer glasses came striding into the café, walked straight up to Gabi and handed her a box file.

'Sorry I'm late, it's all there,' he said.

'Niels!' said Gabi. 'That is *so* good of you, staying in late. Thank you! And you've missed an incredible party, too. Come on, sit down, have a drink. Let me introduce you. *Love* the new glasses by the way.'

She moved her chair to one side to make room for him.

'Sorry, guys, I've got to get on,' said Niels. 'And the bike's not locked.' He took a few steps back towards the door. 'But thanks anyway. Cheers, and good luck for tomorrow, Gabrielle,' he said.

He had mounted his bike and was gone before anyone could edge in a syllable about how daring it was to leave it unlocked, even for a few seconds, in this part of Amsterdam.

'Quite a whirlwind!' said Posthumus.

'He's only been with us three months, and already I don't know what I'd do without him,' said Gabi.

'Big day tomorrow?'

'Sort of. I'm on a discussion panel before lunch, and I need to be well briefed.' Gabi tapped the box file. 'I suppose I shouldn't be partying, really, but I've been on such a high all evening,' she said.

'You've landed yourself that celebrity?' asked Posthumus.

Gabi caught Christina's eye and smiled. '*Possibly*. No names for the moment. Let's just say Christina managed to fast-talk us into the VIP enclosure, and that went very well. She's an amazing operator, and she's been a complete star. She even sacrificed a hot date when we ended up staying longer than we thought we would.'

'Well, if it pans out how we're hoping, it will have been worth it,' said Christina. 'Besides, it looks like it's all sorted with Ben. We're having lunch tomorrow instead.'

'Well done you!' said Gabi. 'Glad to hear it!' She turned to give Posthumus a playful glance. 'The tiger lady is having a cougar moment,' she said.

Christina laughed. 'Jealousy! Jealousy!' she said. 'He's not *that* much younger than me.'

'That sounds exciting, who's this?' said Anna, coming back to sit at the table again.

'Did you ever know Ben Olssen?' said Gabi. 'Drop-dead-gorgeous Ben, my intern back when I was at Greenpeace? He and Christina have a bit of history.'

'It was only a little fling!' said Christina, pretending to kick Gabi under the table.

Posthumus ran his fingers back through his hair, over temples beginning to fleck with grey.

Anna shook her head. 'I don't think I remember a Ben,' she said.

'Oh, you'd remember him if you'd met him!' said Gabi. 'He's clever, too. A bright young economist with his head screwed on right. It seems he's over for the conference, and desperate to pick up where he left off.'

'Or so we hope,' said Christina, once again checking her phone. 'Maybe he's gone off the boil, after all. I've been trying all evening to pin him down to time and place for tomorrow, but he hasn't replied.'

Posthumus shifted back slightly in his chair, and suggested another drink. As they were all on wine, he proposed that they get a bottle.

# THURSDAY

## 19 April

# 2

On the first day of Earth 2050, anti-globalisation groups held demonstrations outside the Stock Exchange and on the Dam. There were violent clashes with police, and an Occupy movement camped out in front of the old Beurs. On the second day, Thursday, there was a midday march from the Dam, along the Amstel and on to the Dutch National Bank. Posthumus watched, standing at the office window, as the last wave swept around the tower of the Munt – all that remained of the seventeenth-century City Mint – and on down the Amstel. Their chanting and the crashing of improvised percussion completely engulfed the delicate sound of the tower's carillon as it struck one o'clock. Posthumus narrowed his eyes. Time was when he could have read the banners, even from here across the river. Time was when he would have *been* there, marching and chanting with them.

Posthumus took another mouthful of the leftover salad he'd brought in for lunch. It always tasted better the next day, when the preserved lemon rind had seeped its flavour into the fat little balls of pearl couscous. Twenty-five years ago, his demo days would have been. More, even. That sounded *so* long, certainly way longer than it felt. The big anti-nuclear protest after Chernobyl; the riot that broke out when police tried to evacuate the Spuistraat squat. Posthumus stepped back from the window, and half sat on his desk. It certainly didn't seem a quarter of a century since he was out there on the street, shouting slogans with others from the squat; or here, just around the corner, throwing stones and kicking up such a racket at the opening of the new, scandalously expensive city hall and opera house that the police panicked and ushered the queen in through a side door. Ironic: here he was now, *working* for the city almost next door to the spot from which they'd blasted Beatrix with heavy metal, through the biggest amp and speakers they could find. Whatever had happened to that wild young man?

Posthumus stared out, across the Amstel. Well, Willem, for one. His brother's death had made him jump tracks. And life itself, he guessed, which managed to dilute ideals in a way that you swear in your twenties you'll never let happen to *you*. Not that he'd always been fully committed to whatever it was he'd been shouting about. It just went with the territory: the squat, Amsterdam in the eighties. Posthumus scraped up a final spoonful of salad. Gabi was different. She had stuck at it. Gabi had been quite a firebrand back then. Later, she'd channelled her energies in a more mainstream direction – Greenpeace, and then Green Alliance – but she'd always had a cause, had some direction, and she had stayed with it. Posthumus had lost touch with her over the years, though Anna had kept up contact. It wasn't until Cornelius started writing poems for the Lonely Funerals that Gabi had come back into Posthumus's line of vision. And he could see that she had become one of those people who actually make a difference in the world.

Posthumus took his empty lunch bowl to the kitchenette across the landing to give it a rinse. Downstairs, the outside door banged, and there were voices in the entrance hall. Maya and Sulung were back from their house visit. Late. Posthumus smiled to himself. Not that he could expect an apology from Maya for returning the department car after the appointed time. She came thundering up the stairs, with Sulung tagging along behind her.

'Bloody demonstrators! We were stuck for ages on the Raadhuisstraat,' she said.

Posthumus put his hand out for the keys. When it was the other way round, and he was late, he invariably had to endure a verbal scorching.

'I'm surprised you even tried to come through town, what with all the traffic warnings on the news this morning and last night,' he said to her, with a wink to Sulung as he passed.

Maya stormed into the office without a word. Posthumus pocketed the keys. He hadn't arranged an exact time with the undertakers, simply said that he would drop by in the afternoon. He'd give it another half an hour. By then the bridge would be open again, the traffic would have thinned, and it would be an easy drive.

A few stragglers from the demonstration – who with their dyed Mohicans and slashed clothing could themselves have been beamed in from the eighties – hung about on the corner, as Posthumus crossed the bridge over the Amstel and headed south past the Munt tower. The call had come in from the Salvation Army that morning. An overdose: a regular from their hostel in De Wallen, Frans Kemp, a known user, had been found the night before last in a doorway near the Warmoesstraat – in the little dead-end alley around the corner from De Dolle Hond, it turned out. The caller had sounded kindly, but resigned. The poor chap had nearly OD'd once or twice before, she said. Helpers at the Sally Army had seen it coming, and had done all they could; but sadly, with Frans, it had really just been a matter of time. There hadn't been much paperwork, the body had already been released, and would be taken to the undertakers around noon. They knew of no relatives. Frans had been a loner, and had left nothing at the hostel. Posthumus had decided he might as well see to the case right away. He had little else to do, and whatever the client had on him when he died was probably all there'd be to work with in putting together some sort of commemoration for the funeral.

Posthumus drove out through the solid, respectable southern suburbs. On an overcast day like this, the brown brick apartment blocks looked squat and sombre. Over the old Olympic Stadium, Art Deco floodlights stood steely hard against the grey sky; in the Stadionsgracht, the water seemed to absorb rather than reflect light. Posthumus crossed the canal and turned down towards Olympia Funeral Directors. A small group of mourners stood at the main door, waiting to go in to a chapel of rest. Posthumus went round to the side entrance, greeted a hearse driver who was standing smoking against the wall, and buzzed on the intercom to go inside.

'Pieter Posthumus, municipal Funeral Team, I'm here to pick up Frans Kemp's effects.'

'Pieter, hello, it's Hendrik. I think he's only just arrived.'

'No problem. I can come up and wait.'

'You could bring whatever he had up with you, if you don't mind. That would speed things along.'

'Fine,' said Posthumus.

'Go straight through, I'll let them know you're coming. Then I'll see you upstairs.'

The door clicked open. Posthumus walked through the loading bay, where wreaths and bouquets of flowers lay, carefully labelled, for the afternoon's funerals, then down a bare corridor to the underground mortuary. One of the morticians met him at the door.

'I'm working on Mr Kemp now,' she said, holding up gloved hands. 'Sorry, I'm on my own today. His effects are through here.'

Posthumus followed her through to the icy-cold laying-out room. The lights were hard and bright, and there was a soft hum of machinery. He didn't often come to this part of the building, but each time he did he was struck by the complete absence of any odour – not the sweet, acrid smell of death, no chemicals, nothing. He guessed it was all sucked out by powerful fans.

There were two bodies. A large woman, one of her legs swollen and blue-black, and the client: skeletal, his skin an unreal white, with red and black sores on his arms and across his belly. Posthumus turned away.

'It's all in the corner,' said the mortician. 'The hospital inventory's on top.'

With her chin she indicated two black bin-bags each with a hospital seal, and a clipboard with a sheet of A4 attached.

'It's signed in, but the bags will have to be checked and processed through admin,' she said.

'Of course,' said Posthumus. 'I'm taking them upstairs, I'll give Hendrik a hand.'

There wasn't much. Hendrik Nieuwenhuis gave Posthumus a coffee, and they ran through the inventory together – for form's sake, really, in a case like this.

'Never any harm in keeping the admin all tight and correct,' said Hendrik.

He spoke in a permanent tone of hushed condolence. Posthumus had never known him put a foot out of place: always perfectly groomed, his tie impeccably knotted, his shirt crisp and new-looking. He carried with him the faintest hint of cologne.

'My sentiments exactly,' said Posthumus, as Hendrik slipped on a pair of surgical gloves, and dipped into the first of the bin-bags. Posthumus held the inventory at arm's length to read it. He had to admit the time had come. He really was going to have to get his eyes tested.

'Clothes,' said Hendrik. 'I imagine we can dispose of these.'

He took out each item in turn, holding it up between thumb and forefinger. His movements were precise, defined: like a dancer's.

'Trainers, woollen hat, jeans, black T-shirt, jersey . . . torn,' he said.

Posthumus ticked off each entry on the list, with a 'Check'.

'Good heavens!'

Hendrik was holding up a very smart, full-length camelhair overcoat, which had clearly been lying on the ground, but was otherwise in pristine condition. He checked the inside panel, as Posthumus glanced down at the inventory.

'Armani,' they said, in unison.

Posthumus held Hendrik's gaze for a moment.

'Stolen, probably,' said Hendrik.

Posthumus nodded. Café terraces all over town already had tables out under heaters. Nicking a coat left folded on a chair while someone was distracted was a classic.

'Possibly,' he said, 'though it could be from a clothes bank or something. We should hold on to it, anyway. If nothing transpires, I might be able to sell it. Every little bit helps.'

The department had been feeling the pinch of budget cuts. Recently, the director had been making noises about having to find independent funding for Cornelius's poetry fee.

'Anything in the pockets?' Posthumus asked.

Hendrik felt around and shook his head. He put the coat to one side, and the rest of the clothes back into the bin-bag.

The second bag contained a grimy backpack, with a rolled sleeping bag belted on to it. Posthumus read aloud from the hospital inventory: 'Drug-injecting equipment, a quantity of narcotics and a Nokia mobile phone retained by the police.'

'There's not much else,' said Hendrik. 'Another jersey, a couple of pairs of boxer shorts, a plastic bag with a toothbrush, a few folded bin-bags, glasses . . . one lens missing.'

He unzipped the front pocket of the backpack.

'And a wallet. That's everything,' he said, producing a frayed canvas wallet, with a red cord wrapped a number of times around it.

'It should contain Kemp's ID and €161.35,' said Posthumus, consulting the inventory.

Hendrik unravelled the cord, and dropped it on to the table. The old wallet fell open in his hands, and he began to count the money.

'All correct,' he said. 'Together with the ID. Quite a sum, for . . . a man like Mr Kemp.' He glanced over at Posthumus. 'You'd like to check for yourself?'

Posthumus shook his head, and picked up the red cord, with a slight frown.

'Probably . . . you know,' said Hendrik.

He mimed putting a tourniquet on his upper arm. Distaste flickered very briefly over his face. Posthumus ran the cord through his fingers. It was a loop of strong cotton ribbon, about a centimetre wide: one of those straps that delegates to a conference wear around their necks. At intervals, all the way around it, was printed 'Earth 2050'. The fastener that would have held a name tag had been broken off.

'Not a very warm welcome from Amsterdam to a conference delegate,' said Posthumus, handing the lanyard back to Hendrik. 'This, I imagine, belongs to the man who is now missing that coat. As does most of the money.'

Hendrik examined the strap. 'Do you think we should file a report?' he said, with a flutter of concern in his voice.

Posthumus shrugged. 'To say what? Dead junkie steals coat from unknown conference delegate?' he asked.

He noticed Hendrik suppress a wince at the undignified 'junkie'. It amused Posthumus to give the funeral director's formality a wicked tweak from time to time. But he always relented.

'I'll be ringing the police when I get back, to see when they'll release the phone,' he said, with a smile. 'I'll ask about it. Like as not somebody's reported the theft, but I doubt anything will come of it. They'll have their hands more than full at the moment, with the conference and the demonstrations.'

Hendrik wrapped the lanyard loosely back around the wallet. 'Shall we set a date for Mr Kemp?' he asked. 'Four thirty on Monday afternoon is still free.'

Posthumus pursed his lips. 'That's possible,' he said. 'It depends on when the police release the phone. But they probably only want to check the call log for dealers, and from what the Salvation Army officer said, I doubt I'll find any leads on it for family or friends. So let's go for Monday. You'll call a cemetery?'

'St Barbara's, by preference?' said Hendrik.

Posthumus nodded. They both liked the old cemetery out west.

'It doesn't give Cornelius Barendrecht much time for the poem,' he said, 'but I'm sure he'll come up with something. Not that he has a great deal to work with.'

Posthumus handed over the inventory, and witnessed Hendrik's signature on it. He would drop in to brief Cornelius before going back to the office. It was on the way.

'I'll take the wallet and the coat, if you'd like to draw up a receipt,' said Posthumus. 'And you can make specific mention of the lanyard, if you want. I've no real interest in the rest.'

Hendrik dropped the coat into the bin-bag that the backpack had come in, and moved to a computer to type out the receipt. Posthumus put the wallet into a brown envelope from a pile on the table, picked up the glasses with a lens missing, and slipped them in, too.

'You might as well add in the glasses,' said Posthumus to Hendrik. 'You never know what might inspire the Great Poet's mind.'

Down in the car park, Posthumus took the coat out of the bin-bag again, to fold it more carefully. He held it by the collar, and gave it a shake. It certainly was a fine garment. And there was nothing wrong with it that a good dry-cleaning wouldn't put right. Even tight-fisted old Bart in the Waterlooplein flea market would pay well for this, and every little bit helped the Funeral Team budget. Posthumus felt the fabric between thumb and forefinger. He'd buy it himself, come to that: why bother with Bart? Posthumus held up the coat so that the shoulders were parallel to his own. He felt a twinge of conscience: he couldn't bluff himself that this wasn't stolen property. He really ought to make some sort of an effort to find out if anyone had reported the theft, or whom the coat might belong to. Automatically, he ran his hands through the two empty inside pockets, then noticed a third, smaller, button-down pocket, a little way further down the right-hand inner panel. He felt inside. It was just large enough for a discreet billfold. Nice idea. The pocket was also empty . . . though not quite. Posthumus's fingers picked up a change in texture. The flap that would normally button over the top of the pocket had been pushed down inside. Behind it was something rougher and stiffer than the silk lining. Posthumus curled a finger around it and pulled it out. A business card. He held it at arm's length and read:

FUTURA CONSULTANTS
*Strategic Planning and Development*
Ben Olssen

A phone number: +1, the US. Maybe it was a mobile. Posthumus hesitated a moment, and rang it.

'Hello, Ben Olssen here. Sorry I can't—'

Voicemail. Posthumus hung up. He wasn't going to waste a fortune on transatlantic calls to strangers. But the *name*. Hearing it rather than reading it brought familiarity. Placing it didn't take Posthumus very long. He tapped into his address book, and made a call

'Cornelius, hello,' he said. 'Are you at home? We've a client for Monday afternoon, if that's enough time for you. There's very little to go on, but I can be with you in five to ten minutes . . . and is Gabrielle there, by any chance? I was hoping to get in touch with Christina.'

An hour later, young Lukas was standing beside his father at the front door, as Cornelius said goodbye to Posthumus.

'And you'll get Christina to phone me?' said Posthumus to Cornelius, taking the three steps down to the pavement in two hops.

'As soon as they're finished at the conference,' said Cornelius. 'Such gallantry! Every inch the gentleman!'

His blue eyes were bright over the tops of his half-moon glasses. As Posthumus walked over to the department's diminutive Smart car, parked a little further up the road, he heard Lukas ask, 'Papa, what is gallantry?'

Posthumus had driven for barely five minutes when the phone rang. He glanced at it: Private Number. Posthumus smiled, rapidly ducked the Smart car into a space between two parked cars, cleared his throat, and answered the phone just before it went to voicemail.

'Hello,' he said, hoping his voice sounded low, relaxed, with just the hint of a smile.

'Pieter Posthumus?' said a male voice. 'Detective Inspector Flip de Boer.'

A prickle of panic condensed in the top of Posthumus's gut. Why, after all this time, did a surprise encounter with police still catapult him back to his years living in the squat, and the arrest? The hours of heavy questioning, after police thought he'd been one of a group who had set light to a tram, until Anna stepped in with a good lawyer to get him off the hook . . .

'Mr Posthumus? Are you there?'

'Yes, sorry, good afternoon. I'm parked in the car. Just switching off the engine. How can I help you? Is it something to do with Zig Zagorodnii?'

Back in February, de Boer had given Posthumus the nudge that had helped him work out the story of poor Zig's death, stepping a little beyond official boundaries to do so. Posthumus had found himself warming to the man, despite himself.

'No, I'm calling you this time in your professional capacity,' said de Boer. 'I'm glad I caught you. I've just spoken with Olympia Funeral Directors. Apparently you have the coat that the deceased Frans Kemp was wearing.'

Again that tightening in the gut.

'I'm on my way back to the office now,' said Posthumus. 'I was going to see whether the theft had been reported, but I think I may have traced the owner. I was just checking.'

There was a silence on the other end of the line.

'You know who the coat belongs to?' said de Boer eventually.

'Ben Olssen?' said Posthumus. 'I found a business card in an inside pocket. Of course, Olssen may have given the card to whoever owned the coat, but it was in the kind of little pocket where you'd keep some separate cash and personal stuff, you know, in case you were pickpocketed or something. Is that who reported the theft? It turns out I know someone who might know him, so I thought I'd ask, and maybe return the coat directly—'

Posthumus realised he was speaking a little too fast. De Boer interrupted him.

'Mr Posthumus, will you be back at the office soon? I can be there shortly after five o'clock. If you don't mind waiting, I'd like to talk to you.'

# 3

Flip de Boer replaced the handset of his landline, rolled his chair back from his desk and stood up in a single motion. 'Ben Olssen.' That was quite feasible.

The man they'd had in hospital since Tuesday night seemed barely able to move, was slipping in and out of consciousness, and had difficulty breathing. They hadn't been able to get much sense out of him at all, but the fevered muttering that a nurse had picked up on while she was putting on the ventilator mask was in English and what she thought was Swedish. Olssen was a Swedish name, wasn't it? De Boer picked up a sleek tablet from his desk, placed one of the earphones in an ear, and listened again to the recording that the quick-thinking nurse had made on her phone. Van Rijn downstairs could speak some Swedish, apparently. As soon as he got back, de Boer would see if he could confirm the language and make any sense of what the man was saying. In the meantime . . . he closed his eyes as he listened: the nurse gently prompting the man to give his name. De Boer noted that the man appeared to respond to both English and Dutch questions. That didn't necessarily mean anything, he could simply be reacting to the sound of a human voice. But de Boer couldn't hear anything that sounded like 'Ben' or 'Olssen', only the name that the nurse had picked up on: 'Hubert', 'Humbert' or 'Hubbard', something like that. She'd said they were old English names, so that's what they'd been working on. It was all they had to go on. He put the tablet and headphones back on the desk. There'd been no ID on the man, no phone, nothing. Nor did he match up with anybody reported missing in the past few days.

De Boer walked to the window and leaned against it, both arms stretched above his head, one fist gently drumming on the glass. For the hundredth time since the case came to him he cursed the fact he hadn't been at the crime scene. Not that he could blame anyone. Not the bus driver, who had first seen the man lying under the arches; nor the ambulance boys – there hadn't been any sign of violence, and they thought the man had had a heart attack, or was yet another tourist who had overindulged in some substance he wasn't used to. The bus driver hadn't seen any assailants. The ambulance had blocked traffic in a narrow lane of the underpass, so when they couldn't revive the man on the spot, they'd rushed him straight to hospital. De Boer checked the times. The bus driver had phoned at 20.42; depot records indicated that the previous bus would have gone through at about 20.25. So he had a time frame for the attack . . . though it could have been earlier: traffic moved fairly swiftly in the underpass, and the arches obscured drivers' view of the walkway.

De Boer stared out across the IJ Tunnel Bureau car park, towards the early rush-hour traffic beginning to thicken on the road into the tunnel. Nor could he really have a go at the uniformed lads from the Beurstraat Bureau. When the hospital contacted them in the morning with the information that the man had no ID or possessions, they logged it as a callous street robbery. They had too much on their hands, with the Occupy lot camped out on their doorstep, and the demonstration, to deal with it immediately. It wasn't until later in the day on Wednesday, yesterday, that the case had landed on de Boer's desk at Serious Crime, after tests at the hospital revealed there was something coursing round the man's veins that they did not understand at all.

De Boer turned from the window, tugging at the bottom of the polo shirt that had ridden up over a stomach that had been beginning to push at his belt when he first got the job ten months earlier, but which, after careful attention at the gym, was now six-pack flat again, and as hard as his chest and arms. He might be in a job usually filled by an older man, but he was determined not to look like one, even though that probably added to the aggro he was getting from those he had over-taken on the way up. He drummed his fingers on the desk. Still no sign of van Rijn. Remaining standing, de Boer picked up his tablet and sent van Rijn a copy of the audio file, asking him to call immediately if he understood any of it. Then he emailed Hans on his investigation team to get him to check the Amsterdam residents' registry and also hotel registrations for a Ben Olssen. Hans was already on to the hotels – but without a name, and with only a hospital-bed mugshot to give them, there had been little chance there. Hotel staff would be run off their feet at the moment. Nearly every room in town was taken because of Earth 2050, and, besides, conference delegates were always in and out of each other's beds like rabbits. A guest not returning for a night or two barely warranted any attention at all.

De Boer closed down the desk computer, slipped his tablet into the hard briefcase his wife had given him to celebrate his promotion (not quite what he would have chosen himself), and walked over to the door. The coat had been the only break they'd had. CCTV so far was a blank. Literally. Construction work had nixed the cameras behind the station, hoardings obscured part of the front end of the underpass – not that a pedestrian should have been there in the first place – and nothing covered that narrow side-lane inside. But they had managed to locate a poor-quality shot from further along the Piet Heinkade of what appeared to be the man, it was too grainy to be sure, entering the tunnel, carrying a pale brown overcoat, followed by someone in a hoodie. It had been Bas at the Beursstraat Bureau – good old Bas, who'd been with him through thick and thin – who'd dropped him the gem about the dead junkie. The lad on the beat who had found the poor bugger had thought the expensive-looking coat a bit out of place and had mentioned it to Bas some time during the turmoil that must have reigned at the Beursstraat Bureau on Tuesday night and Wednesday morning. Bas had put two and two together and come up with 150. It was a long shot. A *very* long shot. But one that looked as if it might have paid off.

De Boer took a black bomber jacket off a hook behind his office door. He'd had to catch a train in that morning, but he wanted to pick up the coat himself. He would get someone to drive him over. De Boer hesitated a moment, then, with the jacket held under one arm, tucked his shirt into his jeans. He remembered this Posthumus bloke. Liked him. And it seemed typical that he had spotted something that no one else had. De Boer had been impressed by Posthumus's reasoning back on the Zagorodnii case. The man was sharp. Posthumus had imagination, and an eye for detail. He could do with a man like that instead of some of the paint-by-numbers lads he had on his team.

A minibus filled the parking bay Posthumus usually used across from the Burials Department offices, pretty much blocking access to the gangplank of a houseboat moored in the canal alongside. When he could, Posthumus parked the little department car very precisely in the spot beside the boat, so that no other vehicle could squeeze in, and the area around the gangplank was free. He found a space further down the canal, and as he walked back past the boat gave a resigned shrug to the woman washing dishes in the kitchen. Posthumus crossed the street and pushed at the door of the small gabled building that housed the department, his forehead slightly furrowed. Flip de Boer was on the Serious Crime squad. If he was involved, then it must mean that the coat was more than simply stolen from a street café. Perhaps evidence of a crime that the dead Frans Kemp had something to do with? De Boer hadn't said anything about putting a stop to the burial. But maybe that's what he was coming to talk about.

Posthumus went inside. Alex was sitting at Reception, on the phone, her tumble of black hair today uncharacteristically done up in a chignon. She imitated Posthumus's scowl as he entered, then immediately flashed him a grin as she carried on speaking. Posthumus could hear that she was still ploughing through the list of calls the director ('Himself Upstairs', Alex called him) had given her that morning, trying to raise sponsors for the Lonely Funerals poems. He felt a twinge of guilt that he, too, should be doing something to help, but if anyone could put the case adroitly and charm money out of people it would be Alex. And he knew that she had added to the list on her own initiative – and probably with names more likely to be of use. He gave her a wave, and a thumbs-up, and went up to the Funeral Team office on the first floor. Maya brushed past him on the landing, clearly leaving for the day.

'I need to go across to City Hall,' she said, with a combative edge to her voice.

At a quarter to five? Posthumus gave her a bland smile and said nothing. Inside the office, Sulung sat at his desk. He was slumped forward slightly, looking at a spot a little to the left of his computer. He didn't acknowledge Posthumus's coming in to the room.

'Nice and quiet,' said Posthumus, going over to his own desk.

Sulung made no response. It was only a couple of months since his wife had died, and it was clear that he was still in bad shape, though he bound his feelings up tightly. Posthumus shot him a sideways glance. Dealing with funerals day in and day out was no job for someone who was grieving. Not for Sulung, anyway. He had never been completely on the ball, but his work was really going to pieces now. Posthumus had quietly taken to checking through files, covering Sulung's mistakes, to protect him from the wrath of Maya. He put down the bin-bag and envelope he'd brought in from the funeral directors, pretended to attend to something on his desk for a moment, then stepped across to the window, half turning to look out across the Amstel.

He waited for a while, then said, almost as if talking to himself, 'It stays tough, doesn't it?'

There was a long silence. Eventually, Sulung spoke.

'People keep saying that it's going to get easier,' he said. '"A little better day by day." But it doesn't. It just gets worse and worse. This time of day, especially, the thought of going home . . .'

He tailed off. Posthumus turned around to face him. It was the first time Sulung had said anything directly about how he felt.

'You know, it looks like it's going to be a lovely evening, the sun's breaking through a bit,' said Posthumus. 'I'm waiting for a late appointment, but it won't take long. Why don't you hang around, and we could go and sit on a terrace somewhere afterwards, or go for a walk?'

As he spoke, he could hear Alex's heels clipping lightly up the stairs from Reception. She came bursting in through the door.

'Boys! Guess what!' she said, but grasped the situation in an instant, and with barely a beat said, 'No, *wait*. I'm going to make it a surprise. You're going to have to hold tight till tomorrow.'

And she was gone. Even Sulung gave a smile.

'OK,' he said. 'You're on.'

They could hear Alex greeting somebody as her heels beat a tattoo back down the stairs.

'That's probably my late appointment,' said Posthumus to Sulung, taking the camelhair coat out of the bin-bag. 'It's a police inspector coming to collect this.'

Using the bag as a protective layer, he placed the coat on top of his desk, carefully neatening the folds, then gave his fingers a quick clean with an alcohol wipe. He looked up as DI de Boer knocked lightly on the open door and came into the room.

Posthumus greeted the detective, and introduced Sulung. De Boer nodded across the room to Sulung, and shook Posthumus's hand. Posthumus had to admit that he didn't look like your average cop: the stylish bomber jacket, the neatly tucked-in Ralph Lauren polo shirt – although the hard attaché case didn't quite suit the image.

'I've just learned what they call your department over at City Hall,' said de Boer, with half a smile.

'Despatches and Disasters?' said Posthumus.

The official name of 'Department of Emergencies and Internment' generally proved a bit too much of a mouthful.

'It could be worse,' said Posthumus. 'They could tweak the acronym and call us DIE.'

The detective grinned immediately. Posthumus waited for the usual quip to follow, about his own name. It didn't. De Boer went up a notch in his estimation. Posthumus indicated the coat.

'That's it,' he said, and fished Ben Olssen's card out of his own shirt pocket, holding it by its edges. 'And this is the card: Ben Olssen, US dial code. I've tried the number a few times, it's a mobile but it goes straight to voicemail.' He handed the card to de Boer. 'I'm afraid my prints will probably already be on it,' he said, as he did so. 'I'm presuming your presence here means there's something more to all this than meets the eye.'

De Boer was silent for a moment. 'I would like to talk some more with you, yes,' he said.

De Boer shot a quick glance towards Sulung. Posthumus caught the detective's eye, and gave a very slight nod. He indicated the chair in front of his desk, and took a seat himself. De Boer re-angled the chair so that its back was no longer to Sulung, and sat down.

'What do you know of this Ben Olssen?' he said.

'I think he may be known to a friend of mine, or at least to his wife and an old school-friend of hers,' said Posthumus. 'If it is the same man, then he's over for the Earth 2050 conference. Some years ago, he worked with my friend's wife, Gabrielle Lanting, at Greenpeace.'

'And this friend of yours?' said de Boer.

'In a sense he's also a work colleague,' said Posthumus. 'Cornelius Barendrecht . . . the poet?'

De Boer didn't appear to know the name.

'He writes elegies for some of our funerals,' Posthumus continued.

'But you haven't established whether or not this coat belongs to Ben Olssen?' said de Boer.

Posthumus explained that he knew only Cornelius's telephone number, and that he was waiting to hear from Gabi or Christina as to whether Olssen had had a coat stolen, but that they were all probably still busy at the conference.

'Has any of them had contact with Olssen in the past few days?' said de Boer.

'I would presume so, although it's an enormous conference. I think he and Christina had a lunch date yesterday. And they were in touch on Tuesday night. She spoke to him, or at least received a text, that I do know.'

De Boer's telephone rang. He apologised, said he had to take the call, and turned away from Posthumus to answer it. Posthumus glanced over to Sulung, and raised his eyebrows slightly. Sulung shrugged. De Boer took the phone from his ear, looked at the screen, and raised the phone again.

'Looks like a match to me,' he said. 'Good work, Hans. I'll call you in fifteen minutes.'

De Boer terminated the call, and turned back towards Posthumus. His expression had changed: his eyes seemed more relaxed, yet his lips were tight, his jaw more firmly set.

'In answer to what you said when I came in, yes, it would appear we do have a more serious issue here than opportunistic theft,' he said. 'There is a man at present in the OLVG Hospital in an extremely serious condition. We were not able to identify him, though we did have a possible CCTV shot, from a distance, of a man who appears to be him carrying a pale brown overcoat. And then thanks to you, Mr Posthumus, we also had a name to work with. That call was from one of my officers. He has just been sent the copy of a passport from guest-records at a hotel in the city centre. The photograph is clearly that of the man lying in the OLVG. Ben Olssen.'

The detective's voice lost a little of its edge.

'I haven't known you long, Mr Posthumus, but it would seem that yet again I owe you one,' he said.

Posthumus let the remark pass. Yes, he had in effect solved de Boer's case for him a few months back, but he had done that for Anna, not for the detective.

'We will have to confirm Olssen's identity properly,' de Boer continued, 'but I'm told electronic room-key records show that he has not been back there since Tuesday evening, so what you say about him making phone contact then is interesting. I think we can work with the assumption that this is our man.'

'And he is so ill that he cannot confirm his own identity,' said Posthumus, more as a statement than a question.

'I'm waiting for a report on further tests from the hospital,' said de Boer. 'The results will, I suspect, confirm that we're dealing with a serious assault, if not attempted murder.'

Posthumus leaned back in his chair. This was not going to be easy news to give to either Gabi or Christina. And he guessed he would have to do it – now that he'd started the process by mentioning the coat to Cornelius. So much for his attempts to get into Christina's good books.

'Clearly there's a personal issue here for you, because of your friends,' de Boer said. 'But there are further professional implications, too. This . . .'

There was the briefest pulse of a pause. Posthumus could sense de Boer's mind flick back and re-engage.

'This Frans Kemp,' de Boer continued. 'If the coat indicates some connection between the two men, we may need the body. I'll be wanting a post mortem.'

'The funeral's scheduled for Monday,' said Posthumus. 'They're already working on him.'

De Boer cursed softly. 'Bloody sped through the system.'

Posthumus caught what he was saying. 'Apparently Kemp had a long case history, so an overdose wasn't unforeseen,' he said. 'But as with any death like this, he'll be buried in a shallow grave, should you require exhumation. Or I can put a hold on it right now. There'll still be somebody at the undertakers, it's only just after five.'

'Now would be good,' said de Boer. 'And best if they stopped any embalming, if that's still going on.'

Posthumus looked over to Sulung. 'Would you mind? It's Hendrik Nieuwenhuis at Olympia.'

Sulung picked up the handset to phone.

Posthumus turned back to de Boer. A serious assault, he'd said, but why did you need tests to confirm that? Surely any signs of an attack would be obvious. He rapped a forefinger on the edge of his desk. 'Poison!' he said.

De Boer looked at him sharply. 'I would prefer it if you kept that to yourself for the moment,' he said.

Posthumus flattened both palms on his desk, and held de Boer's gaze. 'I'm going to have to tell Gabrielle and Christina *something*,' he said.

'I'd prefer to speak to them myself,' said de Boer. 'As soon as possible.'

Posthumus didn't drop his eyes. He had been here before, with Zig's murder in the guest-house, when his interference nearly caused the biggest rift he'd ever had with Anna. Now he felt that he was somehow the cause of upsetting Gabi and Christina, when all he had really wanted to do was help. That wasn't logical, he knew, but the least he could do was break the news himself.

'Christina will probably be calling me herself this evening, anyway,' he said. 'With them in and out of conference meetings, that may be before you've been able to speak to her. I'll have to say something. I've mentioned the coat to Cornelius, they're bound to ask. And they've as likely as not already noticed he's not around, especially if he didn't make lunch yesterday. Besides, I feel an obligation . . .'

Posthumus tailed off, but continued to look directly at the detective. De Boer owed him one. He had said so himself. De Boer was silent.

'If it's an alibi you need, I can provide that,' Posthumus went on. 'They were both with me until quite late on Tuesday night.'

De Boer gave a single shake of his head. 'We know the attacker was a man,' he said. He was quiet another moment and then went on: 'Very well, but I trust that as a fellow professional you will keep information to a minimum. I don't need to tell *you* that much of what we have just said is not in the public domain.'

Posthumus nodded. 'What can I say to them?' he asked.

'You can say that Olssen is in hospital, that he is extremely weak and has severe respiratory problems. And that I'd like to speak to them both, to find out what more they may know about him.' De Boer handed Posthumus a business card. 'You still have my number? I'd like them to give me a call tomorrow morning,' he said.

'All sorted,' said Sulung, from across the office. He replaced his telephone handset. 'They're short-staffed today, and someone else had to be given priority for a viewing, so they're still working and had only just finished stage two,' he said.

'So, viscera still in place, and blood probably not yet drained,' said Posthumus for de Boer's benefit.

He gave an enquiring glance to Sulung, who confirmed that with a nod.

'Good,' said de Boer.

Posthumus leaned over his desk, looking intently at the detective. 'Poison, but clearly not something that is easily – or immediately – identifiable,' he said.

De Boer gave him another warning glance, but this time edged with a grin. Posthumus rolled his chair back from the desk, and swivelled slightly to look out of the window.

'And Olssen must have been found somewhere where he could have been relieved of his coat and all his possessions,' he said. 'Outdoors? A park? It can't have been anywhere very busy.'

De Boer did not answer him. Instead, he asked, 'What else was there among Kemp's possessions?'

Posthumus swivelled back to face him. 'Nothing much. Hardly anything at all. There was his drugs paraphernalia and a mobile phone apparently, but those were retained by the officers who found him. That would be the Beursstraat Bureau.'

'They've already been sent over,' said de Boer.

'Besides that, not a lot,' said Posthumus. 'An old wallet that I'm pretty sure was Kemp's, though with a bit more cash than I might have expected, over a hundred euros.'

He reached across for the envelope he'd brought back from the undertakers, and emptied the contents on to his desk.

'That small button-down pocket inside the coat, where I found the business card,' said Posthumus. 'I'd warrant that's where the money came from, too.'

De Boer looked down at the frayed canvas wallet. 'That certainly looks more like it belongs to a junkie than a conference delegate, but I'll take it anyway,' he said.

He flipped open his attaché case, and took out a large evidence bag and a couple of smaller ones. Posthumus noted that apart from a tablet, there was little else inside the briefcase. De Boer held open the larger bag and nodded at the coat.

'Would you?' he said to Posthumus. 'You've handled it already. And then the rest, into the smaller bags?'

Posthumus didn't buy that for a moment. So the detective was squeamish about touching the coat, was he? But he obliged. De Boer thanked both him and Sulung, and took his leave.

Posthumus gave his hands a squirt of sanitiser gel, and walked over to Sulung's desk.

'Well, well, that turned out to be a more eventful day than seemed likely at first,' he said, rubbing his interlaced fingers together.

They heard the downstairs door bang shut.

'Now: how about that walk and a drink?'

Posthumus's mobile rang. He quickly waved his hands dry, and took it out of his pocket. He didn't recognise the number, but it was most likely Gabi or Christina. Cornelius's message must have got through by now. He braced himself, and took the call.

'Hello, Mr Posthumus?'

It was a young man's voice.

'Niels Klaver here . . . Gabrielle Lanting's assistant?'

Posthumus made a move towards the window. De Boer might still be in the street outside.

'Hold on a moment, Niels,' he said. 'I have someone here who wants to talk with her, or at least he's just left, but I may be able to catch him.'

'Gabrielle's tied up at the moment,' said Niels. 'She's asked me to go through her phone messages for her, she's like non-stop right now. I see there's a text from her husband – you wanted Christina Walraven's number? Something about a coat?'

Posthumus grimaced. He didn't want to do this through Niels.

'Things have changed somewhat,' he said. 'I really ought to speak to them. Could you put one of them on the line, preferably Gabrielle.'

'No can do, I'm afraid. They're in a sort of meeting.'

'A *sort of* meeting? When's it going to finish? This is important.'

'It's more of a drinks thing, and later there's dinner,' said Niels. 'We're at the Conservatorium. It'll be going on pretty much all night.'

'A drinks "thing"?'

'I can't really go into details, sorry,' said Niels.

Posthumus sighed. The Conservatorium Hotel wasn't much more than twenty minutes' walk away. To hell with this, he'd go and speak with them face to face. He shot a glance towards Sulung, who was already putting on his jacket.

'Tell them I'm coming over,' said Posthumus. 'I'm sure they can be torn away from whatever they're doing for ten minutes.'

Niels hesitated. He'd clearly picked up on the irritation in Posthumus's voice.

'She could do some time around six thirty, maybe,' he said. 'The actual dinner isn't until seven fifteen, and we'd scheduled then for her to give me a quick catch-up in the lobby before she went in. Maybe she could squeeze you in for ten minutes or so.'

Posthumus glanced again at Sulung. They could take their walk in the direction of the Conservatorium, along the Reguliersgracht. That would be quiet. Perhaps he could even be persuaded to join them.

'Tell her I'll be there,' said Posthumus.

He ended the call, and turned to explain the situation to Sulung.

De Boer heard the door of the Burials Department offices click shut automatically behind him. There had been no one downstairs. The hot young receptionist with the legs had already gone home. He looked up the canal. A car engine fired into life, and de Boer saw the young sergeant who had driven him over pull out of a bay further up the street. He waited.

So, the man in the OLVG was Ben Olssen. And what did Frans Kemp have to do with it all? How did he get his hands on the coat? De Boer tugged at the base of his shirt, untucked it and let it hang loose. The ancient Nokia that had been sent over from the Beursstraat Bureau was clearly Kemp's, with nothing much on the call record except a couple of numbers known to belong to small-time dealers. But he'd have the drugs gear looked at more closely. And he'd have to see what the post mortem threw up, how the junkie had really died, and whether there was a link . . .

The unmarked car pulled up, and de Boer got in. He checked his watch. 'Thanks for waiting,' he said to the sergeant. 'That took a bit longer than I'd thought.'

He twisted round to put the evidence bags on the back seat. 'Could you drop me off at Central Station on the way back, and get these to forensics?' he said. 'It'll save me a bit of time.'

It would be good to get home early. The domestic danger lights were already flashing. De Boer could sense another series of late nights coming on, with cancelled family appointments and the inevitable uphill that earned him. If he made it in time for the five fifty-two, he'd be home by a quarter to seven. Or . . . if he caught the six twenty, instead, then there'd be time for a bit of a walk around outside the station. What had Olssen been doing in the underpass? Did *that* have something to do with Kemp? Some sort of drugs underworld connection, perhaps?

De Boer gave a wry smile. Trust that Posthumus to jump to conclusions. To the right conclusions, too, mostly. He knew the lads at the Beursstraat Bureau found the man's nit-picking a pain. But then those boys had to deal with him quite a lot. With the red-light district on their beat, they notched up a high body count, of the sort that ended up in Posthumus's in-tray: windows girls nobody wanted to acknowledge, the odd tourist who dropped dead after overdoing it, junkies like Kemp. But Posthumus had been on the wrong track about Olssen being attacked somewhere quiet. That was what was so perplexing, especially if this was more than a simple assault, and de Boer was pretty sure that it was. Trying to do someone in, even in that dark lane of the underpass, shielded by the arches, was incredibly risky. You'd have to be quick, pull a smooth operation. Not the sort of thing he imagined Kemp would be capable of. Or even, if it was an underworld liquidation, something you'd entrust him with. A disposable sidekick, maybe? Why – and how – did he end up dead? And even if Kemp's death was just an overdose, Olssen's was certainly more than robbery gone wrong. He'd have to look into Kemp a bit more . . . and find out for sure just what was the matter with Olssen.

The car had crossed the bridge over the Amstel, and edged into heavy traffic on the Rokin. A banner from the afternoon's demonstration was still strung along the canal railings. De Boer toyed with the pack of cigarettes in his jacket pocket. Maybe none of this had anything to do with Kemp at all. Maybe it was about Earth 2050. Olssen was a delegate, wasn't he? And he was staying at the Krasnapolsky, on the Dam, in the very thick of things, with Occupy camped out almost on the doorstep. What side was he on? Not the demonstrators', surely, if he was at a swish place like the Krasnapolsky. He needed to know more about Olssen. De Boer took out his phone. He had said he'd phone Hans back, more than fifteen minutes ago now. But first he checked his text messages and email. Nothing yet from van Rijn about the Swedish. He looked up. They had barely moved since coming on to the Rokin, and there was a bottleneck further up, where cars and tramlines came together because of building works: the interminable North–South metro line construction, this time. The young sergeant nodded to the blue light balanced on the dashboard then up to the roof of the car.

'Shall I give it a whirl?' he said.

De Boer shook his head. 'I'll walk,' he said. 'It'll probably be quicker.'

He got out of the car, and began walking up towards the Dam. Behind him he heard a short blast on the siren as the sergeant hung a U-turn and headed back to the Bureau.

Posthumus had said that Olssen made contact with one of the women on Tuesday evening. He'd look into that, see whether it was a voice call – anyone who'd got their hands on the guy's phone could have sent or replied to a text. De Boer's phone rang. He looked at the screen. It was Hans. De Boer took the call.

'Hans!' he said. 'I was on the point of ringing you. What's up? You got anything more on Olssen?'

'I'm at the Krasnapolsky,' said Hans. 'Can you get over here? You've got to see this for yourself.'

# 4

Marty Jacobs rubbed at the itch in his groin with the flat of one fat palm. The run-in with Henk's boys had been over a month ago now, yet his hand still hurt a bit. He had that to say for Henk de Kok: when Henk did something, he did it properly. Or at least his boys did. And Marty, now, was one of Henk's boys. 'A trial by fire,' Henk had called it. Marty didn't quite get that. The boys hadn't done him over because of the fire, but because he'd fucked up with Marloes and the guest-house. But that – and Henk had made this clear – that was all now behind him. Marty had paid his price.

Since then, Henk had been good to him. He'd even taken back 'Martin Jacobs Management', the company he'd set up for Marty. It still existed on paper, but Marty didn't have to hassle with any of the tax and the legal side and shit. That was all sorted. Marty half suppressed a leaky belch, and fingered the wad of notes in his pocket. In fact, he'd just collected the rent from one of his sets of windows. Most of it went to Henk, of course, but he got his cut. And respect from the girls. They had to respect him these days. Marty Jacobs was someone, when he walked through De Wallen. Maybe he'd get himself a nice black leather jacket, like Henk always wore.

Marty rocked back on his chair till it touched the wall. Its legs creaked dangerously. He surveyed the room. Milord was empty. Almost. Just the three old guys who seemed to come every Thursday afternoon, staring glumly at the lap-dancer. Better than going down the Day Centre, Marty supposed. The girl was going through her routine in a bored sort of a way. She knew she wouldn't be getting any money out of those three, but the after-work crowd would be there any minute, slipping in between knocking off and going home. Marty gave a wheezy giggle: 'Slipping in'. He must remember that. Say it to Henk some time. Marty let the chair thud back on to the floor. This was his world now. Jacobs Butcher's would have to do without him one of these days. He already took some mornings off. You should have heard his mother going on about that! Dried-out old lizard, having to get up early herself for a change and do some work, instead of lying on the sunbed all morning sucking on ciggies. She'd been sour enough when he was all beaten up and couldn't work. The moment he started getting better, it was back with the nag, nag, nag, at full fucking croak: 'Lazy sod', 'Useless lump of nothing', the usual shit. Talking about him to customers as if he wasn't there. Marty folded his lower lip up over the moustache he had been growing for the past few weeks. It was coming out flecked with grey, even though he was only thirty-two. He chewed at it a little. The old lizard had gone quiet soon enough when he told her he was working for Henk. Very quiet. Yes, that had shut her up, all right. She hated Henk. She had just glared for a long time, then lit a ciggie and gone upstairs wearing that sour smile of hers. He'd always told himself that one day he'd show her, and he had. And she didn't even know the *half* of it.

The middle-aged couple who did the live sex show came in, and went straight through to the back. They always kept them-selves to themselves, those two. They were a real couple, married even, but how they did it again and again, night after night, amazed Marty. Viagra, he supposed. Or acting. Marty waved his empty glass as a waitress passed. *He* was on another level. A real somebody in Henk's organisation. Especially now, after what (to himself at least) he liked to call his 'mission'. The job had been his chance to prove himself, to show what he was worth, Henk had said. But once again Marty felt a sudden spear-stab through his gut, and the feeling that he was going to be sick. He put down his glass and quickly wiped away the sweat he could feel breaking out below his hairline. It kept coming back, this feeling of panic, every time he really thought about what had happened. He couldn't help it. They had actually *killed* a man, for Chrissakes. Marty tried to look normal, to slow down his breathing. It was fine, it was all *fine*. Mission accomplished.

The waitress was standing over him. Marty hesitated a moment, then ordered another Coke. And even if it wasn't fine, it wasn't *him* who had actually done the guy in. All he'd done was block the way, and then take the stuff, like he was supposed to. It was the foreign geezer who had actually *done* it. And *he* had scarpered, fucked off straight away to Schiphol and back to Lapland, or wherever he came from. But still . . . the words 'accessory to the crime' kept coming into his head, from some TV series or other. He called the waitress back, and changed his order to a tomato juice and some crisps.

'With a spoon,' he added. 'And vodka in the tomato juice.'

He didn't normally do this when he was out in a bar, but it was his favourite: crushing the crisps into the tomato juice and eating the mush. He wouldn't scrape out the last bits with his fingers, as he *really* liked to, but it would calm him down. The vodka, too. That was new: a Marty Cocktail. But he would make sure he was finished before Henk came.

Marty shifted his weight in his chair, and drummed on his knees with the flats of his hands. Yes, mission accomplished. He stopped drumming, and held tight. Sort of accomplished. 'Just make sure you burn the fucking hard-drive!' that Alexi geezer had screamed at him, before disappearing out the other end of the underpass. But Marty didn't know how. He had thought he was supposed to give the phone and laptop and stuff to Henk, but Henk didn't want to know about it. 'No idea what you're on about,' Henk had said, looking at him hard. 'I've nothing to do with what you've been up to, get it? Just as long as it's sorted.' Marty had destroyed the passport and cards and things, but the laptop and phone . . . they were beautiful. New-looking, expensive. The phone had driven him mad at first, ringing and beeping all the time, until he'd thrown away its little card. But he couldn't work out how to open the back of the computer, and besides, he didn't even know what a hard-drive looked like. He had tried both the computer and the phone first, but they needed passwords. Still, he'd made sure his mother had seen him with them, let her think they were his. He'd even thought of taking the phone to one of those shops where, he was sure, they could unlock it. Marty couldn't bring himself to smash it up.

The tomato juice arrived. Marty took a large gulp, and then thumped on the crisp packet to smash the contents. But all that stuff was evidence, wasn't it? Again, the spear-stab. He'd get rid of all of it, really he would. Tonight, as soon as he got home, or as soon as it was dark enough, he'd put the phone *and* the computer into a bin-bag, maybe with some stones or something, and when no one was looking he'd drop the bag into a canal. That's what he'd do. That would destroy the hard-disk, surely? Marty shook shards of crisps on to the tomato juice, till they reached the rim of the glass, then picked up the spoon to start mixing them in. But then there was the junkie . . . If Marty thought about the mission too much, it all seemed a bit of a mess.

'*Interesting*. Hungry, are you?'

Marty looked up. For a large man, Henk de Kok moved very quietly.

'Just an experiment,' said Marty, pushing away the glass so that it almost fell off the table.

'Feeling adventurous, are we then, Fat Man?'

'No, no . . . I mean, yes,' said Marty. 'If I need to be.'

That was quick. He'd saved himself there. Almost tripped up, but that was the right answer. Henk said nothing. Marty remembered his joke from earlier.

'I see those three old guys have slipped in again,' he said.

It didn't work. Henk didn't even smile.

'I might have something for you, Fat Man. Another little adventure that needs more bulk than brain. That's if you've been doing your work properly.'

Marty didn't like that 'Fat Man'. One day, he'd mention that to Henk.

'The rents?' he said instead. 'Yes, all here, all done. Record time.' He pulled the thick wad of notes from his jacket pocket.

'Not here, idiot.'

Henk's voice was flat. He might have been saying, 'Not today, thanks,' to a caller. But Marty caught a glint in his eye at the sight of the notes.

'Bring it to my office later. How much?'

Marty told him. 'It's all there, down to the last euro,' he said. 'Even old Agnes, and the lot near the church.'

Marty was proud of that. She was a tough cookie, Agnes. Had been at it for years, and always had some story when it came to the money. She was one of the few who would dare.

Henk signalled a passing waitress, who flinched slightly.

'Get the Fat Man some whisky,' he said, with a scowl at the Marty Cocktail. 'On the house. We can't have him slurping that crap in the bar.'

'You just remember that,' said Posthumus, one hand firmly on Sulung's shoulder. 'And dinner at my place on Sunday, right?'

'Thanks, mate,' said Sulung, and stepped up into the tram just as the doors closed.

The walk from the office had been intense. Posthumus had mentioned Willem, and then found himself getting deeper into his own feelings of guilt about his brother's death than he'd intended. He'd talked to Sulung about Willem in a way that he'd hardly ever done with Anna, or even with his niece Merel, who in these past few months had helped him to begin to get a hold on it all at last. But that had given Sulung the opening he needed, and he'd guardedly opened up about his wife, how he was plagued by the idea that he hadn't done enough for her. They had stood a long while talking, leaning against the parapet on the bridge over the Prinsengracht, where canals stretched in four directions into the evening haze. Now Posthumus was late. It was going on for a quarter to seven.

Posthumus crossed rapidly from the tram-stop into the courtyard that screened the entrance to the Conservatorium Hotel. Through a glass wall he could see Christina and Gabi sitting on a sofa in the vast lobby. The irritating assistant was with them. Gabi gave Posthumus a wave as he walked on towards the foyer.

Stepping out as if to greet him, a doorman politely blocked his way. 'Are you a guest with us tonight, sir?'

'It's OK, he's with me,' said Gabi, coming up behind the doorman, ushering Posthumus past, linking her arm through his.

'It's all because of you-know-who,' she said, dropping her voice. 'What happened to you? We haven't got very long. I was just about to send you a text.'

'Problem at work, sorry,' said Posthumus. 'And I-know-not. Who?'

They'd reached the sofa where Christina was sitting, straight-backed, designer-clad, and tapping out a text. Niels was zipping up his jacket with one hand, speaking into his phone in the other.

'Just sort it, OK?' he said, with a roll of his eyes that took in Posthumus, somehow making him complicit in whatever idiocy he was encountering at the other end of the line.

Posthumus gave him a nod. Christina finished the text with

a flourish, sprang up, and pecked Posthumus three times on the cheeks.

'Still Dutch enough for *three* kisses, even after all those years in London,' said Posthumus.

'Good-looking Dutch men help me to remember,' said Christina, lowering her chin and giving a pretty good imitation of the look Lauren Bacall made famous.

Posthumus faltered, set a little adrift.

'*This* is who,' said Gabi.

She showed him her phone. Posthumus looked at a photo, seemingly taken by Gabi herself, of her and Christina standing on either side of someone who seemed vaguely familiar. All three were beaming. Posthumus smiled, but said nothing.

'You don't know who it is, do you?' said Gabi. She gave Christina a look of exaggerated disbelief.

'You haven't seen the *Harry Potter* movies?' said Christina.

'The first one, I think,' said Posthumus.

'Wasted! *Wasted* on you!' said Gabi, pocketing her phone with a laugh.

'But I take it this means you've been successful with your celebrity-nabbing for Green Alliance?' said Posthumus.

Gabi put a finger to her lips. 'Not clinched just yet, but almost. We'll be sorting it out over dinner tonight,' she said.

She turned to Niels. 'That all looks super-fine,' she said. 'Thanks for staying on. We can sort the rest out tomorrow.'

'And by then I'll have had a word with Bill, depending on what time-zone he's in,' said Christina.

Posthumus wondered if she could possibly mean Clinton or Gates.

Niels gave a mock salute. 'Cheers, all,' he said, and stalked off towards the main door, causing a waiter to step back, a tray of glasses tinkling in his wake.

'Come on, sit down, we've time for a very quick drink,' said Gabi to Posthumus.

She summoned a waiter, and Posthumus ordered a wine, to join them in their round. He perched himself on the prim-looking designer chair that stood at right angles to their sofa.

'So what's the big mystery?' said Gabi. 'Niels said it couldn't wait, and Cornelius said you had a surprise. Something about a coat?'

Posthumus felt a flush rise up the back of his neck. Of course, Cornelius would still be playing along.

'I'm afraid things have changed a bit since I spoke to Cornelius,' he said.

He could see that Gabi had picked up on the serious tone in his voice. She put down her glass.

'I do have a coat, yes,' said Posthumus. 'It belonged to Ben Olssen.' He shifted uneasily on the hard seat.

'Ben?' said Gabi. She cocked her head quizzically to one side, then for a moment she seemed to freeze. 'Belonged? Oh my God, he's dead!' she said.

Christina looked confused, then she brought her fingers to her lips. 'Of course . . . your job,' she said. She slumped back into the sofa.

'No, no, he's fine,' said Posthumus. 'At least, not dead. When I said "belonged" I only meant he no longer has the coat. I got it off a junkie who died of an overdose the day before yesterday. I worked out the coat probably belonged to Ben, but when I spoke to Cornelius I didn't know the full story.'

'And what is the full story?' said Christina, her face pale. 'How did a *junkie* get his coat? Where's Ben?'

'Ben's in a bad way, I'm afraid. He's been attacked. He's in hospital. I think the junkie probably stole the coat.'

'But how in hospital, where?' said Gabi. 'What's happened?'

'He's in the OLVG, he can't breathe well and he's apparently very weak,' said Posthumus.

'We must get to see him and find out what's wrong,' said Christina.

She made a move to get up. Gabi's brow crumpled in desperation.

'Oh no, not now, not tonight,' she said. She put one hand on Christina's knee. 'I'm sorry,' she said. 'That's an awful, selfish reaction, I know, but I *so* need you here! *Please.*'

She looked across the lobby, to where a small group of people were beginning to gather at the foot of a stairway leading to a door on the mezzanine level.

'Ben's delirious, he can barely speak and apparently is making hardly any sense,' said Posthumus. 'I doubt that he would know you were there, even if you did go tonight. The police haven't been able to get anything out of him. If I hadn't found the coat they wouldn't even know who he is.'

'The *police?*' said Gabi.

She moved to hold Christina's hand. The urgency in her voice was reflected in both their faces. Posthumus hesitated.

'Look, I don't really know how to put this,' he said, 'but it seems there's something strange about the attack. I don't know much more than that, I don't think the police do, either, but the investigating detective wants you both to give him a call in the morning. They're trying to find out what they can about Ben.'

He reached into his pocket for de Boer's card, and gave it to Gabi.

'Until then, there really isn't much you can do,' he said. 'I'd say that what you seem to have ahead of you tonight is more important.'

He glanced quickly at Christina.

'In the long run, more important for more people,' he went on.

'This is dreadful. Poor Ben,' said Gabi.

She sank back into the sofa. Christina was sitting straight again, some colour had returned to her cheeks, but her voice sounded distant. She was staring through the glass wall of the atrium, beyond the courtyard itself, it seemed.

'He was trying to warn me about it,' she said.

Gabi and Posthumus looked at her.

'Or he was worried about something,' Christina went on, speaking more clearly. 'He was really insistent that we meet up on Tuesday night, even when I said it wasn't that convenient. He just wouldn't take no for an answer, said there was something he had to tell me. That's why we were meeting at the station café of all places, straight off the train from the cocktail party.'

She gave a faint laugh, but Posthumus could see she was blinking back tears.

'And I thought he was just being keen,' she said, 'that he'd been carrying a torch for me all these years. When I didn't hear from him yesterday, I presumed he was mad at me for standing him up . . .'

Her voice trailed off. There was a stir at the other end of the lobby. A small group was going up the stairs to the mezzanine floor, among them the person Posthumus had seen in the photo with Gabi and Christina. He noticed how throughout the lobby people were casting glances in that direction, or pretending not to look.

'If that's your dinner date, it looks like you should be going in,' he said to Gabi.

Christina stood up, smoothed down her dress, and lightly touched her hair, and the corner of one eye. 'I need to freshen up quickly,' she said.

Gabi rose, too. She rested a hand on Christina's forearm. 'Thank you, Chris,' she said. 'I'll cancel my morning appointments. There's nothing hugely important, just a panel appearance at a fringe forum. So if you're free, we can go out to the hospital.'

Christina gave her a quick hug. 'I won't be a minute,' she said. 'Meet you on the stairs. Bye, Pieter.'

She walked off to look for the Ladies. Posthumus watched her go, recalling the expression about shooting the messenger.

Gabi took out her phone. 'Sorry about this, Piet,' she said. 'I need to phone Niels about tomorrow, then I'll have to desert you.'

Posthumus nodded. His wine still hadn't arrived, but as he looked around for someone to cancel the order, he saw a waiter walking towards them with a single wineglass on a tray.

Gabi got through, and held her phone to one ear, hugging herself tightly with her other arm as she spoke. 'Niels? Sorry to be on to you again, just when you thought it was all over for the day, but I'm going to have to pull out of that Oil or Water? panel tomorrow morning. Something awful has happened . . .'

The lobby of the Krasnapolsky Hotel swarmed with people wearing Earth 2050 conference badges around their necks. There was no sign of Hans; he was probably up in Olssen's room. De Boer was about to identify himself to Reception and ask to be taken up, when a uniformed officer, whose face he recognised from the Beursstraat Bureau, signalled to him from beside the concierge's desk.

'Room 256, sir,' the officer said, walking up to de Boer. 'I've been called back to the Bureau, but one of the concierges will show you. He's just come off duty, and he spoke to Olssen on Tuesday.'

A large, middle-aged man stepped out from behind the desk. A drinker, de Boer noted: clothes too tight, potato face, skin a raw-scrubbed reddish-pink. The concierge introduced himself. His pale blue eyes looked as if they'd been left out too long in the sun.

'Jonas Keizer,' he said, without shaking de Boer's hand.

The two men walked across the lobby towards the lift.

'You spoke to Olssen on Tuesday?' said de Boer.

'Mid-afternoon some time,' said Keizer. 'About four, I should think. He wanted to know of a place he could meet someone near Central Station that evening. I suggested Café Eerste Klas, it's right on the platform.'

De Boer nodded. The concierge pushed the button to call the lift.

'Did he say anything else?' asked de Boer.

'Not then, he was on the phone to someone, and then he picked up an umbrella from our stand and left the hotel,' said Keizer.

The lift was crowded. They rode up in silence.

'Not then, you said? You spoke later?' said de Boer, when they were alone again in the corridor.

'Just after seven. He was on his way out, and came to the desk to ask if I could recommend a computer repair firm.'

'And that's all?'

'We talked a bit about Helsinki,' said Keizer. 'He'd just arrived from there. My mother was Finnish, and I've still got family around the place. But he wasn't exactly conversational. He seemed in a hurry, edgy. But what's all this about?'

Keizer bristled with a sudden edge of alcoholic ire, irritation bringing a deeper flush to his face.

'I've already said all this to your boss,' he said.

De Boer gave a terse smile. Hans was older than him, and this wasn't the first time someone had thought that de Boer was the deputy. Women DIs, the few that there were, had the same problem. But Hans was one of the rare older officers at the Bureau who didn't have a problem with de Boer's age. They had reached the door. Keizer gave it a rap, and Hans opened it immediately.

'Good evening, boss,' said Hans, right on cue – but there was a twinkle in his eye, so he'd probably heard Keizer through the door.

60

'Thank you, Mr Keizer,' said de Boer to the concierge. 'That will be it for now, but we'll probably be in touch again in the next day or two.'

He stepped past Keizer into the short passageway that led between a bathroom and a built-in wardrobe to the main room.

'Any news from the OLVG about Olssen?' Hans asked, closing the door behind de Boer as he entered.

De Boer shook his head. 'Nope. Which means he's still not making any sense, and the only news on the poison is that it's a neurotoxin of some sort. They'd have been in touch if there was any change.'

'Well . . . take a look at that,' said Hans, as de Boer reached the end of the passageway.

De Boer did. The room had been completely trashed. A figure eight, turned on its side, was sprayed in red paint on the far wall. De Boer's eyes flicked about, snapping what he saw and burning it into his mind, like an old-fashioned flash camera: bedding crumpled in a heap, pillows and quilt out of their covers; mattress at an angle, the two single halves of the double-bed base yanked apart; a large photo of Amsterdam pulled from the wall, lamps smashed, minibar cupboard forced, the little fridge hauled out and on its side, open with bottles scattered on the carpet; a hardcover suitcase upended, its contents in an untidy pile, sifted through, ripped. De Boer glanced back over his shoulder towards the wardrobe.

'Empty,' said Hans. 'I don't think he'd unpacked yet.'

'And the safe?'

'Open and empty,' said Hans. 'And it hasn't been forced.'

So, either Olssen hadn't used it, or whoever opened it knew what they were doing.

'And the room has been like this for two *days*?' said de Boer.

'Whoever it was hung the Do Not Disturb notice outside,

and they left music on and the shower running lightly, with the bathroom door shut,' said Hans. He gave a little chuckle. 'Good trick,' he said. 'Even when the room-maid did get a bit suspicious and peeked in, that put her off. And from the main door you can't see much, anyway, only the heap of clothes.'

'Music, did you say?' said de Boer. He looked past Hans to the device at the door into which guests had to insert their key card to switch on the electricity. A plastic card poked out of the slot.

'Albert Heijn Bonus Card,' said Hans. 'The slot works on pressure, rather than any magnetic reading.'

'CCTV?'

'Nothing in the corridor. There's one focused on the lift doors, but that might as well be Central Station.'

'We'll have a look at it anyway. You've called forensics?' said de Boer.

The supermarket loyalty card would be a start, at least.

'I thought I'd wait till you got here,' said Hans.

De Boer hoped his sigh wasn't audible. Sometimes even Hans needed a bit of a boot up the arse.

'Can you do so now?' he said.

De Boer took a step into the room. There'd probably be hundreds of fingerprints everywhere, but nothing at all in the places that mattered. He looked again at the wall. He'd seen that red sideways figure eight sprayed on walls around town recently. It was the mathematical symbol for 'infinity', apparently, but one of his younger colleagues had said he thought it was also a gang ID tag, that he'd seen people with it tattooed on their hands, in the hollow at the base of the thumb. Interesting. He couldn't rule anything out, not just yet. Including the more commonplace reasons for a mess like this.

'Burglary?' he said, before Hans had begun to phone. 'Somebody looking for something, maybe?'

'Well, there's nothing valuable of Olssen's here. Apart from the suitcase, clothes and toiletries, there doesn't seem to be anything that doesn't belong to the hotel,' said Hans.

So, either whoever had trashed the room had helped them-selves . . . or Olssen had his valuables on him when he was attacked. Drugs? De Boer lifted the suitcase with his foot, so that he could see inside. The fabric dividing-pocket had been ripped out, and the case had no compartments. He lowered the case back to its original position, and looked about him again. The destruction in the room seemed wanton. As if a rock group had been on the rampage. Or as if it had been done somehow to punish Olssen, to teach him a lesson, to frighten him. Yet there was something about it – the bedding ripped from its covers, the print pulled off the wall, the fridge hauled out of its niche – that made him wonder whether whoever had been here was looking for something.

De Boer's eyes moved to the writing desk against the inside wall. What had once been a complimentary bowl of fruit lay smashed, the contents scattered. A dried-out apple core and a blackening banana skin lay on a small plate, with a large bottle of mineral water knocked over beside it. There was water in the bottle. Whoever had taken a swig had resealed it after-wards. De Boer waited for Hans to finish the call.

'I want the fruit and the water sent for analysis,' he said. 'The apple core and banana, too, and the toiletries. Toothpaste, mouthwash, shower gel: his own and the hotel's. Anything he's used, any medication he was taking. And I want chemical swabs taken everywhere.'

De Boer looked at his watch. The five fifty-two train had long gone. He wouldn't even make the six twenty now.

Marty's tomato-juice-and-crisp cocktail stood untouched on the table. He was on his third glass of whisky: on the house. He smiled quietly to himself. The girls couldn't bullshit Marty

Jacobs that they hadn't been busy. He walked about. He watched. And Marty had it all, every last cent. He hadn't slipped out even a tenner for himself. No way. You didn't cheat Henk. Not when it came to money, you didn't. And Henk was pleased. 'Whisky on the house', indeed!

Marty felt good. He felt a bit more relaxed about his mission. He hadn't even known who the bloke in the underpass *was*, for Chrissakes. So nobody could pin anything on *him*. Maybe he would keep the phone, after all. Dump the computer, but keep the phone. He looked at his watch. It was past dinner time and he was hungry. The food at Milord, if you could call it that, was shit. And expensive. He slugged down the rest of the whisky, pushed himself up off his chair, and padded a little unsteadily towards the exit. Henk would be in his room behind the ticket office. He could put his head in and drop off the rent money on the way out.

Marty nodded graciously to the old geezer who sold tickets, swung past him, gave a single rap on Henk's door and pushed it open. Henk was standing. He was on the phone, and if it hadn't been Henk de Kok, Marty would have said he looked frightened. Anxious at least.

'What do you mean it didn't work?' Henk was saying. 'That's not my fault, that's *him*.'

Henk paused, listening to the person on the other end of the line. He had noticed Marty come in. Marty fumbled for the wad of money and put it on Henk's desk, then he raised one hand in a limp wave, and took a step back.

'I've said, you have *nothing* to worry about there,' said Henk. He thrust one hand deep into the pocket of his black leather jacket. 'I also have an interest in that.'

He was giving Marty a look that Marty couldn't quite work out.

'No, no problem. That element is . . . disposable,' Henk said.

# 5

Posthumus sat alone with a full glass of wine in the lobby lounge of the Conservatorium Hotel. The hubbub around him died down, as the star's retinue – Gabi and Christina among them – ascended to the mezzanine and disappeared through a dark glass door. Gabi gave him a little wave as she went.

Posthumus took in the space about him. He had been meaning to drop in for a look at the new hotel for months, to see if all the hype about the designer makeover of the former music conservatory was justified. It was good to see that the beautiful nineteenth-century brickwork and tiling had been retained and restored. And the vast atrium certainly made a mark, in a city that usually went for the cosy and small-scale. He checked his watch. It was just after seven fifteen, and he wasn't meeting Merel at the Schreierstoren till eight thirty. Clinks of cutlery came from behind a glass room-divider, which was laden with gleaming white porcelain and backed by a bristle of leafy bamboo. He'd treat himself to a quick bite here first, why not? He stood up, and carried his wine with him to a table at the brasserie.

'Sir?'

The waitress had been standing over him for some time, as he sat, one hand on the closed menu in front of him.

'Sorry, lost in thought,' Posthumus said.

He ordered, took a sip of wine, and leaned back in his chair. Could it have been true, what Christina said, about Olssen trying to warn her about the attack? That was the word she had used, 'warn'. Was she also in danger, or did she just mean that Olssen was frightened, knew something bad was about to happen? Posthumus wondered exactly what Olssen did for a living, why he was in Amsterdam for the conference. The card he'd found in the coat pocket had said something about a consultant for 'Strategic Planning and Development', but that could mean anything – though not saving tigers, like Christina, surely. That was hardly likely to land you in such hot water, although Posthumus had read that there was big money involved in tiger body parts, and in rhino horn, that sort of thing. He frowned, and took another sip of wine.

And then how did Frans Kemp fit in? Was Olssen smuggling drugs, or caught in a deal that went wrong? The idea didn't quite fit: Posthumus couldn't see someone whom both Gabi and Christina knew and liked being involved in anything that shady. A joint or two, maybe, they'd probably all done that at some time or another, but that was it. And as far as Kemp went, one look at his wasted body at the funeral parlour and you could see he was a victim of the drugs world, not a big player. Posthumus was sure of that.

A basket of bread arrived. Posthumus straightened it slightly, so that it wasn't at an angle to the edge of the table, then took a piece. He could not imagine Kemp attacking anybody, let alone with a sophisticated poison – and he knew from DI de Boer's reaction that he'd been correct in his reasoning about the poison. But if the police hadn't been able to identify Olssen, he must have been found with no possessions on him at all: no phone, no wallet, no ID, nothing. The most logical reason for that would be that everything was taken in one go.

And apart from the coat, Kemp had nothing on him that could conceivably be Ben Olssen's. The broken spectacles maybe? They didn't look particularly special. And more money than you would expect to find on a junkie. A payoff of some sort? But then what had happened to the rest of Olssen's belongings?

Posthumus broke off a piece of his bread, but put it down again without eating it. De Boer hadn't reacted, back at the office, when Posthumus suggested the attack must have happened outdoors, or in a park. But he had mentioned CCTV . . . so, not a park; yet he'd said the footage was from a distance, and poor quality . . . so, somewhere not adequately covered by cameras. Christina said that Olssen had arranged to meet her at the café at Central Station; Kemp was found nearby, in De Wallen, on the same night. So the attack most likely happened around there somewhere. And with no witnesses, apparently. Where on earth, near Central Station, could you attack someone and make off with his coat and belongings without anybody seeing, and with hardly any CCTV coverage? If Olssen was with one of the window-girls perhaps, with Kemp as some sort of go-between? But then coverage in the red-light district was good, both on the streets and in the corridors inside. Or so people who argued that the women who worked the windows were safe were always saying. Again, Posthumus frowned.

'Your scallops, sir.'

With lemon risotto. Posthumus poked at a courgette flower with his fork. It was rare for him to be so abstracted as he ate. He toyed with a scallop. Almost every working day, he constructed the stories of lives – from the books, the photos, the music collections of his clients, from their letters, the pictures on their apartment walls – finding a shape, building up a portrait that he could use at the funeral. Mostly, he found, even among the saddest or humblest of them, that there was an eloquence in the way the elements hung together. You couldn't always spot it at first, but it was there, after a little prodding and some thoughtfulness: a clue, a way in, that helped you compose the whole. Maya at the office said he was a time-waster, but Cornelius understood what he was going on about – it was what Cornelius did in writing his elegies. But occasionally the elements jarred, the parts just would not fuse. And when that happened, Posthumus couldn't ignore it, he couldn't let things go, not until he had found the flaw that was preventing his pulling everything together. It was almost physical, the sensation that got hold of him, and he was feeling that discomfort now, thinking about Ben Olssen. There was surely more to this than mugging. If what de Boer had implied was true, that there was no other sign of violence, then the poison must have worked pretty swiftly to enable Olssen to be so easily relieved of his possessions. But *why?* What was the point of it all?

Posthumus worked methodically through his meal (not too bad, though he would have gone a little easier on the lemon zest) and placed his napkin on the table. Or maybe the deed *was* the point. Did somebody perhaps *want* to take everything from Ben Olssen, anything that might give information about him, and leave him anonymous and senseless? Posthumus felt a prickle at the top of his spine. And leave him *dead?*

Posthumus paid the bill, and walked out swiftly to catch a tram.

Merel stood waiting on the small raised stairway at the door to the Schreierstoren. The sky had cleared completely now. The dumpy tower with its pixie-hat roof rose behind her against a backdrop of darkening pink and blue, like softly backlit glass, hinting at long summer twilights soon to come. When she saw

Posthumus, Merel tossed her head back and ran her fingers dramatically through her hair.

'I feel like one of the wailing women up here, waving to departing ships,' she said.

Posthumus laughed as he mounted the stairs. 'Actually, the "schreiers" doesn't refer to weepers at all,' he said. 'It probably comes from an old word "scray", which meant "astride", because the tower straddled two quays.'

'*PP!* Don't be such a pedant,' said Merel, pecking him on the cheeks. 'And what's that all about then?' She pointed to a gable-stone above the door, dated 1569, depicting a weeping woman.

'A bad year for Amsterdam trade, apparently, and she is the spirit of the city bewailing her lot,' said Posthumus.

'Where's your *romance*, PP? Even if it *isn't* true, I prefer the other story, of women gathering here to wave farewell to their men, as they sailed off in those tiny ships to the edge of the known world, for years and years, maybe never to come back at all.'

Merel remained looking out over what for centuries had been Amsterdam's Eastern Docks.

'Bit different these days,' she said.

Traffic tore past within touching distance; buses rumbled over a low, flat bridge to stop at Central Station, or to disappear into the railway underpass; streams of bicycles flowed in both directions, on either side of the road, and beyond them, two tourist boats chugged by, through the former harbour. In front of the station stretched the jumble of sheds, hoardings and heavy machinery that served the interminable underground burrowing of the new metro line; across the water, in edgy contrast to the old city, rose glittering skyscrapers of the new music conservatory, the public library and other bravura buildings fast growing up on the Eastern Islands.

'Not much romance, I'll grant you,' Merel said, turning back towards the Schreierstoren door. 'Is it OK to go in? There seems to be some sort of function on.'

A 'Private Party' sign stood in the doorway.

'It's fine,' said Posthumus. 'The manager's expecting us. It was an early evening drinks thing, and should be winding down. It's OK for us to have a look around.'

Posthumus had had the idea of hiring the bar that now occupied the little tower to throw a party for Anna's fiftieth birthday; she had once mentioned that she'd walked past it all her life, but never been inside. But when he dropped in to check it out, he'd found the interior rather too redolent of the tower's medieval origins – dark, brick-lined and brown. So he'd asked Merel along before making a final decision, to hear what she thought, and whether she had any ideas about brightening the place up a bit. He tried to put the business about Ben Olssen to the back of his mind.

Together, they went inside. A few guests with Earth 2050 lanyards around their necks were still hanging about. The manager greeted Posthumus from the bar.

'Your daughter?' he said, with a smile to Merel.

'Niece,' said Posthumus.

'I can see the family resemblance.'

Posthumus wondered whether the image of Willem that flashed before his mind was the same as the one that Merel (who was just a girl when he died) must have. A man frozen for ever at the same age as she was now.

'I'll be with you in a minute, feel free to look around. Can I offer you a drink?' said the manager.

With a glass of wine each, Posthumus and Merel wandered away from the bar.

'I see what you mean about the brown,' said Merel. 'It's

cosy enough, but hardly festive, especially for a June party, when the weather might be good.'

Posthumus followed her through a door to a smaller room, surrounded by windows, and with two water-level terraces built out over the canal behind the tower.

'Now *this* is a different story,' said Merel. 'How many people were you thinking of?'

'I don't know, about forty, fifty.'

'Then enough space for everyone out here and on the terraces, if the weather's good, or inside if not.'

Merel wandered over to the windows.

'*And* I've just had an idea,' she said. 'Do you know what would be fun? I've got this friend who's a set designer and sculptor, who did these brilliant floating installations for Gay Pride. I could ask him to make something for outside on the canal, maybe in here, too, to liven it up, make it really special for Anna. Maybe something with Velvet Underground, or using vinyl.'

Anna's passionate belief that no music recording could ever beat the atmosphere of vinyl drew banter from her friends, but her fervour for New Wave music had spawned an LP collection of archive quality.

'We could do something with album covers, maybe, drape everything with velvet, have plates made out of old records,' Merel went on.

'Come on, be serious,' said Posthumus.

'I am! I'll speak to Kamil. That can be my gift.'

Posthumus beamed at his niece as she fired off a few more ideas. God, how she reminded him of Willem when she enthused about something. He went in to confirm the booking with the manager.

When Posthumus returned, Merel was sitting at a table looking out across the water, seemingly lost in thought. He joined her, expecting another torrent of ideas, but what she said took him by surprise.

'I met up with Aissa today.'

For a moment, Posthumus was silent. The aftermath of his investigations into the death of a young man drowned in a canal a year earlier, and Merel's subsequent newspaper exposé of shady doings in the secret service, had blown apart Aissa's family life, just as a friendship between the two women was beginning to grow. It had been a delicate time for Merel, and a painful one for Aissa, but Posthumus suspected that both women wanted to attempt a repair.

'And?' he said, after a while.

'It went OK. Better than last time, anyway.'

'I'm glad to hear that,' said Posthumus. 'Really glad. Is there any news of Najib?'

Aissa's brother had fled the country, and had only written once, to say he was in Pakistan.

'Well, good and bad I suppose,' said Merel. 'At least he emails Aissa from time to time now. He's still not coming back to Amsterdam, but he's left the madrassa and gone to India. He's in Bangalore doing some computer job. It all seems a bit obscure, and Aissa is still worried.'

'At least he's back in touch,' said Posthumus. 'That's a step, anyway.'

'But he won't really let on why he went to Bangalore, or who he's with, and he simply won't answer any questions about Amsterdam. And all they have is a Hotmail address.'

Posthumus frowned. 'And Mohammed?'

He had liked Najib's father, and it unsettled him that Mohammed saw what had happened as some sort of betrayal on Posthumus's part.

'He's still devastated. If you ask me, it's Aissa who's holding everything together.'

A knocking sound came from one of Posthumus's pockets. 'Text message,' he said, in response to Merel's quizzical look.

'Read it,' she said. 'Don't worry about me.'

'Do you mind? It could be important.'

Posthumus explained about Ben Olssen, and what had happened earlier in the day, and took out his phone. Cornelius. Posthumus opened the message.

My wife is dining with a film star; my son is at a sleepover, and what am I doing with such delicious freedom? Sitting at home reading. Do you incline to De Dolle Hond?

Posthumus smiled, and turned his phone towards Merel. 'Shall we go on to De Dolle Hond?' he said.

Merel read the message and laughed. 'Cornelius is the only person I know who would use a semi-colon in a text message,' she said. 'But no, you go on, I should be getting back. I've an early start tomorrow. Mum's coming up from Maastricht to Den Bosch, and I said I'd spend the morning with her.'

Posthumus let the remark slip by. He might at last be dealing with his feelings of guilt about Willem's death, but Merel's mother still refused to speak to him, and he wasn't ready to deal with that yet. That Merel was now back in his life was enough.

'I think I might join him,' he said. 'I've an ADV day tomorrow, so what the hell.'

The regular day off that Dutch employment law insisted on meant he could sleep in. He texted a 'Why not? I have tomorrow free. See you there' to Cornelius.

Niece and uncle finished their drinks, and took their leave. As he waited for Merel to unlock her bike, Posthumus looked across towards Central Station. Where, he wondered, had Ben

Olssen been attacked? He gave Merel three goodbye pecks, and as she cycled off turned back along the canal, down the side of the Schreierstoren, for the five-minute walk to De Dolle Hond.

Anna gave Posthumus a wave from behind the counter as he came in. De Dolle Hond was busy. Little Tina had come from Anna's B&B next door, and was helping out behind the bar. Posthumus looked around. Not many familiar faces. The fragments of conversations that reached him as he walked up to the bar were all in English, in various shades and guises. There was somebody sitting on his usual stool. Anna laughed as she caught his glance.

'Over there,' she said, nodding to the far corner of the room, and handing him a glass of the New Zealand sauvignon that she kept especially for him, which she must have begun pouring the moment he walked past the window outside. On the low platform where once Paul's band had played, Anna had, after the fire that had ravaged De Dolle Hond, installed a large communal table. Now it bore a RESERVED sign.

'For regulars,' said Anna, as Posthumus took the wine. 'We can't have Earth 2050 entirely disrupting our lives.'

Posthumus crossed to the table, edging past Mrs Ting, who was, as ever, silently working the fruit machine. He gave her a smile and a nod, which she returned, but still with not a word. Even after the fire, when she had helped clean up, had brought them soup, and effected a seemingly miraculous repair on the large Delft vase, now restored to the shelf above her head, Mrs Ting never spoke. He and Anna still didn't know her real name.

'Happy winnings,' he said, as he passed.

Marie, who ran the new boutique around the corner, was sitting at one end of the table with her girlfriend (he couldn't recall her name), and John from the snack bar on the Dam. Posthumus greeted them, but took a seat at the other end, thus raising one of those subtle barriers that are not impolite, but fully understood in a small, crowded city. The others acknowledged it, and returned to their conversation. Posthumus sat quietly, looking appreciatively at the stretch of wall near the kitchen door, where a craftsman from England had reworked the charred wood panelling so beautifully that you could barely tell the new from the old. Posthumus ran his forefinger along the edge of the tabletop in front of him, stopping when he came to a kink in the wood, and tapping it. Poison. He let his finger rest in the sharp V-shaped crevice. Poison just did not match up with a mugging. It didn't fit. If you poisoned somebody, you generally wanted to kill them. And you didn't do it out in the street. He pushed hard at the V. Ever since his conversation with de Boer that afternoon, an image had been passing through his mind. Something odd, to which he hadn't really been paying much attention, as if it were out of focus and needed another turn of the lens to bring it properly into view.

For years, from back when he was an investigator with the municipal corruption unit, long before he worked with the Funeral Team, Posthumus had on quiet evenings at home amused himself with memory games. He had honed his mind to retain ideas, to make associations, to create interconnections. He attached single images to entire events, concepts, or significant facts: useful symbols that could be economically stored, to be used when needed, to trigger off a train of recall. Sometimes, one of these images was unexpectedly sparked, brought back to life by an incident in the outside world. When that happened, Posthumus knew not to ignore it. He continued gazing at the wood panelling, urging the shape that had been hovering in his head all afternoon into sharper focus. A man on a bridge. In London. Dressed as no Englishman had dressed for decades: in a bowler hat, and carrying an umbrella. Posthumus raised his eyebrows.

'Charon, dear Charon! May I enter your world, or entice you back to ours?'

Posthumus looked up. Cornelius was standing over him, shrugging loose an overcoat. Posthumus noticed Cornelius's nickname for him cause a flicker of confusion at the other end of the table. Cornelius picked up on that, too. He turned to Marie.

'The ferryman, my dear, the Stygian ferryman,' he said.

Posthumus had the impression this left Marie none the wiser.

'You got here quickly,' he said, as Cornelius pulled out a chair beside him. For the second time that evening, Posthumus pushed Ben Olssen to the back of his mind.

'A girdle round the earth in forty minutes!' said Cornelius. 'Well, from Zuid in fourteen.' He sat down and leaned back in the chair. 'A glass of fine red, I think,' he said.

Posthumus smiled, and rose to fetch Cornelius a drink. It was rare for the poet to volunteer a round, but Posthumus was beginning to accept that as part of a package that he otherwise rather liked. He knew that Cornelius didn't earn a huge amount, and didn't like using his wife's money for his own diversions. At the bar Anna gave Posthumus priority, but was too busy to chat. He returned with a glass of wine for Cornelius and a top-up for himself.

'What on *earth* is going on here?' said Cornelius, waving an arm over the busy bar.

Posthumus caught the glint in his eye. On a side street at the edge of the red-light district, De Dolle Hond drew an odd clientele – a ragbag of locals who'd been coming for decades, the occasional working girl, strictly off duty, ditto the odd copper from the Beursstraat Bureau nearby, and now and again curious tourists – but seldom so many out-of-towners in one go.

'Exactly,' said Posthumus. 'An Earth 2050 visitation.'

'It's the same all over town,' said Cornelius. 'There's no respite, even at my own hearth, alas.'

'Gabrielle seems incredibly busy with it all,' said Posthumus.

'Battling on all fronts,' said Cornelius. 'She's desperate to present cogent, convincing arguments to the moguls and mandarins in the halls, yet finds calm reason undermined by what's going on out on the streets. And for their part, those on the streets accuse her of selling out, of betraying the cause. There's no end to it.'

'It must be hard for her,' said Posthumus. 'She's really made a mark with Green Alliance, in the mainstream, but I guess she must know many of the hardliners personally, from the old days.'

'And now spends endless hours arguing with them. My Gabrielle is a driven woman. As is her *most* assiduous young assistant.'

'Do I detect someone feeling a little left out?' said Posthumus.

Cornelius laughed, took a sip of wine and settled more comfortably into his chair. 'Young Lukas and I are feeling somewhat sidelined, yes,' he said.

'Even when we were younger, Gabi always gave her all, headlong,' said Posthumus. 'And she really meant it. People like Anna and me, we're the ones who have sold out. Gabi's just become more pragmatic about how she's going to achieve what she wants.'

'Ah, but pragmatism entails moderation, and moderation has no place, they say, in the current situation. All solutions have of their nature to be radical, or they are not real solutions,' said Cornelius. 'I must say, I can rather see their point and I suspect, at heart, that my wife does, too.'

Posthumus placed his wineglass carefully on a cardboard coaster, and with his fingers on the stem rotated the glass back a few degrees. He let go.

'I'm afraid I've indirectly added to her troubles this evening,' he said.

He filled Cornelius in on what had happened since they had met earlier in the afternoon, outlining what he'd told Gabi and Christina about Ben Olssen, but holding back on the thoughts that had been bothering him.

'That's most unfortunate,' said Cornelius. 'I don't recall meeting the young man, but I know Gabrielle was fond of him when he worked with her. The fair Christina, too, from what I gather. Are they much upset?'

'Christina more so. Gabi too, but she had to focus on tonight.'

'Ah, the famous face who may soon front the Green Alliance. I'm not convinced that will help the cause. It may even worsen her standing with the hardliners. You know, falling in with celebrity culture and other heinous crimes.'

'It wouldn't mean much to *me*,' said Posthumus. 'I didn't even recognise who the celebrity was.'

Cornelius chuckled.

'Still, I'm glad the news didn't throw her off her stride,' Posthumus continued. 'And Christina seemed OK about staying for the dinner, too, to keep the cogs oiled. They're going to the hospital as soon as they can tomorrow to see how he is, and if there's anything they can do.'

'And you, my dear Charon, you find your gallantry regarding the coat cruelly thwarted, or at least misplaced.'

Posthumus gave a light shrug.

'Was that what might be termed a rueful smile?' said Cornelius. 'I thought you were hoping for the lady's favour.'

'Not really,' said Posthumus. 'Simply responding to a little flattering flirtation. In a way that now seems inappropriate.'

'Flirtation seems something of a modus operandi with the dear damsel,' said Cornelius, looking at Posthumus over the tops of his glasses. 'A bit of a flibbertigibbet if you ask me, a spoiled little rich girl, albeit an attractive one, playing at jobs while living off old man Sybrand and the family bank.'

'The bank?'

'Walraven, my dear Charon, *Walraven.*'

'Of course. I didn't make the connection,' said Posthumus.

The Walraven Bank. One of those gracious family banks, founded back in the Golden Age, quietly residing in a patrician mansion on the Herengracht. Old money.

'And Christina didn't mention it,' Posthumus went on, with a glance to Cornelius that carried something of a reprimand.

'Oh, they sold up back in the eighties, the family kept only a minority interest,' said Cornelius. 'Sybrand was the baby brother; went into the diplomatic corps. Besides, I think it all took a bit of a tumble in the financial crash, so there's not much to boast about.'

'I doubt she would,' said Posthumus.

'Ever the gentleman. But I would have thought you a man drawn to women of a little more personal substance.'

'Oh, there's substance to Christina, I think,' said Posthumus.

'More than Daddy's money, and a PR job saving furry animals?'

'That's unfair. She gets things done. She seems to have landed Gabi a patron.'

Cornelius opened his hands in submission. Then he raised his glass. 'Here's to gallantry, and the gentle art of allure,' he said.

'I quite agree! To real gentlemen,' said Marie, joining in from across the table.

'And kind ladies,' said John, giving his toast just an edge of double entendre.

'How delightfully old-fashioned,' said Cornelius. He patted his pocket as his phone rang, and took it out. 'Gabrielle.' Cornelius listened for a second or two. 'My darling! That is excellent news,' he said, beaming. He dropped the lower part of the phone away from his mouth. 'Celebrity on board,' he said to Posthumus. He raised the phone back to speak, and listened a while, his expression clouding slightly. 'Oh, but I can't,' he said. 'I have that meeting with the people from the LIRA Fund, to discuss a subsidy for the funeral poems. It really wouldn't look good to cancel.' Cornelius was silent for a moment. He gave Posthumus a teasing glance. 'Perhaps Piet will oblige,' he said. 'He has a day off tomorrow. I'm with him now.' Cornelius listened a little longer and then held out the phone. 'She wants to speak to you,' he said.

Posthumus put the phone to his ear. 'Gabi! It sounds as if congratulations are in order,' he said.

'Isn't it marvellous,' said Gabi. 'I'm absolutely over the moon. But here's the thing, we have to meet up tomorrow morning to make a more formal announcement, and for a photo-shoot, so I absolutely have to be there . . .'

Posthumus could hear a woman, it sounded like Christina, saying something in the background.

'Nonsense, Chris,' said Gabi. 'Piet will go with you, I'm sure . . . would you, Piet?' She was speaking to Posthumus again. 'Christina's just spoken to that policeman whose card you gave us, and he said he'd arrange for us to go and see Ben in the morning outside visiting hours. But now this photo call's scheduled for the same time, and I feel really bad deserting her after all she's done to help. She doesn't even know how to get to the hospital.'

'I can go in a *taxi*, for goodness' sake!' Christina's voice was clearer now, and sounded closer by.

'I'm not taking "No" for an answer, Christina!' said Gabi.

'Piet, it will be awful for her to have to go to the hospital alone. Is there *any* chance you could go with her? You're sort of involved with it all, in a way, anyway.'

'I'm a grown-up girl, Gabs. Honestly, it's no problem!' Christina's voice again. Gabi clearly ignored it.

'You would need to be at the hospital by nine thirty,' she said to Posthumus. 'Christina's staying at the Hotel Estheréa, on the Singel.'

Bang went his lie-in. Posthumus couldn't readily think of an excuse. Not since Cornelius already knew that he had the morning off, the old rogue. Also, part of him felt in some way responsible for the situation; and there were worse ways of spending his time than an hour or two with Christina, and he wanted to help. Besides, he had to admit, he was curious to know more about Ben Olssen.

'Tell her I'll be there at nine,' he said.

Posthumus ended the call. 'You old stirrer,' he said, as he handed the phone back to Cornelius.

'A driven woman, my wife, as I was saying,' said Cornelius. 'Nothing stands in the way of work.'

'That's not what I meant.'

Posthumus smiled. He wondered how de Boer had taken to being called at ten o'clock at night.

'*Hoi*, Mr P, more drinks, gents?'

Tina had come across from the bar, and was picking up their empty glasses.

'I think "Mr P", here, owes me one,' said Cornelius.

'Vice versa, I should think,' said Posthumus. 'I'm the one who's had his lie-in tomorrow blown out of the window.' He looked up at Tina. 'Same again, I think, Tina. I have a tab,' he said.

'Yep, I know that,' said Tina. '*And* a special bottle, what the others don't get.'

Posthumus smiled. 'It's a surprise, seeing you behind the bar,' he said.

Tina glanced over her shoulder towards Anna, and leaned forward conspiratorially. 'I don't think she wanted me to,' she said, dropping her voice, 'but it got crazy busy, and that Simon guy what usually helps out couldn't come in, so here I am. And I haven't made no mistakes yet, neither.'

'Good on you,' said Posthumus. 'Didn't I tell you things would turn out all right?'

Tina nodded. 'And you're still OK for tomorrow, Mr P?' she asked.

Posthumus didn't answer immediately.

'You haven't forgotten?' said Tina. There was a note of panic in her voice.

Posthumus had forgotten, truth be told. He felt his free ADV day ebbing slowly away. 'Of course, of course, but it will have to be some time around lunch,' he said. 'You'll be next door?'

Tina nodded.

'I'll text you when I'm coming, OK?' said Posthumus.

Tina went off to fetch their drinks.

'And that?' said Cornelius.

'I'm going with her to register her address with the council,' said Posthumus. 'Anna wants everything above board, and she hit the roof when she heard Tina hadn't registered properly, but the poor girl's got a thing about officialdom.'

'Even with something as everyday as that?' said Cornelius.

Posthumus shrugged. He understood it, that fear of the hidden machinations of authority.

'Honestly, Charon,' Cornelius went on. 'Where *do* you keep the white horse?'

Posthumus laughed. 'Just for that, you are *definitely* buying the next round,' he said.

# FRIDAY

## 20 April

# 6

Posthumus woke up naturally at half past seven, earlier than he had expected to. He showered, spiralled down the metal staircase in his bathrobe, zapped out a quick wake-up espresso in the kitchen, then went back upstairs to dress. Early spring sunlight was warming the apartment. The old roof-beams of what three centuries ago had been a canalside warehouse creaked and cracked at the first touch of the new season. On days like this, Posthumus was sure he detected a faint waft of spices, released from deep within the wood.

Up in his bedroom, he picked out a blue-grey cashmere-knit shirt, slightly darker trousers, and a pair of Church's loafers (Christina might appreciate that touch). He'd be warm enough with the goatskin *Trachten* jacket he'd found for next to nothing at the Waterlooplein flea market. Perhaps a light scarf for a touch of colour. Back downstairs, he fixed a quick breakfast, and as he had time to spare, took his coffee and muesli to the front of the long apartment, opened the large arched windows – which reached all the way to the floor, having once been doors through which goods were hoisted – and pulled up a chair to sit looking out over the canal.

It was quiet outside. Amsterdam rose late. Posthumus had removed the low safety rail the builders put across the window during the apartment conversion, so his view was untrammelled. The gabled houses, the hump-backed bridge (cluttered with locked bicycles), the houseboats and the canal itself seemed poised, absolutely immobile, as if in a photograph. The trees were still only hesitantly in leaf, but there was the first hint of a light that gave colour to the bricks and gables, rather than draining it away, as it seemed to in winter. A solitary walker crossed the bridge.

Posthumus's mind lighted again on the image he had managed to bring into focus before Cornelius had arrived at De Dolle Hond the night before: a man in a bowler hat, with a rolled umbrella, on a bridge in London. And on what the image, stashed away on the back shelves of his mind, stood for. Posthumus gave a grin. Anna sometimes said that the trivia, the odd moments, the scraps of information that he had stored away were his equivalent of any other man's garden shed: filled to bursting with boxes of things that might come in useful one day. And *this* one threw a little light on what could have happened to Ben Olssen.

Posthumus swung off his chair, took his breakfast things back to the kitchen, and went to the computer at his workspace under the spiral staircase. There was no need to try to dredge it all up himself. He tapped a few words into Google. That was it. Waterloo Bridge. Posthumus clicked open a website. Interesting. He scrolled down. *Very* interesting. He read on for a while, then turned off the computer, fetched his goatskin jacket, locked up the apartment, and descended the three flights of stairs to the street door. It wasn't far to the hotel, but he hated being late.

On the bridge outside, Posthumus leaned over to unlock his bicycle from the railings, and for a moment was pulled up short by the sight of his hands on the heavy metal U-bolt and keys: their backs no longer smooth, but like onionskin paper, with wrinkly bags around the knuckles of the long fingers. His *father's* hands. When the hell had *that* happened? He let out a short, plosive sigh, mounted the bike, and rode off down the side of the canal.

It took a little over ten minutes to cycle to the Hotel Estheréa, on the Singel canal. Posthumus was a good quarter of an hour early as he walked up the short flight of stairs from the street into the lobby. A couple of receptionists stood at a counter in front of an old-fashioned rack of room keys, each key with a heavy wooden tag. Posthumus glanced around the lobby-lounge. Lots of plush and pink. Patterns on every fabric, different paper on every wall, fake cherry blossom, real orchids and crystal chandeliers with frilly shades. Not quite Christina's style, he would have thought, but there was something tongue-in-cheek about it, curiously endearing – décor that careered towards kitsch, then made a last-minute dash for irony. He decided not to call up to the room, but to wait until nine, as they'd arranged. As he crossed to a sofa, he almost collided with Christina coming out of the lift. She looked displeased.

'You're early,' she said.

It sounded like a reprimand. Posthumus pulled back a little, his neck stiffened.

'I was going to wait before calling up to the room,' he said.

The words came out clipped, terser than he'd intended. Christina put a hand on his shoulder and gave him three pecks on the cheeks.

'Sorry, sorry, *sorry*,' she said. 'Bad night. And I'm feeling a bit off this morning.'

Posthumus walked with her to the reception desk, to hand in her key.

'You wouldn't happen to have an aspirin, would you?' Christina asked the receptionist. 'I seem to have run out.'

'Certainly, madam,' said the receptionist, bringing out a small first-aid box from under the counter. 'Can I get some water for you?'

'No need, I have a bottle.' Christina tapped her large

handbag. Not the Hester van Eeghen she'd had the first time Posthumus met her, but just as stylishly geometrical.

'We can take pretty much any tram from around the corner, then a seven will get us there,' said Posthumus.

'Good heavens no, I phoned last night to order a cab.'

'It's already waiting for you, madam.' The receptionist nodded to a short, square man standing patiently to one side.

'Let's go then,' said Christina, ushering Posthumus towards the door. She nodded curtly in response to the taxi driver's greeting as they passed him, and Posthumus checked the man knew their destination.

'Very distinctive décor,' said Posthumus as they walked out of the hotel. 'Sort of Old Amsterdam meets opera-set bordello.'

Christina laughed, and seemed to relax a little.

'My room is the same,' she said. 'It breaks every design rule in the book, but I *love* it. I'm on a WildCat budget, and they made the booking, otherwise I'd never have thought of staying in a place like this.' She paused at the foot of the hotel stairs, to allow the taxi driver to edge past them. 'Usually I top up the allowance and stay somewhere nice, but *everywhere* in town is full at the moment. But this is a delight, I'm really glad I ended up here.'

The driver was holding open the door of a black Mercedes, parked half up on the pavement to allow other cars to pass on the narrow road. It had taxi number plates, but no sign on top: a car from the sort of private-hire company that probably wasn't entirely within the WildCat budget either. Christina got in and slid to the other side of the back seat, reached into her bag for her water, and took the aspirin the receptionist had given her. Posthumus got in after her. Christina replaced the water bottle, pulled her handbag close to her side, and crossed one arm over her belly, leaning back against the head-rest, her eyes closed. She breathed out slowly.

'This must all be very upsetting for you,' said Posthumus, as the car pulled off.

'I just wish we knew what was wrong with him!' said Christina.

Posthumus held back on airing any of his own speculations. Best get to the hospital and find out for sure, rather than needlessly distress Christina. He resisted the impulse to reach over and give her a reassuring squeeze of the hand.

'OK if we go via Stadhouderskade?' said the driver to the rear-view mirror. 'It's further, but it will be quicker. The Dam is hell at the moment.'

'Fine,' said Posthumus, also to the mirror.

Christina straightened up and looked at Posthumus. 'I'm sorry,' she said. 'This whole Ben thing has completely thrown me, and I don't really know why. It's so silly. I mean, I was fond of Ben, back when we were all at Greenpeace. And intrigued about seeing him again after so long. But the fling we had together, well, it was just that. A fling. And it was ages ago.'

'While you were at Greenpeace?'

'No, later. But still some years back. A mad conference weekend in Venice, then a few more heady weeks. And yet here I am, I don't know, I just feel so . . .'

Posthumus looked at her. 'Unsettled?'

Christina turned her head away.

'It's really not surprising, you know, feeling like this. You're having to cope with something that's come completely out of the blue,' said Posthumus.

The driver hooted at a young couple walking in the middle of the narrow canal road as if it were a footpath, muttered something about 'Bloody tourists', and surged forward, narrowly missing a cyclist.

Posthumus flashed a look of annoyance into the rear-view mirror, and continued: 'We don't expect things like what's happened to Ben to happen to someone we know. And when they do, sometimes it reminds us of our own vulnerability.' He was wary of slipping into platitudes, or of echoing phrases he'd heard on the counselling course he'd had to take when joining the Funeral Team. He paused.

Christina glanced his way and gave a weak smile. 'And here you are, caught up in it all,' she said. 'It seems so bizarre, your ending up with Ben's coat.'

'Not really,' said Posthumus. 'It's not unusual. It goes with the job. I'm glad I could be of some help . . . in a way.' He felt himself colour a little.

'Things like this are *always* happening?' The smile grew. Christina raised her eyebrows and widened her eyes.

Posthumus shifted a little in his seat. She was mocking him, however gently. The driver skimmed through the last millisecond of an amber light, turning south on to the wide, busy Raadhuisstraat.

'It's a small place, Amsterdam,' said Posthumus, 'and we all live on top of each other. In many ways it's like a village. So, every now and again it happens that my clients are not complete strangers to me.'

'Doesn't that feel a bit like prying? Looking into their lives and all that?'

'It can feel a little like that,' said Posthumus. 'Like when I discovered that a neighbour, someone I didn't know but used to see at the market, had committed suicide and left a note to explain to whoever found him, but didn't want the rest of the world to know why.'

'That's happened? How gruesome.'

'As I said, it goes with the job. You learn what to keep quiet about, and what not.'

'Anne Frank House, just up there,' said the driver. 'Westerkerk, where Rembrandt is buried.' They were crossing

the Prinsengracht, passing the church with its towering stee-
ple topped by a gaudy yellow crown.

Posthumus and Christina stared at the back of the driver's
head. Was the man on some sort of Amsterdam-tour autopi-
lot? They glanced at each other, and ignored him, driving on
in silence over the bridge.

After a while, Posthumus spoke again. 'Last night you said
an odd thing,' he said. 'You said you thought Ben was trying
to warn you about something.'

Christina turned to look at him. He did not go on.

'Sharp memory,' said Christina. 'I guess that also goes with
the job.'

Posthumus acknowledged that with a small sideways nod.
'What did you mean "warn"?' he asked. 'About something
that might happen to *you*?'

'No, no, not at all,' said Christina. 'Perhaps warn is the
wrong word. It was more like Ben really *had* to tell me something. He was so insistent on meeting *then*, it had to be on
Tuesday night. At the time I didn't think it *so* odd.' She gave a
little downward grimace of the lips. 'I guess I'm a bit of an
egotist. I took his "I really have to see you" as flattering. But
now, with hindsight . . .' She looked out of the car window.

'But what was it, do you think, the urgency? What could it
have been about?' said Posthumus.

'I don't know, but I can't help blaming myself. All I can
think of is that he was trying to tell me about it, and that if I
had made it in time to meet him in the café as we arranged,
maybe this wouldn't have happened.'

'Don't go losing yourself down *that* slippery path,' said
Posthumus. They passed a tram stop, and Posthumus glanced
at the little crowd clustered beside the shelter. Would it have
happened anyway? Was whoever attacked Ben Olssen so
intent on doing so that Christina would not have stood in the

way? Or might have got dangerously in the way? The taxi crossed a busy junction, and turned left into the rush-hour traffic on the Nassaukade, the main feed-road around the edge of the historic centre.

'What does Ben do, exactly?' asked Posthumus.

'Now? He advises companies, countries even, on energy policy, I think. And is also something of a lobbyist. Gabi knows more, she's followed his career more closely. Last time I saw him, he was still with Shell.'

'From Greenpeace to Shell? That seems an odd career path.'

'Lots of people said he'd sold out. Ben's line was that he could encourage greener practices from inside the camp, by speaking the same language.'

'And had he? Sold out, I mean,' said Posthumus.

'It wasn't entirely empty talk, but most people didn't buy it, and some never forgave him,' said Christina. 'And in truth, he was doing it for the money. He said he was tired of trying to eke out a life on student-level wages.' She looked out of the car window again, one hand pressed to her cheek. 'Poor Ben,' she said.

'Do you think all this might have something to do with the conference?' asked Posthumus.

Christina shrugged slightly.

'Someone with a grudge, or a point to make?' Posthumus went on.

'I heard he was involved with fracking,' Christina said, facing him. 'Passions are running high about that.'

'Rijksmuseum,' announced the taxi driver as they passed.

'We are both familiar with the city landmarks, thank you,' said Christina, with such a sharp edge to her voice that the driver glanced at Posthumus in the rear-view mirror, and raised his eyebrows, as if in sympathy. Posthumus ignored him. Christina put her head back against the headrest, and closed her eyes. Her hands were spread flat against her thighs, fingers stiff and raised. Posthumus sat in silence. After a while, Christina relaxed a little, and gave Posthumus a rueful smile.

'This temper!' she said. 'My father used to call me his "little firebird".'

'I'm used to it,' said Posthumus. 'Been there before.'

It was true. Anna might be a good listener behind the bar at the Dolle Hond, but her temper and intolerance of fools were something of a family trait. Posthumus had learned to ride the outbursts early on in their time together.

Christina fell silent, and looked back out of the window.

'That time in Venice, it was . . . it was one of the best times of my life,' she said, eventually. She gave a half-laugh, half-sigh and turned again to Posthumus. 'God, listen to me. Cliché, or what? "In love in Venice and the best time of my life."'

'Still,' said Posthumus. 'Venice . . .'

'And then New York, it was a whirlwind!'

'He lives there?' said Posthumus. He remembered the US dialling code on the business card he'd found in Ben Olssen's coat.

'Now, yes. Not then. It was an extended business trip,' said Christina.

'He's American?' said Posthumus.

'Swedish, actually, but he's lived everywhere, speaks just about everything.'

'Including Dutch? That would be a novelty.'

Christina smiled. 'A little, I guess, from when he was working here. But you know how it is at a place like Greenpeace, everyone from all over the world, and English by default. Ben and I always spoke English together, so I'm just as much to blame. It's odd, you know, after so long in the UK, my Dutch feels like it's slipping away, almost as if it's become my second and not my first language. I often speak it at home with Daddy, even. Madness.'

Posthumus had noticed the occasional hesitancy in the way she spoke, the way she lapsed into English from time to time. They were nearing the hospital. Christina took out her phone and checked for messages. The journey from the hotel had been the longest stretch Posthumus had seen her not tap-tapping on a screen. He resolutely kept his own phone in his pocket.

'OLVG Hospital,' said the taxi driver, turning in to a small car park. He jammed on the brakes, throwing both Posthumus and Christina sharply forward against the front seats. An old woman using a wheeled walking frame had stepped out almost into the path of the car. The driver muttered something that sounded like 'Demented old bat'.

'*What* did you say?' said Christina, flaring suddenly, and pushing herself back into her seat. 'Did I hear right?' The driver said nothing, and gave Posthumus a sullen look through the rear-view mirror. 'Don't you *dare* use that as an insult,' said Christina. Her voice was quiet, each word frugally measured. 'Dementia is a *dreadful* disease.'

The driver turned and mumbled something to Posthumus, but Posthumus was looking carefully at Christina. There was a note of urgency in her voice. Of panic even. The old woman banged on the bonnet of the Mercedes, and walked slowly on. The driver rode on a few metres, and came to a more gentle halt. Posthumus reached for his wallet, and looked for the meter. There was none.

Christina waved the wallet away. 'I'm using them the whole week. I have an account,' she said, opening her door, and getting out, without another word to the taxi driver.

Posthumus walked with her up a long pathway to a double glass door. There they had to wait. It was an airlock-style security door, and a young man had just entered the interim chamber from the other side. Christina held her arms tightly around her and kicked at the ground impatiently. The doors slid open. Again a wait, in the chamber, before they were eventually released into the hospital lobby. To their left, just around a corner, was a large revolving door, clearly the main entrance.

'Can you believe it?' said Christina. 'That *idiot* driver!'

'I don't think they can drop off in front of the hospital,' said Posthumus.

'He could have told us,' said Christina. A long reception desk with a row of computers, only two of them manned, stood directly in front of them, but Christina stormed over to an information board opposite, skimmed it in a second and announced, 'First floor, in the Lichtstraat, wherever the hell that is. It had better bloody be in this building.'

She seemed all set to go straight up, but Posthumus walked over to the reception desk. Olssen was in Intensive Care, after all, and they were outside visiting hours. It would be best to announce themselves.

A plump girl, with too much make-up, dull eyes, and facial expressions she seemed to have learned from television, looked up at him from behind a computer.

'We're here to see Ben Olssen,' said Posthumus, and spelled the surname.

The girl tapped a few times on the keyboard. 'No visitors.'

'We have special permission,' said Posthumus. Christina had come up behind him.

A single tap. 'Impossible. He's in ICU.'

'If you could perhaps speak to them, I think you'll find we're expected,' said Posthumus.

The inside corners of the girl's eyebrows went up, and her lips simultaneously gave a slight downward curl. She did not touch the computer. 'Come back after three.'

'For Christ's *sake*, woman, just tell us how to get there!' said Christina.

Posthumus was aware that people at the espresso bar across the foyer were looking in their direction.

'I think I can help.' The voice came from behind them.

Posthumus turned round. It was DI de Boer. Posthumus greeted the detective, noting his faint look of surprise.

'Gabrielle Lanting couldn't make it,' said Posthumus. 'So I've come along.' He introduced Christina. She was looking a little embarrassed.

'I'm sorry,' she said to de Boer. 'It's been one of those mornings when small irritations pile up. Then the slightest thing can set me off. It's a girl thing.'

De Boer nodded. He flashed his police ID at the receptionist. 'This has been arranged,' he said, and without waiting for a response turned to Christina and Posthumus. 'This way,' he said, walking towards the lifts.

The receptionist said nothing, but looked as if she were about to roll her eyes the moment their backs were turned. Posthumus fell in alongside Christina and de Boer. Christina was already firing questions at the detective.

'The first thing I can tell you is that there is a very strong possibility that Mr Olssen will recover,' said de Boer. 'I feel confident that he will soon be well enough to give us a statement. We're following various lines of enquiry, and are hoping that he'll be able to shed some light on what happened.' He pushed the button to call the lift. 'I've just been on the phone to the toxicology lab.' He turned to Christina. 'You know that Ben Olssen was poisoned?' Christina shook her head. De Boer gave an approving glance to Posthumus, acknowledging his professional discretion. 'We'll probably find that he still has difficulty breathing and is under sedation,' de Boer went on, 'but I think we can safely say he is no longer in danger.'

'So it wasn't ricin,' said Posthumus, almost to himself.

For a moment the detective seemed to drop his guard. 'What makes you say that?' he asked, turning quickly to face Posthumus.

Posthumus mentioned the incident he had dredged up from the back of his mind that morning. Something from the Cold War years. All very cloak-and-dagger, like a spy thriller. Someone – a Russian agent, probably – had poisoned a Bulgarian dissident working for the BBC, one Georgi Markov, as he waited at a bus stop on Waterloo Bridge in London, in broad daylight, in the rush hour. The assailant had injected Markov with ricin, using a device hidden in an umbrella. Markov had developed an extremely high fever, and had breathing difficulties. Poisoned in public, and breathing difficulties: that's probably what had tweaked at his memory, set him off thinking of bowler hats and umbrellas, Posthumus explained. De Boer looked at him nonplussed. The lift doors pinged open, and the three of them stepped in. They were alone. De Boer pushed the button for the first floor.

'Sometimes, Mr Posthumus, your mind unsettles me,' he said. He looked Posthumus intently in the eye. 'The method was not dissimilar, though the poison involved was a neuro-toxin, an engineered version of the poison found in puffer fish.'

'That's *dreadful*,' said Christina, her face taut and pale.

The lift had arrived at the first floor. Christina walked out ahead of them.

'Not the *fugu*?' said Posthumus. The stories of dedicated gourmands who expired after eating the Japanese delicacy fascinated him. 'But that's usually fatal, isn't it?'

De Boer held the lift door back from closing, and for a moment did not move out. 'Not in a small dose. In this case, barely any TTX, as the toxin is called, has entered Mr Olssen's system, though the little that has may account for his semi-paralysis and breathing difficulties,' he said. He waited a moment, and then continued, speaking quietly to Posthumus. 'The toxin was injected into the side of Olssen's waist in a titanium pellet, which seems to have malfunctioned. It seems that Olssen was saved by his "love handles", as people call them. Apparently, burst fat cells closed the holes in the pellet and contained the poison. Luckily, a scan picked up the pellet, and it was removed before it could do further damage.'

The two men followed Christina to the small ICU reception desk, just to the right of the lift.

'Enough poison was released to knock him out pretty much instantaneously, or at least to weaken his muscles, and lower his heart rate dramatically,' de Boer went on. 'He collapsed, had trouble speaking, and seemed to be suffering from chest pains, which is why the ambulance team thought he was having a heart attack. But, as I say, although there is no antidote to TTX, he should, with care, be able to recover from the amount in his system. Isn't that right, sister?'

De Boer looked over to the nurse at Reception, who nodded, recognising him.

'We have every hope, Inspector,' she said. 'He still can't breathe without the ventilator, but he's getting a little stronger. We're trying him on NIV for a few hours.'

De Boer looked perplexed.

'Non-Invasive Ventilation,' said the nurse. 'Through a face mask, rather than tubes in his throat. It means he might be able to speak.'

Christina walked on, to a room with a glass wall through which Posthumus could see, on a bed among drip bags and computer screens, a handsome man in his thirties, lightly tanned and with a wave of brown hair spreading on to the pillow. Christina paused at the door for a moment, and then went in. De Boer and Posthumus moved to follow her.

'Sorry, only two at a time,' said the nurse.

Posthumus's eyes flicked from the nurse – friendlier than the downstairs receptionist, but just as firm – to Christina, standing at some distance from Ben's bed, as if immobilised.

'Someone she knows should be in there with her,' he said to de Boer.

The detective walked with him to the door of Ben's room. He opened it to let Posthumus through, turning to speak over his shoulder as he did so.

'If he's going to say anything, I want to be there,' he said to the nurse, 'and I'd like Mr Posthumus to accompany me.'

'I'm sorry, sir, but that's strictly—' said the nurse.

'Call someone, if you need to,' said de Boer, following Posthumus in.

The hiss and click of the ventilator, and intermittent peeps and pings filled the silence of the room. Ben Olssen lay frail, fragile, tubes running in and out of him, computers and glossy apparatus surrounding his bed like a bank of attendant mourners, his eyes closed.

'He looks so small, all this *machinery*,' said Christina, her voice barely audible. She stood just inside the door, as if Olssen's bed somehow emitted a force-field that repelled her.

'Everything's controlled automatically these days,' said de Boer. He spoke with reassuring warmth, but still Christina did not move.

'He . . . he doesn't look human, in among all that . . .' she said, but trailed off.

Posthumus put his hand lightly on the small of her back. 'Perhaps if you said something to him?' he said.

Christina shook her head. It looked as if she were blinking back tears.

'It might help,' said Posthumus.

Christina took a step forward and leaned towards the bed. She spoke softly in English. 'Ben? Ben? Are you OK?' she said. She straightened up again. 'God, just listen to me, what a ridiculous thing to say.'

Ben Olssen stirred slightly. He turned his head towards Christina, his eyes still closed. His hair was lighter than Posthumus had first thought, but damp on the pillow. Beads of sweat seemed to bubble up from his forehead and temples.

'Ben, oh Ben, I'm so sorry,' said Christina. 'So, *so* sorry. I should have been there.'

Ben's lips moved silently beneath the ventilator mask, as if he were practising a foreign word. Christina reached out and touched his hand with her fingertips.

'Rest,' she said. 'Don't even try to talk.'

Ben's head tossed on the pillow, in Christina's direction, as if trying to locate the source of her voice. His eyes flickered open, then shut again. An arm twitched, threatening to loosen a drip tube. An odd, plaintiff bleat came out of him. Too small a sound for a man. Christina drew back a little.

'I can't do this,' she said. She turned and spoke softly to Posthumus. 'I just can't see him like this. I'm sorry, I just can't. We shouldn't have disturbed him. It's unbearable.' She gripped Posthumus's forearm tightly and looked across at de Boer. 'It was a mistake coming here, I'm sorry. Can we just leave him be, *please*?' She glanced back at Posthumus, her eyes full, and walked hurriedly out of the room.

Ben tossed his head again at the sound of the door. Posthumus was about to follow Christina, but de Boer restrained him, and nodded back to the bed. Ben's lips were moving again. His voice came weakly from behind the mask. De Boer stepped towards the bed, and bent low.

'What is it, Ben?' said de Boer. 'What are you trying to say?'

The words were almost inaudible, at first just a soft ffff, then 'Felix', or so it sounded, then Ben appeared to make more of an effort: 'Far . . . fara.' Or maybe it was 'Farda'. Nothing more.

'*Fara,*' said de Boer, straightening up. 'It's part of what he's said earlier, that and some English-sounding name, "Humbert" or "Hubbard" or something, but it never makes any sense.' He turned to face Posthumus. 'I had someone at the Bureau listen to a recording. It's the Swedish word for "danger".'

'An espresso for me, thank you,' said de Boer to Posthumus.

'Just some water,' said Christina.

Ben had said nothing more before an irate nurse had returned with the ward doctor, and Posthumus and de Boer had left his room. Christina joined the two men again in the espresso bar downstairs. She had fastened her hair back, and freshened her make-up, but sat leaning against one of the tall, round tables without her usual straight back or hard edge of energy. Posthumus went up to the counter to order the drinks.

'Don't you have any leads *at all?*' Christina was saying as Posthumus returned.

'We've had almost nothing to go on until now,' said de Boer. 'We were hoping you and Ms Lanting could fill us in a little on who he is, what he does.'

'I'm sorry, I really don't know any more than what I've just told you,' said Christina. 'I wish I could be more helpful, but it's a while since I last saw him. Gabrielle should be able to help you more with what he was up to workwise, and as for family, as I say, I've a feeling both his parents are dead. There's a brother, I believe, in Sweden, but I don't think they're very close.'

'And he gave no intimation of why he wanted to see you on Tuesday?' said de Boer. 'Apart from the obvious, I mean.'

He gave Christina a smile. Posthumus placed the drinks carefully on the small tabletop, in between Christina's and de Boer's phones and a bright plastic object soliciting donations for Clini-Clowns.

Christina shook her head. 'He wouldn't say at all. Just that it *had* to be that night. But it was all texts, you know, short. We didn't actually speak.'

'And the last you heard from him was just after eight o'clock.'

'Agreeing to meet for lunch the next day, after I'd said I really wasn't going to make it that night.'

Christina tapped a few times on the phone in front of her.

'Eight seventeen exactly,' she said, swivelling the phone to face de Boer. Posthumus glanced at the screen as de Boer read. The last few texts were a succession of one-liners, all from Christina: 'Still up for lunch today?', 'Guess lunch is off. You that peeved?', 'Thought you desperate to meet? Talk to me!'

With a 'May I?', de Boer scrolled back through the corre-spondence, made a note of the number at the top of the screen, and slid the phone back across the table to Christina.

'I called once or twice, but it went straight to voicemail,' said Christina.

'I imagine this is the same phone that's on his business card,' said de Boer. 'In which case we've been trying that too. Sometimes thieves pick up, but so far no luck. And we're wait-ing for authorisation to run a trace on it, in case geolocation is activated. You never know.'

De Boer checked the time.

'I need to go,' he said, downing his coffee. He spoke again to Christina. 'As you've probably gathered, this is now an investigation of attempted murder. We need all we can get on Ben Olssen's background, so we're going to need statements from both you and Ms Lanting. You have my card?' Christina nodded. 'If you could come down to the Bureau as soon as possible. Meantime, if you could think of anything, *anything*, that might help explain this: people he might be involved with, organisations that might be antagonistic to him, something that might give us a link, that would help.'

Christina picked up her phone to check her diary. 'I don't know about Gabi,' she said, 'but I'm pretty busy with the conference from half past eleven onwards. I could do it now, though, if I could be back at the conference centre soon after eleven?' She looked across at de Boer.

'I'll give you a lift,' he said. 'One of my colleagues is contacting Ms Lanting.'

They both rose to go, taking their leave of Posthumus. Christina leaned over and squeezed his hand.

'Thanks for coming,' she said. 'And sorry I've been so off.' She said nothing about a taxi.

Posthumus shrugged lightly, and said goodbye. He gathered their empty cups to take to the bar. Then he went out to catch tram seven, back to fetch the bicycle he'd left locked outside Christina's hotel.

# 7

Tram seven, tram five, then a dwindling creep to a complete halt. Posthumus glanced at his watch: ten thirty. He craned his neck to look up the aisle through the front window. Tram after tram stretched in a line up the middle of Leidsestraat. Friday shoppers thronged in both directions on either side. Eventually somebody persuaded the driver to open the doors. Leidsestraat was pedestrianised, with even cyclists officially banned, so the driver's mumbling about rules and safety just didn't hold. Posthumus filed out with the others, and began to walk. It wasn't that far to the hotel: up to the end of the street, on to the northern side of the Singel canal and past the Spui.

As he reached the Spui, Posthumus saw the cause of the problem. A protest occupation was under way on the small separated patch of the square, almost a traffic island, in front of the Athenaeum bookshop. A tent had gone up beneath two banners bearing the slogans 'Don't Frack with Nature' and 'You Can't Drink Money'. A scraggly bunch of people, mostly young but with quite a few oldies among them, surrounded the tent, linking arms and chanting slogans. The slender, impish statue of a street urchin, *Het Lieverdje*, stood on his pedestal at the centre of it all, as he had during many a demonstration in the 1960s, this time with a placard reading 'Frack Off' thrust into the crook of one arm.

The protest, probably an offshoot of what was going on nearby at the Dam and in front of the Beurs, seemed light-hearted, rather in the spirit of the 1960s demos around *Het Lieverdje*: zany 'happenings' which heralded the counter-culture. But it seemed to have taken the police by surprise, and their response was heavy-handed. Officers in crash helmets, carrying shields, numbered almost as many as protesters; a few had dogs, and a riot van blocked the street. Posthumus stood aside as he heard the clip-clop of horses' hooves from behind, and a couple of mounted police pushed by. Suddenly, the protesters broke ranks. Groups of them ran off in different directions, causing a flurry as the police decided which to follow; then they stopped, and retreated to a single body again, around the tent, only to divide into other groups and rush off in different directions. The protesters whooped and cheered, like children playing a game; the police were stern-faced, taking it all very seriously.

Posthumus grinned. Some things didn't change. It seemed only yesterday that he was living in the squat, just a little further up the Spuistraat, playing much the same cat-and-mouse game with police. Sure the issues were serious, or at least some took them seriously, but you could be resolute about something and still have a sense of fun. What was going on here was about something beyond, or rather below, the issues, something more fundamental. It was about openness and rigidity, imagination and control, about the vision of youth and the grip of adulthood. Posthumus felt like giving a little whoop himself. How come he instinctively still always took the side of protesters against authority? Well ... perhaps not so much these days. He straightened his left arm and looked down at the middle-aged hand that had taken him by surprise earlier that morning. Look at him now. He touched the hair at his temples. Flecked with grey. People jostled against him, he felt the jab of an elbow in his back. The crowd in the street was getting thicker. The intensity of the moment's connection to his 1980s life was gone. The immediacy of the past dissolved into nostalgia. Posthumus moved to double back, away from the action, and across the bridge to the other side of the Singel canal, but the push of onlookers blocked his path.

Instead, he decided to make his way around the edge of the main part of the square, which was quieter than the patch around *Het Lieverdje*, and then on past his old squat on the Spuistraat, and down an alley to the bridge over the Singel where he'd locked his bike. He weaved through a couple of rows of onlookers, and round against the railings of the university admin buildings on to the square, where customerless stallholders from the Friday book market looked over at the demonstrators, bemused and perhaps a little nervous. Some had packed up – or, more likely, hadn't unpacked yet – and stood beside boxes of their wares. Posthumus nodded to one or two whom he knew by sight. He crossed the square around the top of the market, past a café terrace where people were sipping coffee, taking in the spectacle as if it were a theatre performance.

A sharp crack and a sound of crashing glass came from the direction of *Het Lieverdje*. Whoops and cheers instantly became yells. Louder, and more of them. And the world began to move. Fast. A surge outwards from *Het Lieverdje*, criss-crossing darts of booksellers and coffee drinkers, a charge back into the throng, and then, with a shellburst of louder shouting, a thundering on the cobbles as columns of police stormed down streets and alleys all round, converging on the square. In front of Posthumus, somebody stumbled, fell flat, picked himself up and ran off, blood already dribbling down his face.

'Piet! This way!'

Posthumus felt a hand grab his elbow, and yank him off the square, through a brown wooden door and into a short, dark tunnel. The door slammed behind them, and they emerged into a quiet garden courtyard. The Begijnhof. It was one of Posthumus's favourite parts of town. Even when the world outside swarmed with shoppers rather than exploded in full riot, the medieval courtyard, with its diminutive gabled cottages, grassy central green, and little church, was a haven of village-like calm. Today, the transition seemed surreal, like something from *Alice through the Looking-Glass*. Posthumus turned and blinked a few times at the man who had tugged him in.

'Prissy Piet! I *thought* it was you, sneaking around the outskirts and away!' said the man.

It was a good two decades since anyone had called Posthumus by that nickname. Gradually the figure before him edged into familiarity, as if he were slowly coming into focus.

'Bin-Bag!' said Posthumus.

He couldn't remember Bin-Bag's real name, if he'd ever known it. Bin-Bag had always been just Bin-Bag, named for the inventive sartorial measures he took against the rain.

'I'm sorry,' said Posthumus, 'but "Bin-Bag" is all . . .'

Bin-Bag laughed. 'It's Freddie, now, mostly,' he said. 'But there're a few around still call me Bin-Bag. From the old days.'

Posthumus wondered whether he had aged as visibly as Bin-Bag – Freddie – whose skin seemed cracked and hardened by cold nights, his hair faded and straggled.

'Freddie, then,' he said. 'Thanks for the rescue. Quick thinking.'

'Didn't want to see you all messed up,' said Freddie. He took a step back. 'So . . . Prissy Piet, still the snappy dresser.'

'Piet will do,' said Posthumus. 'Freddie.' He had never liked that nickname; he'd laughed along with it all right, but it hurt.

'Chill, chill!' said Freddie, giving Posthumus a soft punch on the shoulder.

The two men stood facing each other. Beyond the courtyard, the clash between police and demonstrators still raged.

'You part of it?' said Posthumus, indicating vaguely back down the tunnel.

'Not really. But there're a few of them staying with us, from Greece and Denmark and the like. I walked down for a look, then found Spuistraat blocked behind me by rozzers.'

'You still at the squat, then?'

'Yep, same place, same life,' said Freddie. 'You, last I heard, had gone a bit soft. Job with the council, and all.'

'You could say that,' said Posthumus.

No, not the 'same life' at all for him. Willem's death, and his own feelings of guilt about it, had knocked him into a different channel entirely: back to college, that first proper job, buying the apartment. But was that selling out, 'going soft'? Was Freddie sticking to principles, or simply in a state of stasis? The silence that had fallen extended a second or two too long beyond a natural pause.

'So . . .' said Posthumus, but couldn't take the sentence anywhere. Three tourists came out of the church, the only other people in the courtyard. Posthumus thought he heard an 'awesome': Americans, probably, here because the band of dissenters who became the Pilgrim Fathers once worshipped in the church. The tourists came towards Posthumus and Freddie, heading to the outer door.

'I wouldn't go out there, not yet,' said Freddie, in English.

His explanation of what was going on outside caused a flutter of panic.

'We could go out the top way, that will probably be OK,' said Posthumus. 'There's an exit on the other side of the court,' he added for the benefit of the tourists. 'It leads to an alley that will take you back to the main shopping street.'

'Where you off to?' said Freddie to Posthumus as they walked.

'My bike's on a bridge on the Singel,' said Posthumus.

'I'll walk with you.'

They shed the grateful group of tourists, and walked on back towards the Spuistraat, talking of the old squat days. The conversation was hesitant at first, feeling its way along a long-forgotten path, but, warmed by nostalgia, it was soon in easy, energetic stride: who was still around, and who had disappeared from view, did Piet remember the time that, and did Freddie know what had happened to ... and then what about the time Piet had handed the placard he was brandishing to an advancing policeman, and the policeman had automatically taken it with both hands, giving Piet the chance to scarper ...

An old favourite hangout, Bar Scruff, stood along the way. Well, almost along the way. And, after all, Posthumus owed Freddie a drink after Freddie's nifty thinking on the Spui, so why not?

'And, you never know, old Kees might be there,' said Freddie. 'He still goes in quite a lot.' They had been talking of Kees Hogeboom, patriarch of the squatters' movement back in their time. Kees was the one who knew the legal ins and outs, where the next empty property to squat could be found, what to do if things went wrong. And he was still going strong: the wise old man of political activism and the alternative scene.

'He's got to be in his seventies at least, eighties, even,' said Posthumus.

Kees was old enough to have been at the original happenings around *Het Lieverdje*; he had taken part in the student occupation of the university buildings in '69, and been at the heart of protests in the eighties, when what remained of the Jewish Quarter was being razed to make way for an opera house. He had also been a lodestone in Posthumus's own forays into that world. Kees was the one who had actually read the books they were all constantly citing, who instilled ideas, and nurtured young minds: a father-figure, whose commitment had never waned. Gabi still worshipped him, Posthumus knew. She said Kees had set her on her path, and kept her on it. And the old man was still making a mark, rapping on the windows of mainstream politics. Posthumus had read a piece on him – still living on his houseboat in the Amstel, white-haired now but as shaggy as ever – in a news-paper magazine in the run-up to Earth 2050. The twinge of nostalgia for his youth that Posthumus had felt earlier in the morning sharpened into a pang. Kees had been a rock, after Willem's death had set Posthumus completely adrift. He hadn't seen the old guy in ages.

But Kees was not in the bar. Posthumus looked around. It was years since he had been to Scruff. The place had changed, edged (hadn't they all, except a handful like Kees and Freddie) into conventionality. The graffiti that once covered the walls had become stylised murals, the old hotchpotch of furniture, salvaged from the street, was now carefully mismatched vintage. Yet the clientele hadn't quite followed the same trajec-tory, and gave the bar an atmosphere reminiscent of the scruffs and sundry stirrers who had inhabited it in the past. Freddie took a seat on a scuffed leather office chair, and Posthumus went to the bar to fetch drinks. When he returned, Freddie had got out a new iPad, and was gazing at the screen. Posthumus gave a soft chuckle. The way Freddie dressed had not changed a bit. Well, maybe the bin-bag had been aban-doned, but Posthumus could swear that the motley jumper Freddie had on was the same one he had been wearing for the past twenty years. Yet he was clearly on the cutting edge when it came to technology. Posthumus put down the drinks, and eased himself into a captain's bentwood chair. That's what came of living a life with younger people around you. Even Cornelius was kept on his technological toes by little Lukas.

'It's changed quite a bit in here,' said Posthumus as he sat down.

'Like the whole of bloody Amsterdam, becoming yuppie-fied,' said Freddie.

He waved a hand at the iPad, now flat on the table. Two heads moving on the screen. Posthumus recognised the face of the minister of housing, but couldn't hear the interview.

'Chip, chip, chipping away at controlled rents in the centre,' said Freddie. 'Soon there'll be no one left in Amsterdam but fat-cat expats and yuppies. And tourists. Up goes the "Visitors Only" sign; "Disneyland City, nice, neat and pretty". Amsterdam's becoming like friggin' Bruges or Venice.'

'Or even worse, like The Hague,' said Posthumus.

Freddie laughed. 'Fuck help us, no!' he said.

'But I guess it's where all the money is coming from, not just those big rents, but the companies that come here,' said Posthumus. 'There's a hell of a lot more money about, you've got to admit. Everyone's richer than they were back in our day.'

'Speak for yourself,' said Freddie. Posthumus looked hard at the iPad, and back to Freddie. 'OK, OK,' said Freddie. 'But still, what are these companies doing such wonders? Media, advertising, new technology. And who's driving them? Blokes that used to hang out with us, who came to Amsterdam from all over the world because it was rough, and cheap, and creative, and set you thinking, and because everyone else round you was doing the same. And where are people like that now, the ones who should be shaking things up and pushing things forward?' Freddie made a slicing gesture across the front of his throat. 'Gone,' he said. 'High rents.'

'That's not entirely true,' said Posthumus. 'I read all the time of kids barely out of college with new ideas, exciting start-ups, new ventures.'

'*Entrepreneurs*,' said Freddie, dropping out each syllable separately, with a sour twist. 'But the real guts is being pulled out. Amsterdam's getting ironed out nice and flat. Rich, smug, all the *same*. They just don't get it, do they, the politicians? They don't realise they're slashing the city's wrists, draining away what's always made it *live*.'

'I don't know,' said Posthumus. 'Amsterdammers are an unruly bunch, resistance is in our genes. We'll make our point, if they start to get too pushy.'

'Well, we're certainly making it this week,' said Freddie. 'And not just us, there're guys from all over the planet in town, making a point about a hell of a lot *more*. It's the best showing we've had in years.'

'Quite as international as Earth 2050 itself, by the looks of things,' said Posthumus.

'Well it's an international battle, these days, isn't it?' said Freddie. 'We're not fighting governments any more, but corporations, the big blokes with the money who really control the show, and they ain't got no borders, that lot. Do you know that if you ranked the world's top one hundred economic entities, forty of them would be corporations, not countries? Wal-Mart comes in ahead of Norway. And they've got governments stitched up, anyway, with their lobbyists and fat donations.'

Posthumus could hear the voice of Kees here, and prepared himself for the full exposition, but Freddie stopped in mid-flow.

'*Yes!*' he said, holding up one hand as if to stop Posthumus interrupting. 'Have a look at this.'

Freddie had been glancing back and forth at the iPad screen all the time they'd been speaking. Posthumus looked down just in time to catch a photo of a ravaged hotel room, as the screen cut to a presenter talking into a mike outside the RAI conference centre. Freddie tapped the screen to turn up the volume, and angled the iPad to give Posthumus a better view. Three speakers at Earth 2050, maybe four, had had their hotel rooms trashed over the past few days. The vandalism hadn't happened all at once, and the speakers were staying in different parts of town, so it was only at a panel session that morning, when they were all on the same platform, that the connection had been made.

'They're all evil bastards, fracking Führers,' said Freddie, with a little smile, and a sharp glance to Posthumus. 'This will shake them up a bit.'

'And the first you knew that this had happened to all of you was this morning?' the presenter was asking.

'Well, three of us for sure,' said the interviewee. 'The fourth speaker hasn't shown up, and we can't get hold of him.'

'Ben Olssen,' said another voice, as the screen flipped to pictures of the four panel speakers. 'I've been trying for days.'

'Ben Olssen!' said Posthumus. Freddie stared at him. 'He's a friend of Gabi's,' said Posthumus. 'And he's more than "shaken up a bit".'

Marty whipped the lump of stewing steak off the scales before the customer could properly focus on the flickering digits on the display screen.

'Four euros eighty,' he said, with a scowl up at the clock on the wall.

His bloody mother was late down again. Typical. It was gone half past twelve, she should have been down half an hour ago. He wanted his lunch. *And* the Kester cow would be in any minute, spewing gossip and bile as she did every bloody day at this time. She was *still* whingeing on about being banned from De Dolle Hond, and that was months ago now. Marty surprised the customer with a subterranean chuckle. And no bloody wonder. The thought of Irene Kester, more pissed than usual one night, landing herself in such hot water never ceased to amuse him. The idea of her roaming the city on bail, with a trial and a couple of years in the nick hanging over her head, delighted him even more. But he had no intention of having to listen to the old bint himself. Let alone the two of them: his mother, Blonde Pia (or so customers called her) and Battleship Irene yakking on all morning like a fucking soap opera. 'Blonde' ha ha. She hadn't had her own hair colour since she was six. It wasn't even her own *hair* any more, some days. As soon as she was down, he was off, whether she liked it or not.

Marty left the next customer standing, and clumped to the walk-in refrigerator at the back of the shop to fetch more steak. Yes, off. To one of those shops where he could get the underpass guy's phone unlocked. He patted the flat shape in his trouser pocket. The computer was still up in his room, in a bin-bag together with a brick he'd found in the yard. He'd meant to dump it in a canal last night, but what with dinner and those whiskies at Milord, he'd fallen asleep on the sofa. Then up before six this morning to see to the shop while his mother was still in bed snoring – like a wrinkled, dried-up orange lizard with her bright red talons poking out over the bedclothes. Marty took his time, kicked the fridge door closed behind him with his heel as he came out, and placed the meat in the vitrine, before glancing wordlessly at the customer he'd left waiting.

'Half a kilo of mince please,' she said. Her voice had an acid edge.

Marty ignored that. He covered his spread hand with a sheet of plastic from the roller, then plunged it in to the tray of mince. It had been one of his father's party tricks: to come up with the correct measure, to the nearest five grams. Just another of the things his mother went on about, another of the ways Marty would never measure up to Mr Perfect, Mr The-Man-Marty-Was-Not-And-Never-Would-Be. Marty thumped the mince on the scales with such violence that the customer started. Four hundred and thirty grams.

'That will be fine,' said the woman.

Marty wrapped the mince. He couldn't stop thinking of the bloke in the underpass. He hadn't done *anything* himself, not really. Just blocked his way, and taken the stuff. Whatever had happened to the bloke was nothing to do with *him*. Really. But still. Marty shifted from foot to foot and felt a shudder slide like an eel down his spine. Maybe he should put the phone in the bag with the computer after all.

'Two euros forty,' he said, pushing the mince across the top of the vitrine, and taking the money.

And the junkie? He hadn't seen him lying there. For an instant he again saw the junkie's startled face, heard the little cry of surprise at a coat that seemed to have dropped from heaven. Marty gave a wheezy chuckle as he handed back the customer's change. No danger there. The poor sod wouldn't have had a clue.

The shop was empty now. Marty came out from behind the counter and plodded across to the door. He looked out. The Kester woman was rounding the corner at the far end of the street. Marty reversed back through the door, and began to cross in front of the shop window to get to the intercom to call his mother from upstairs. He'd had enough of this. Soon he'd have enough money to get out of here, to rent a place of his own, and never have to work in this fucking place any more. Leave her to it. He would be out of here, all right. For ever.

'And it takes the *press* to tell us what is going on!'

Flip de Boer felt the exasperation in his voice tip into anger. Couldn't anyone just do their job, for once? Four speakers

from the same conference panel having their rooms vandalised, and the police taking almost as many days to tumble to
the fact.

'The incidents occurred separately, over the course of three
days,' said Hans, bristling to the defensive. 'One of them wasn't
even reported, the hotel came to some private compensation
agreement, wanted to keep the incident under wraps. Another
was out of town, in Zaandam, so not on our patch. No one, not
even the victims, made any links till this morning.'

Hans had a point there. And de Boer didn't want to piss
him off entirely. Hans was one of the few men at the IJ Tunnel
Bureau who wasn't trying to kick him in the balls. He softened
his tone.

'But we've been talking about Olssen and his room all day,'
he said. 'It's not as if other officers round here didn't know
about it. You'd think somebody's radar might have pipped as
reports started coming in from the other bureaux. Who's the
liaison officer for Earth 2050?'

'Ed Maartens,' said Hans.

De Boer said nothing. That made sense. Maartens was one
of the older men who had wanted de Boer's job.

'Well, I want the initial reports, photos of the rooms,
descriptions, all the details available. From now on all three
cases are in the Olssen file,' said de Boer. 'Hans, I want the
local bureaux to put someone on to providing protection for
each of those other delegates. They'll squeal like pigs that
they're overstretched, but tough shit. We don't want three
more Olssens.'

Hans nodded. He was standing up against the wall, near the
door of the incident room. The others were . . . well, de Boer
wouldn't quite say sprawled, but certainly sitting easy on
chairs around the room. He was pleased to see arses shift a
little, and backs straighten as his glance swept past.

'And I want those other delegates interviewed,' de Boer went on. He nodded the job towards a junior member of the team. 'We should warn them of a possible danger, and advise them to be vigilant. For the moment all they need to know is that Olssen appears to have been the subject of an assault. And I want more on his background. Schmidt, will you look into his conference schedule, his phone records, the works. And don't anyone give me any bullshit about this being Friday.' He had noted a fidget of discontent. 'You've got all afternoon.'

Did he really have to spell this out? De Boer looked around at the team he had managed to put together. Not the brightest bunnies in the Easter basket. Funny how the other DIs somehow always had the men he wanted already working on something. Still, he would make do with what he had. Getting the best out of them was part of the job, wasn't it?

'We've had bugger all to go on, but we're now actually getting somewhere,' he said. 'We're still waiting for the forensics report. Murat, can you see if there's a chance of speeding that up? End of the day if possible. These trashed rooms could well provide the lead we need. I want to know who vandalised them, and how they got in. The incidents were spread out, so could this have been an individual? Or is there a group behind it, some sort of anti-fracking movement? So: CCTV, checks on hotel staff, any links we can find. Hans, will you take on this side of the investigation?'

Hans looked pleased.

'We do know something already,' he said. 'All three delegates mention in the news reports that a sideways figure eight was sprayed on their room wall. You know, like the one in Olssen's room, that we've seen sprayed around town and thought might be a gang ID tag?'

'The infinity symbol,' said de Boer.

'Yes. Apparently it's being used to stand for sustainable energy, a sort of shorthand slogan, but doesn't belong to any specific organisation.'

'Good to know, thank you, Hans,' said de Boer. 'Further fuel for the anti-fracking idea.'

'There's more,' said Hans. 'The Albert Heijn loyalty card that was used in Olssen's room to keep the electrics going was registered to a Mrs Beatrix Orange, at number one the Dam.'

A quick curl of laughter went round the room. Some joker, registering as the queen, with the royal palace as an address. De Boer smiled.

'And that raises a question we should all be considering,' he said. 'If something links all this with Olssen, then what causes a step-up from playful protest, to vandalism, to attempted murder?'

He looked around the room. Blank faces. De Boer suppressed a sigh, and got down to the original business of the team meeting.

'First thing I can tell you is that Olssen appears to be out of danger,' he said. He filled the team in on what he'd learned at the hospital that morning. 'But that makes the case no less serious,' he said. 'We are still looking at attempted murder.'

He tapped his laptop to activate a projection on to the large screen behind him.

'So, what do we know about Ben Olssen?' he said, as an image of the hotel photocopy of Olssen's passport came on to the screen. 'Swedish. Resident in New York. A consultant of some sort, specialising in strategic planning with a company called Futura Consultants, working with large international clients and governments. He would appear to be involved in fracking deals. Know what that is?'

A couple of the officers looked blank.

'Getting oil and gas from shale rock. Google it. It's controversial, what a lot of the rumpus this week is about, and most likely central to the case. Olssen has had connections with some controversial fracking disputes in the US. I'm looking into that, ditto his travel record which at first glance throws up some odd places: Liberia, Uzbekistan, Belarus. Think about it.'

De Boer's glance ran round the room, clocking each pair of eyes.

'But, bear in mind that Olssen is a victim not a suspect,' he said. 'Although he is recovering, he is now sedated and still incoherent. We have a recording taken when he was first admitted, which amounts to little more than delirious babble, although according to van Rijn downstairs, he does appear to say the Swedish word *fara*, meaning "danger". He repeated this at the hospital this morning. We couldn't pick up much more from the recording, except possibly an English name, Hubert, Humbert or Hubbard, but a download of the whole thing is on file.'

De Boer held back from saying 'Listen to it'. He had to leave them some room for initiative.

'Olssen also appears to understand some Dutch,' he went on. 'The reason for that is that he lived in Amsterdam between 2000 and 2004, first as an intern with Greenpeace, and later working for Shell, a move that apparently lost him friends. We need to look into that, and to see if any of the old names come up among current anti-fracking activists. We do know of two people with whom Olssen does appear to have maintained contact, one Gabrielle Lanting, resident in Amsterdam and currently head of Green Alliance, and a visiting Earth 2050 delegate, Christina Walraven . . .'

De Boer heard a soft 'phwoar' from the other side of the room, and suppressed the murmur that followed it with a glance.

'Both women gave statements earlier today, which told us not much more than I've outlined now. As far as the women themselves go, we have no reason to regard either as a suspect, but we are running background checks, and have some idea from their statements . . .'

De Boer glanced across at Hans.

'Both Dutch, both from diplomat families. They knew each other as kids when their fathers were posted to London,' said Hans. 'Lanting's parents are now retired, and living in Castricum. We're looking into Green Alliance activities, but the organisation's pretty mainstream, there's no history of any dodgy activist involvement. Walraven's father currently lives in Brussels, she's clearly very close to him; the mother's deceased. There's old family money there. Walraven herself still lives in England, and works for WildCat, saving tigers, as a high-end PR. Celebrity parties, that sort of thing. All very much her scene. Again, lightweight, on the cuddly side of the environmental lobby.'

'Olssen had a date with Walraven on the night he was attacked,' said de Boer, 'but she was at a party with Lanting, and stood him up. Apparently, she was helping Lanting land a patron for Green Alliance, and they had to stay on longer than planned. She's let us see her phone and SMS records, which corroborate this. We should not neglect the fact that if she had not stayed on with Lanting at the cocktail party, Walraven may well have been with Olssen when he was attacked. At the OLVG this morning, Olssen was again mumbling *fara*, and he could have been trying to speak to Walraven, as she had only just left the room. Walraven dismisses any notion that she might be in danger, through her work or for any other reason, but she does say that she has a feeling that Olssen was agitated about something when he made contact. She says he sounded desperate to see her.'

This time de Boer let the male murmur in the room die of its own accord.

'The last communication she had from Olssen was a text sent at 20.17 on Tuesday evening,' he went on. 'Of course, anyone who had his phone could have sent that, and as you know the phone remains missing, as does everything else he may have had with him, bar the coat later discovered on the body of the junkie Frans Kemp. This is currently with forensics.'

De Boer tapped a photo of Ben Olssen's coat on to the screen.

'The coat is not uncommon, but it is distinctive, and people may remember it. Until such time as we can interview Olssen himself, we need to be looking into his activities earlier in the day, who he was in contact with, what he might be involved with that could have led to an attack,' he said. 'We're doing a deeper check on Futura Consultants, but we need to find out if Olssen met anyone else in Amsterdam. We should not dismiss the possibility that this could be criminal activity, and that even if he were to be interviewed, Olssen might not disclose the information. We ought also to look into whether Walraven herself might be in danger. I don't think it is likely, but I don't want to leave any stone unturned.'

De Boer glanced around the room.

'We do have some idea of Olssen's movements after he checked in to the hotel on Tuesday,' he said. 'We have a statement from a concierge at the Krasnapolsky, one Jonas Keizer, who says that Olssen spoke to him that afternoon, asking for recommendations for a café to meet someone close to Central Station later in the evening. That was for the date with Walraven, which was arranged for seven fifteen. Keizer recommended Café Eerste Klas, at the station itself, and Olssen then left the hotel. That was at about four o'clock. He was clearly back at the hotel some time later, because he left at seven, again speaking to Keizer, and this time asking if he could recommend a computer repair firm. A waiter at Eerste Klas who recognised Olssen from the passport photo, says he was waiting alone at the café for about an hour, from a quarter past seven until some time after eight. The waiter says he remembers Olssen because he seemed upset about something and was "quite a hunk".'

No murmur this time. De Boer tapped a few times on the keyboard, and grainy CCTV footage replaced the image of the coat on the screen behind him.

'CCTV cameras in the area behind the station were inoperative, but we do have this, from a distance, showing a man we now know to be Olssen going into the underpass, on the side where pedestrians are forbidden. I don't think there's much to gather from that. There is a narrow pavement on that side, and it's a pain to cross over four lanes of traffic to where you are allowed through. Though we could ask ourselves what Olssen was doing behind Central Station in the first place.'

Even enhanced by the techies, the image wasn't much help. You could barely recognise Olssen, though you could see that he was carrying a brown overcoat, and what appeared to be a laptop case.

'Here we most likely have our attacker,' said de Boer, indicating the figure in a black leather jacket, worn over a hoodie with the hood up, and with a bag over one shoulder, following Olssen into the tunnel, and leaving just over a minute later, walking fast back towards the station. 'But after this, we lose him, I think we can assume it's a him,' de Boer continued. 'Possibly this was a pre-arranged meeting in the underpass, or this man could, of course, simply have witnessed the attack and be getting the hell out of there, not wanting to be involved.

There are witness-request notices currently posted in the area.'

De Boer started a looped slide show of photos depicting the area behind Central Station, and the side of the underpass where Ben Olssen had been found.

'Unfortunately there is no coverage of the other end of the underpass, not for this part of it, anyway,' he went on. 'So, we don't know who came and went there. But the figure we see leaving the underpass does not appear to be carrying anything. Olssen was found without the coat, or any possessions. This brings us to the question of how the deceased junkie Frans Kemp ended up wearing Olssen's coat, and whether he was involved in the attack.'

'I think I have something there,' said the youngest officer in the group. 'I've been going through some of the other CCTV material that's come in, since you widened the scope and asked for footage from further around the underpass.' He held up a memory stick. 'I've got a couple of things on this,' he said.

De Boer indicated the laptop. Perhaps there was a bright bunny in the basket, after all.

'Thank you, Murat, go ahead,' he said.

Murat inserted the stick into the laptop, and tapped the keyboard a few times. A clear image of Frans Kemp, walking in the overcoat, came up on the large screen.

'Hang on a minute, wrong file,' said Murat. 'That's afterwards.' He paused the image.

'Where are we?' asked de Boer.

'On the blind side of the underpass, but a bit further along the side of the railway lines,' said Murat as he tapped. 'A little walkway behind the public library, at 20.40. There's no camera in the walkway, but there's one on each end. A bloke goes in one end, carrying the coat, then out the other, without it. Then a minute later, what you've just seen, Kemp in his glory. There you go, this is the other camera.'

He gave the keyboard a final tap. An image flashed on to the screen, of a large man, walking fast, with the overcoat over one arm, a laptop case awkwardly propped under the other, fumbling with both hands at a wallet as he went.

'Well, I'll be buggered!' said Hans. 'Look who we have here.'

'It's that fat butcher bloke! From the Lange Niezel!' came a voice from one of the other officers. 'You know, a couple of months back. We interviewed him about that fire at that café, you know, what's it called . . .'

De Boer stared at the screen. Yes, he did know. 'De Dolle Hond,' he said.

'That's it!' said the excited officer. 'We couldn't pin anything on him, but he was shifty as hell.'

Murat had flipped to the other file, and rewound, to show the fat man emerging from the walkway, still with the laptop case, but not the coat. It took only a few seconds for de Boer to remember the name.

'Jacobs. Martin Jacobs. Jacobs Butcher's,' he said.

De Boer laid an arm across Murat's back, grasped the top of the young man's shoulder, and gave it a firm shake. He looked across the room to Hans.

'Right,' he said, 'let's bring him in.'

# 8

Posthumus watched Freddie's motley jersey and fuzz of scraggy hair disappear down the street, in the direction of the squat. Freddie had known something about those trashed rooms, Posthumus was sure, probably from others at the squat. But he had seemed shocked to hear about the attack on Ben. Anxious, even. Conversation had faltered a little after that.

Posthumus made his way across to the bridge on the Singel to fetch his bike. Should he inform de Boer? Posthumus felt a tug of loyalties: his old life and the present, pulling in different directions. The detective would already know about the rooms, surely, and he was certain to make a link with the Earth 2050 demos, and possibly with the squat itself. De Boer would manage well enough.

Posthumus unlocked his bike and began to cycle up along the Singel. He needed something more than simply a feeling that Freddie had been waiting for that news report, before he went fingering people from his past to the police. But those other men could be in danger. The sight of Ben this morning had thrown him. The man was seriously sick. And scratching away at the back of Posthumus's mind were those uneasy thoughts of last night: that poison was an illogical weapon if you simply wanted to mug someone, that whoever had done that had wanted to leave Ben anonymous and senseless. Even dead. The junkie Frans Kemp didn't fit that role, whatever way he'd got his hands on Ben's coat. Nor, for all their passion and commitment, could Posthumus see the likes of Freddie and his mates going that far. Yet Ben was involved with fracking, even if only as some sort of adviser, at an international level. Feelings about that clearly ran high. There would be plenty of people from his old Amsterdam life who would not forgive him that. And Christina *had* said she thought he was trying to warn her about something. The bicycle jolted as it hit a bump in the paving stones. Posthumus gripped the handlebars tightly, and frowned. There was so much missing in all this. It was like opening a box of playing cards to find only ten or twelve inside.

Posthumus cycled on beside the canal, towards Central Station. It would be best to avoid the Dam, with all the Earth 2050 rumpus going on at the moment. He trundled over the uneven road. Drifts of papery-winged elm seeds were piled up against tree-trunks and the walls of buildings, and took flight in flurries with each gust of wind. A cloud of them rose around Posthumus as his cycle wheels churned through a mound that had gathered against a roadside skip. A moment of boyish glee surged through him, and he aimed for, rather than avoided, the next pile. The elephants at Artis Zoo went mad for the seeds, he'd been told. He ducked up a narrow alley, behind the heavy dome of the Lutheran Church. He'd cut through here to De Dolle Hond, and pick up Tina to take her to City Hall, earlier than he'd promised. Or, rather, he'd spend some time with Anna first. It would be good to speak to Anna – about Freddie, about this morning, about Ben, about everything. He pulled over, and reached for his phone. Perhaps she might even start opening up at last about Paul, and the fire. Anna's walls were still up, but he wanted to try to ease her out, to get her to talk about her own problems for once. They hadn't chatted properly in days. He missed that. After all these years they were still each other's 'significant other', even when there was somebody else in the picture. Perhaps that was the problem: it was often hard for anyone else to *be* in the picture. Anna still sometimes called him 'my ex', more than a decade after that had first held true.

Anna answered after a few rings. 'PP!'

'You home? I thought I might pick up some lunch, and come round,' said Posthumus.

'Lovely idea! Gabi's here,' said Anna.

Well, so much for the heart-to-heart.

'Where are you?' she asked.

'At the top end of the Singel, near the Lutheran Church,' said Posthumus. He heard the two women talking between themselves.

'Is Small World too much of a detour? Gabi says she loves their spicy salami.'

'No problem at all. Good choice,' said Posthumus. Aussie Sean at Small World had been supplying tour-de-force sandwiches since way back in the time when pretty much all you could get in Amsterdam was limp white bread with mayonnaise-clotted salad. 'I'll be with you in about half an hour,' he went on.

It took Posthumus less time than he thought to pick up lunch and get over to De Dolle Hond. It was just gone half past twelve when he propped up his heavy sit-up-and-beg bicycle against the café window. He picked the Small World bags out of the black milk-crate he had attached, Miss Marple-like, to the front of his bike, as Anna opened the door for him to come in.

'We're here in the café,' she said. 'Upstairs is a mess.'

It very often was. Possessions in Anna's apartment seemed subject to a centrifugal force, until the disorder reached a critical point, then, suddenly, as if the force were reversed, everything was sucked – in an hour or two's intense activity – back into cupboards, bags, files and boxes. Critical peak had clearly not yet been reached.

'Here you go,' said Posthumus, handing the bag over to Anna. 'One spicy salami with Emmental, one avocado with wasabi mayo and roasted veg, one meatloaf with honey mustard, and a beetroot and pear salad on rosemary focaccia, in case anyone is feeling adventurous.'

'We all know who *that* might be,' said Anna, with a grin. 'I'll put these on plates. We can't be seen with takeaways when I won't let customers do it.'

She disappeared into the small kitchen behind the bar: spanking new since the fire but still, despite Posthumus's offers of coming up with recipes and menus, barely used except as a turn-round for ready-made bar snacks.

There were only one or two other customers in the café. Simon, the casual help, was reading behind the bar. Posthumus nodded to him, and walked across to where Gabi was sitting beside the fireplace, sipping sparkling water, with a laptop open in front of her.

'This is a surprise,' he said, as he pecked her on the cheeks. 'I thought you'd be swanning about with your new celebrity, or back at the conference.'

Gabi laughed. 'I'm conference-free till the big general session at two, and our star is somewhere over the Atlantic by now,' she said. 'But the photo-shoot this morning was amazing. I felt quite the star myself, for my own little fifteen minutes.'

Posthumus sat down.

'You're busy?' he asked, with a glance at the laptop. 'You all right for a lunch break?'

'No, no, it's fine. I've just been down at the IJ Tunnel Bureau, giving my statement about Ben, and sneaked in here to use

Anna's WiFi,' she said. 'It was easier than going all the way over to the office, and then back to the conference; thanks, by the way, for this morning.'

Gabi reached over and gave Posthumus's forearm a squeeze.

'Christina doesn't really do gratitude, I know, but I'm sure she appreciated it,' she said. 'We've just bumped into each other, giving statements. She told me how bad Ben looked.'

Gabi's laptop gave a ping.

'I'm sorry, I'm going to have to check this quickly,' she said. 'It's the final draft of the press release with our big announcement.'

'You should have a word with Merel, maybe she could swing some sort of a feature or interview,' said Posthumus. His niece was currently flavour-of-the-month at her newspaper, following a couple of high-profile pieces. But Posthumus could see that Gabi was only half listening.

'Niels has been such a star, he's sorted the whole thing, two steps ahead of me all the time,' she said. 'He's already whisked up a storm on social media, and has all sorts of stuff happening online that I can never quite get the hang of.'

Posthumus was silent. He hadn't really taken to Gabi's pushy young assistant. But maybe it was true, what Merel said about being part of the dying throes of print media and paid journalism. Whatever Niels was up to was no doubt having more effect in an instant than any feature Merel could ever write. Posthumus looked up as Anna came back with the lunch.

'I've cut everything in half, so we can mix and match if we like,' said Anna. 'Something to drink, PP?' She sniffed the air as she leaned over Posthumus to put the plates on the table. 'As it would appear you've already started,' she said.

Posthumus smiled. 'A beer, I think,' he said, turning to catch Simon's eye.

'*Beer?*' said Anna. Her look of surprise was genuine.

'I do *sometimes*,' said Posthumus.

He told them of his chance encounter earlier that morning.

'Bin-Bag!' said Anna. 'Now there's a name I haven't heard in a long time.'

'Well, it's Freddie now, apparently,' said Posthumus. 'But it was good to catch up after so long. We had a couple of drinks in Scruff, for old times' sake. Freddie thought we might bump in to old Kees, but he wasn't there.'

Gabi's face softened, and she shut down her computer.

'Kees was probably holding forth from the floor, at the Oil or Water panel session that I was supposed to be sitting on this morning,' she said, smiling and taking a sip of her drink. 'I should really get over to see the old man, I haven't done so for ages.' She took her laptop from the table, and propped it against a leg of her chair. 'And someone ought to tell him about Ben,' she said. 'Kees always had a soft spot for Ben, he'll want to visit.'

'How does Kees know Ben?' Posthumus asked. His hand hovered over the sandwich he was about to pick up. A twinge of unease prickled through him. 'Did Ben used to hang out at the squat?' Freddie hadn't said a thing about knowing or recognising Ben.

'No, no, they met through Greenpeace when Ben was working with me. They enjoyed each other's argumentative streak, I think. Ben always rather looked up to him, called him the Guv'nor,' said Gabi. 'And Kees was really around for him when Ben was grappling about whether to go to Shell or not. He said Kees was the only one who really understood what he was on about.'

She put one half of a spicy salami roll on her plate. Simon came over with the beer. Posthumus toyed with the glass, but did not drink.

'It all ended a bit oddly with Freddie,' he said. He told them about the trashed rooms.

'But that's *terrible*,' said Gabi. 'The police didn't say anything about that. Do they know who did it? Have the other three also been attacked?'

'It seems not,' said Posthumus. 'But something's going on, clearly. You haven't heard anything? On the grapevine, I mean, people talking about upping the ante.'

'Not a thing, but then I'm pretty out of the loop these days, as far as that sort of activism goes. I could ask some of the younger ones at the office, but most of us see that sort of behaviour as actually harming the cause.'

'Well, they'd better not try anything like that next door,' said Anna, through a mouthful of meatloaf. She put down her sandwich and narrowed her eyes at Posthumus. 'You're up to your old tricks again, aren't you?' she said.

Posthumus hesitated. His inability to let loose pieces lie scattered, his need to make sense, to make a story out of scraps that didn't quite seem to fit together, had caused one of the biggest fallings-out they had ever had, after young Zig had been killed some months back, in the guest-house next door. He looked hard at Anna. But her eyes were shining, and a slight crinkling into crow's feet preluded a smile. In the end, he had redeemed himself.

'Something Christina said has been eating at me,' he said to Gabi. Out of the corner of his eye, he detected Anna give a resigned sigh, then he felt her fingers run briefly through his hair. 'She said that when Ben contacted her, she felt that he was trying to warn her of something, or at least that he had something urgent to tell her. She hasn't said anything more to you perhaps, about that?'

Gabi shook her head.

'Have you any idea what that might have been about?' said Posthumus. 'Who might have it in for Ben?'

'Well, it has to be something to do with fracking, doesn't it?'

said Gabi. 'Given what's happened. But from what I've heard about Ben, he's not entirely in support. He takes a more holistic approach: fracking as a stepping stone, rather than a solution; buying time until we can integrate more sustainable energy sources, rather than a miraculous cure for dwindling oil supplies.'

'People are always exaggerating the figures to support their own arguments about that, if you ask me,' said Anna.

'Well, I think it's water, not oil, that's going to be the next big issue, anyway,' said Gabi. 'But that's beside the point. The point about Ben is that he was the odd one out on that fracking panel this morning, he's not on either side.'

'So potentially an enemy of both,' said Posthumus.

'But enough for him to be nearly killed?' said Anna.

Posthumus pulled his chair closer to the table. He couldn't get the image of Ben at the hospital out of his head. Sweat-drenched, fevered Ben seeming to want to talk to Christina, muttering '*fara*', the word de Boer said meant 'danger'.

'Is there something Christina's not letting on about, perhaps?' he said. 'Or could she be in danger herself for some reason, and too scared to say?'

'I can't think of any reason for her to be in danger,' said Gabi. 'I mean, she's not involved in that sort of thing at all. Even with the tigers, what Christina does is pretty vanilla. Events, parties, the social side. She'd hate me saying this, have a real go at me for putting her down, but really, it's just window-dressing. She talks the talk brilliantly, but she's here for the networking. She only decided to come at the last minute.'

'And she doesn't seem jumpy, or upset about anything?' said Posthumus.

Gabi was quiet for a moment.

'It's true, she hasn't really been herself, these past few days,' she said. 'Not that you'd notice, Chrissie has always been good at putting up a front, but I have been worried. I don't think that's anything to do with Ben, though. It started before that, ever since she's been here. I get the idea it's about her father. They've always been so close.'

'He's some sort of diplomat, isn't he?' said Anna.

'More of a lobbyist, these days,' said Gabi. 'But it's not to do with work. I think he's ill, but Christina just clams up about it when I mention it.'

Posthumus touched the tips of his fingers together. Christina's outburst about dementia in the taxi that morning had struck a chord.

'But she's said nothing about feeling in danger herself?' he said.

'If anything, she *blames* herself for what happened,' said Gabi.

'Yes, I picked up on a bit of that this morning,' said Posthumus.

'How, blames herself?' said Anna.

'Because she wasn't back from the party in time, and if she had been, then maybe it wouldn't have happened,' said Gabi. 'She says if she hadn't insisted that we be good green girls and take the train that night, we wouldn't have taken so long to get back after we'd stayed on late.'

'Self-flagellating crap,' said Anna. 'Tell her not to be such a drama queen.'

Posthumus smiled. The owner of De Dolle Hond's reputation as the doyenne of tough love was well earned.

'Well, anyway, after she made the intros, she only stayed on to support me, to help make it all happen. So, really, if anyone is to blame for that, it's me,' said Gabi.

'That's total nonsense, both of you, and you know it,' said Anna.

There was a rapping on the café window from outside. Posthumus turned around, and saw Tina, staring in through cupped hands. She grinned, and gave a wave.

'Honestly, that girl. She could come in, rather than bang on the window like a street urchin,' said Anna. 'How you convinced me to keep her on, I don't know.'

'Oh come on, she's doing wonders next door, you have to admit,' said Posthumus. He circled a hand over their nearly finished lunch, and signalled 'five minutes' to Tina.

'The poor little thing can't even get down to City Hall on her own to register with the council,' said Anna to Gabi.

'Some people need a few more stepping stones out of the mire than others,' said Posthumus.

'He mollycoddles her,' said Anna, but there was a softer note to her voice.

Gabi leapt up. 'My God, it's almost a quarter past one,' she said. 'I ought to be going, too. I said I'd meet Christina before the main session this afternoon, so that we could go in together.'

She slipped her laptop into her briefcase, and said a hurried goodbye.

'Perhaps ask her again if she has any idea who might have it in for Ben,' said Posthumus, as Gabi was leaving. 'Now that this room-trashing thing has come out.'

'*Honestly*, this man!' said Anna. She gave Posthumus a playful slap on the back of the head, and began clearing away the remnants of their lunch.

Posthumus got up to go. 'Need any help?' he said.

'No, you get going,' said Anna, picking up Posthumus's still-full glass. 'You haven't touched your beer!'

'The mood left me somehow,' said Posthumus.

He gave Anna a peck on the cheek, and walked towards the door.

Outside, Tina was still standing beside his bicycle, stamping her feet for warmth. There was a sound of police sirens from over near the Beurs, and a bit of a flurry among pedestrians at

the end of the street. Probably something going on down at
the Occupy camp.

'We'd better go down the Zeedijk, instead,' said Posthumus.
'You got a bike?'

Tina shook her head. 'I can ride on the back of yours,' she
said. 'Like you're taking me to school.'

Posthumus reached into his pocket for his keys. Crazy kid.
He might have expected she wouldn't have a bicycle.

'All right,' he said. 'Come on.'

He began to cycle slowly towards the Zeedijk. Tina tripped
along beside him, then gave a little jump to sit side-saddle on the
back carrier. She was as light as a bird. It was years since Posthumus had done this. Anna's weight had always caused a notable jolt
as she got on, a straining of the thighs. He hardly noticed Tina
there at all. She giggled and clutched his jacket on either side.

'I never done this,' she said. 'I ain't never really had a dad.'

They passed Mrs Ting on her way to De Dolle Hond, later
than usual, clutching her cotton bag of coins for the fruit
machine. She gave them an enormous smile.

'Right, Jacobs Butcher's. You know the place?' said de Boer to
Hans, getting into the passenger seat of an unmarked car. It
was more statement than question. It was Hans he had sent to
question Marty Jacobs, a few months back, about the fire at
De Dolle Hond.

'And I remember the man,' said Hans. 'Sullen bugger, bit of
a Dumbo. It was like talking to a teenager.'

He pulled fast out of the IJ Tunnel Bureau car park, and
turned hard right, up towards the tunnel entrance.

'So, not the sort to pull off an elaborate poisoning?' said de
Boer.

Hans shrugged, and made a left at the entrance to the
tunnel, along the docks towards Central Station.

'Let's see what the fat boy has to say for himself,' he said.

'A DNA match off the coat would help,' said de Boer. 'There's sure to be something. My guess is that he was dumping it, and the junkie struck lucky. But we need to push him a bit on that.'

Hans reached through the window to put the blue light on the roof, and switched it on. He shot an envious glance at a marked car that sped past in the other direction, all lights and sirens. De Boer could see Hans relished the driving.

'Go easy on the siren as we get there,' said de Boer. 'We don't want him doing a runner.'

De Boer skimmed through his notes from the Dolle Hond fire case as they went. That name again. Pieter Posthumus. Was there anywhere he didn't get to? One or two steps ahead of them all. But in the heat of everything else going on at the time, with the Zig Zagorodnii murder, de Boer had forgotten about this instance.

'From back then,' he said to Hans. 'You remember a man called Pieter Posthumus?'

De Boer had not mentioned Posthumus personally, in connection with the overcoat and the dead junkie.

Hans made the 'puk puk puk' sound of an old hen. 'That meddler from the Burials Department? He's got quite the reputation for pushing his nose in,' he said.

De Boer frowned, and continued. 'I'd forgotten that he'd told me that this Jacobs character had threatened him in the street,' he said. 'Apparently he warned Posthumus that he had "powerful friends".'

De Boer gripped the armrest as Hans performed a sudden U-turn, across the busy junction just before Central Station.

'What the hell?'

'I hadn't thought about all the demos around the Beurs,' said Hans. 'We'd better go round the back way.'

He bumped across a bicycle path, and up the narrow road past the Schreierstoren, along a canal. De Boer's phone rang. He answered, listened, then closed the call with a curt, 'Thank you. Get him to phone me as soon as he knows.'

For a moment de Boer was silent, then he turned to Hans, his face hard set.

'That was the hospital,' he said. 'Ben Olssen died twenty minutes ago.' He flipped his phone over between his fingers. 'This is now a murder enquiry.'

'*Jeez*,' said Hans, making a turn to weave through the alleys towards Jacobs Butcher's. 'I thought Olssen was supposed to be out of danger.'

'The consultant is looking into it now, he's getting back to me.'

Hans's foot hit the brakes. The way up ahead was blocked: a thick crowd of people, blue flashing lights, police cars everywhere.

'What the fuck . . .'

'Afternoon, sir,' said a young officer de Boer recognised from the Beursstraat Bureau. 'That was quick. We've only just radioed your lot.'

De Boer ducked under the crime-scene tape that was stretched across the road, and strode up to Jacobs Butcher's, Hans close behind him.

Marty Jacobs, or what was left of him, lay sprawled on his back, all over the meat in a shattered vitrine. The shop window was in fragments. The top corner of Jacobs's skull was blown away. Blood and brains mingled with animal kidneys in a shallow tray. More blood from the mouth, which sagged beneath a peppery blond moustache, and in a diagonal of darkening blots, across the chest and into the guts. The body was twisted, feet still turned towards the window, torso stretched across the vitrine shelf. One hand gripped into a bowl of mince, as if for support, meat oozing between fat, sausage fingers. De Boer swallowed and cleared his throat, as he felt his bile rise. Behind him, Hans let out a quiet 'Jesus!' From the far corner of the room, a woman sitting on the floor let out an animal howl, ending in a contralto waver. De Boer recognised Irene Kester, from the fire at De Dolle Hond. A policewoman was trying to calm her. Beside her stood a scrawny woman, late fifties, blonde, too much make-up, raisined by sunbed tans, stock-still and silent. Her lips were pursed in a lemon-sucking pout. She stared directly out, through the broken window at de Boer.

'The mother,' said Hans, into de Boer's ear.

'Irene, shut the fuck up,' said the woman, loud enough for de Boer to hear, keeping eye contact.

'Bit of a mouth on her,' said de Boer, turning away from her gaze to speak to Hans.

'You don't know who she is?' said Hans. 'Before your time, I guess. Pia Jacobs. Married Dirk Jacobs, small-time hood here in De Wallen. He was liquidated some time back in the eighties.'

De Boer looked towards the butcher's. Out of a door to one side of the shop, probably leading to an upstairs apartment, came Bas, from the Beursstraat Bureau. He stepped through the window frame.

'Flip! I didn't expect anyone so soon,' he said to de Boer. 'I was hoping they'd send you.'

'And I didn't expect to see *this*,' said de Boer. 'We were here to ask Jacobs a few questions. But it looks as if someone just robbed me of a murder suspect.' Bas raised his eyebrows; de Boer turned to Hans. 'Get on to the Bureau, tell them we're here already. And that this is part of our case.'

'Drive-by shooting,' said Bas, while Hans rang. 'Two men on a motorbike. Hit him through the window, then straight off. North, we think, through the tunnel. We're still looking.'

Helicopters churned overhead as they spoke.

'Forensics?' said de Boer.

'On the way.'

'Hans has told me about the mother,' said de Boer. 'Apartment above the shop?'

Bas nodded.

'And the Kester woman?' said de Boer.

'Regular customer, family friend, witness,' said Bas. 'At least, she saw it from the end of the street.'

'All sorted at the Bureau,' said Hans, putting away his phone.

'Come on, then,' said de Boer.

The three men stepped into the shop. Irene Kester immediately let forth a torrent about motorbikes, men, noise, blood and her weak heart. Pia Jacobs remained immobile, glaring at de Boer and Hans.

'I think we'll all be more comfortable upstairs,' said de Boer.

He nodded to the policewoman, who helped Irene Kester to her feet and towards the apartment door. Pia Jacobs followed, taking a cigarette from the pack she had clutched in one hand. She paused as she passed the men, facing them, as if waiting for one of them to step forward with a match. De Boer felt for his lighter. Hans did not budge. She fixed her gaze on him and he held it. He leaned forward, chin up.

'You know who did this, don't you, Pia Jacobs?' he said.

# 9

Tina's registration was accomplished fairly swiftly, and was all over by a quarter past two. Two pale young women – girls, really – who had greeted Tina as they came in, were still sitting waiting for their number to be called as Posthumus and Tina left. One of them made a remark as they passed. Posthumus missed it, but he felt Tina tense. Two figures from her past, he guessed, from before she had found haven in the guest-house. Posthumus shook free the shudder that snared at the top of his spine, as he recalled the warren of corridors where he'd gone searching for her one night, back at the time of Zig's death. Tina was looking up at him: apprising him like a bird deciding whether to take flight.

'You ain't never done that, have you?' she said, as they emerged from City Hall into the flea market that spread beside it. 'I mean, like with . . .'

Posthumus knew what she meant. He shook his head. Tina was still looking him intently, seeming suddenly decades older than she really was.

'No, no, you wouldn't have,' she said, almost to herself.

She gave a sage nod. Posthumus felt a surge of protective anger against the men, the succession of men, who had violated her, and for a moment sensed himself capable of murder.

'It doesn't ever have to be like that again,' he said. 'You know that. Anna and I will make sure of it.'

They formed an odd, involuntary family, the three of them. Tina looked a little sceptical at the mention of Anna's name, but Anna was coming round. Posthumus held Tina's gaze until she nodded.

'It ain't never really going to go away, though, is it?' said Tina.

It couldn't be easy for her, living on the edge of the red-light district, seeing people who knew her, day in and day out.

'What has happened to us never really does go away, does it?' said Posthumus. 'It will always be there, I know. Our past is part of us, and part of the future, but it's up to us how we make it fit, don't you think?'

Listen to him! He would do well to heed his own advice. Tina shrugged, but she gave him a half-smile.

'It's a bit like what you was teaching me, you know, when you was trying to help me remember the night Zig died,' she said. 'Those memory things you did with your dad, but the other way round.'

Posthumus smiled. 'I suppose it is,' he said. He had taught Tina one of the memory games he'd taught his father, when a viral infection had been ravaging his father's brain, eating away his past, his very concept of himself. 'What we remember and how we forget, both take a little bit of effort, and both are important, you're right,' he said.

They had reached the rack where he had locked his bike.

'Thank you, Mr P. For coming today, and everything,' said Tina.

Posthumus glanced at his watch. It was not yet half past two.

'You don't have to come back with me,' said Tina. 'I'm OK now.'

'I'll come as far as the Nieuwmarkt,' said Posthumus. 'I want to pick up some things for dinner at the market.'

With any luck he might find some early morel mushrooms: market, a bracing swim at the Zuiderbad, and then a perfect morel risotto. With a little quail, maybe? Perhaps Merel was at a loose end, and would like to drop round. They could talk more about Anna's party. Or maybe he'd even dig out some of the old crowd and make a night of it? Meeting up with Freddie had sparked a wish to see some of them again. Posthumus reached for his keys. His phone rang, and he fished that out of his pocket instead. His heart sank as he looked at the screen: Sulung.

'Sorry, I'm going to have to take this,' he said to Tina. 'It's work.'

Any thought of a leisurely afternoon dissolved, even before he'd answered. Tina mouthed a goodbye, and gave a little wave.

'Sulung. What's up?' said Posthumus.

'It's impossible here!' said Sulung. Posthumus sensed an edge of panic in his voice. 'Maya called in sick this morning, Alex has one of her college days off, the temp didn't come in to replace her, the phone hasn't stopped ringing, I'm supposed to go and collect Mrs Dam's ashes, and now the Barendse head has come in!'

'OK, OK, OK,' said Posthumus, trying to suppress a smile as he spoke. The idea of Sulung in a flap, with a human head on his desk, seemed suddenly irresistibly comic. It wasn't there of course, not in reality. The decapitated corpse of Dirk Barendse had been found some months back, in a burned-out apartment. The case had made headlines. When the police investigators released the body to the department before the head, Posthumus had negotiated the mortuary storage fee down from ninety to seventy-five euros per day, and had then persuaded the police to foot the still hefty bill that would build up until the parts could be reunited, and the funeral go ahead. That time had clearly come, but it called for some odd paperwork, which had probably been the last drop that caused Sulung's bucket to overflow on an unmanageable day. Sulung – yet another person trying to build some sort of a future with the broken bricks of the past.

'I'm just around the corner,' said Posthumus. 'I can be there in a few minutes.'

It didn't take long to dig out the Barendse file, and guide Sulung into what he had to do. Posthumus offered to scatter Mrs Dam's ashes himself, as her niece in Canada had asked them to. In his inbox was an email from Alex, headed 'Surprise'. He had forgotten that she'd come into the office with good news just before he'd left with Sulung the previous afternoon, but had said the news could wait.

'That's brilliant!' Posthumus said, as he read. 'Alex has landed some funding for the poetry fee!'

'He's upstairs,' said Sulung, not appearing especially bowled over.

'Who, Cornelius?' said Posthumus.

'Talking to the director,' said Sulung.

'Just finished actually.'

Posthumus turned in the direction of the voice. Cornelius was at the door.

'Excellent news!' said Posthumus. 'Congratulations.'

'A heaven-sent shower of munificence,' said Cornelius. 'Though it's all down to Alex, from what I hear. And there may be even more coming from the LIRA Fund.'

'So, secure for a good few months yet,' said Posthumus.

'Possibly more, according to Him Upstairs, as I believe your honourable director is known.'

Posthumus was relieved: Cornelius didn't know what a close call it had been, with all the cutbacks.

'I thought *you*, dear Charon, had the day off,' said Cornelius.

'Me too,' said Posthumus. 'But I dropped in to help out with a couple of things. Do you feel like a coffee somewhere? I'm nearly done here, then I'll be going off to De Nieuwe Ooster to pick up some ashes.'

'De Nieuwe Ooster? Not the gentle Mrs Dam?' said Cornelius. He began to recite the poem he had written for her funeral.

'That's the one,' said Posthumus.

'I'll come along, too,' said Cornelius. 'I rather took to the old dear. And you'd be doing me a favour. Could you drop me off afterwards at one of those smart new high-rise blocks along the Amstel? Lukas is at a birthday party, and they want a little contribution to the revels.'

Posthumus could guess what that was. On more than one occasion, Cornelius had astonished clientele at De Dolle Hond, and exploded his stuffy image, with hilarious extempore rhyme and rap.

'Of course,' said Posthumus. 'We have an interesting new arrival for you, by the way. A little different from the norm.'

He indicated the Barendse file. While Cornelius read, Posthumus helped Sulung with a few of the other tasks that had spun out of his control that morning: all jobs Sulung would have coped with easily before his wife died. Then he signed out the department car keys, and went downstairs with Cornelius.

They had just reached Reception, when Posthumus heard Sulung run out of the office on to the landing.

'Pieter, Pieter, phone call for you!'

Posthumus's shoulders slumped. Perhaps he could slip out quietly.

'It's DI de Boer.'

'I'll take it down here, can you transfer it?' said Posthumus. Alex's Allure seemed to enfold the Reception phone handset. The Chanel scent stood in stark contrast to the voice that Posthumus heard click through from the phone upstairs.

'Mr Posthumus, I'm afraid I have bad news.'

'Ben Olssen?'

The detective didn't have to say. Posthumus felt it in his gut.

'He died earlier this afternoon. Something appears to have gone wrong with his ventilator. I'm at the hospital now, still trying to get to the bottom of it; it doesn't seem entirely straightforward. But I thought Ms Lanting and Ms Walraven should know. I've not been able to get through to either of them, and didn't want to leave a message with Ms Lanting's assistant. You don't know where they are, do you?'

'I believe they're in session at the Earth 2050 conference,' said Posthumus. 'It'll probably be going on a while.'

'That's what I thought.' The detective hesitated. 'I have my fingers on a few too many buttons at the moment,' he said. 'I'm not sure that I could get out there, or when I'll next be free to phone them, and I wouldn't want them hearing this through the media, if news got out. Do you think you could perhaps see your way to . . .'

'It's the sort of thing I do every day,' said Posthumus. 'Part of the job.' Should he bring up the trashed rooms? Freddie's reaction this morning still bothered him. Perhaps not now. 'So this is a murder enquiry,' he said instead.

'That is the other reason for my call,' said de Boer. 'We have a suspect. We have CCTV footage showing a man with what appears to be Olssen's belongings and that brown overcoat. Or, rather, I should say we *had* a suspect.'

'Frans Kemp?' said Posthumus.

'Martin Jacobs.'

It took a while for the penny to drop.

'*Marty?* Marty Jacobs from the butcher's?' said Posthumus.

Marty was deeply unpleasant, a sly toad of a man, but a *killer*?

'We went round to question him, but arrived too late. Jacobs is dead. He's been shot.'

Posthumus felt for Alex's chair, and sat down.

'Back when we were investigating the Dolle Hond fire, you told me that Jacobs had threatened you in the street,' de Boer went on. 'When I asked if you wanted to press charges, you answered, "Not yet." Can you tell me what that was about?'

De Boer was right. He remembered now. It had been at the Nieuwmarkt.

'I'd almost forgotten about that,' said Posthumus. 'It came completely out of the blue. Something about having powerful friends, I think. But all I can recall is that I thought it had to do with the fire.'

'Well, if anything else occurs to you, will you contact me?' said de Boer.

Posthumus could hear voices in the background at the other end of the line.

'I'll want to talk about this further,' de Boer said, 'but the consultant and ward sister have just come in. Could I call you later?'

'Best use my mobile,' said Posthumus. 'I'm about to leave the office.'

He replaced the handset, and sat staring at his fingers, spread out flat on Alex's desk.

Marty Jacobs. Odd moments came back to him, drop by drop. Marty, foul-mouthed, furious, shouting at him on the Nieuwmarkt. Marty, badly beaten up; why, Posthumus did not know. Tina, who loathed the man, telling him that Marty had been a client at one of the dreadful places she'd worked in, and got off on making girls cry. There clearly was a very nasty side to Marty Jacobs.

'Not good news, I take it,' said Cornelius.

Posthumus stood up. He told Cornelius about Ben and Marty as they walked to the car.

The two tall men, folded into the department's little Smart car, were still discussing Ben Olssen, Freddie, Marty and the whole business when they arrived at De Nieuwe Ooster crematorium.

'Mrs Dam is not quite ready for you yet,' said a willowy young man in a black frock coat. 'If you don't mind waiting.' His hand curved languidly towards a corner of soft chairs.

'We'll go round the back and pick her up,' said Posthumus, taking Cornelius's elbow and steering him out the door before the young man could object.

Posthumus tapped on the door of the low building behind the crematorium furnace, and opened it. He recognised the operative in overalls, who was placing the lid on a funeral urn.

'Queue jump for Mrs Dam?' asked Posthumus.

'No probs. I was just about to do her.'

Posthumus and Cornelius stood to one side as the operative shovelled lumps of charred grit and recognisable bits of bone from a box into the top of a solid, chest-high machine.

'It's those still living we should be concerned about,' said Posthumus, picking up on their conversation of earlier in the car. 'Those three other delegates, and Christina.'

'Ah, I was wondering when we might be getting on to the fair damsel,' said Cornelius. 'Still the autumnal knight on a quest for spring?'

Posthumus gave Cornelius a sour look. It wasn't as if that thought hadn't occurred to him.

'If I *am* having a mid-life crisis, I flatter myself that I would do it in a way that was slightly less clichéd,' he said.

'I'm glad to hear it,' said Cornelius. 'The woman riles me. Good heavens!'

Posthumus followed Cornelius's gaze to the buttons on the crematorium machine: FILL, REFILL, GRIND and EMPTY. The operative pressed GRIND.

'I didn't realise the "unto dust" part of the process needed such a helping hand,' said Cornelius. 'No wonder you Catholics are so opposed to cremation.' He turned back to Posthumus, raising his voice above the noise of the machine. 'Of course, my dear Charon. Forgive me. It's just that I'm getting a little too much of the dear creature at the moment. Surface, surface, surface, celebrity and status. Gabrielle doesn't see her for a decade, and then she's flitting into every corner of our day.'

'But this tiger thing, "saving furry animals" as you rather dismissively put it last night, that's not just surface. There's more to it than you might think,' said Posthumus. 'I've been having a look online. There was a big conference in St Petersburg a few years ago, all sorts of world leaders. Putin's a big fan. And there are huge sums involved in trafficking skins and body parts, in China and India especially.'

'But nothing to do with fracking, surely?'

'There's also big money pouring into conservation,' said Posthumus. 'And it's all very much tied up with the animals' environments, with foresting, with carbon-emissions projects, and who knows, maybe also with fracking. Maybe Christina has crossed someone somewhere, and Ben Olssen knew about it. Somebody Olssen had also antagonised.'

'I really can't imagine she would be that deeply involved,' said Cornelius. 'Or be that important a part of her organisation. Christina's all smoke and mirrors, the mistress of spin. That's her job, and she's good at it, that I'll grant you, she always has been. Gabrielle says that back in London when they were girls, Christina always had everyone thinking that *her* father was the ambassador, while old man Lanting was the lowly attaché. And she's still doing it: the family name, the historic bank, Daddy the prince of power in Brussels, while in the world you and I occupy, dear Charon, the family name is fading, Arabs own most of the bank, and Daddy, much though she may adore him, is a mere lobbyist. Smoke and mirrors, Charon, my dear distracted man. She puffs it all up and plays the game, she's not the sort of woman who would engage enough with the real issues to get herself into danger.'

The grinding stopped. The operative took a container from a drawer at the bottom of the machine, and emptied it into a funnel that deposited the ashes into a brown paper bag.

'It's like buying coffee!' said Cornelius. He looked genuinely taken aback.

'No need to label her,' said Posthumus. 'We're taking her straight out, I'll sign for her here.'

The operative deposited Mrs Dam's remains into a container with a swivelled handle.

'For scattering,' Posthumus explained to Cornelius.

'Whither?' asked Cornelius, as they stepped outside.

'There's an arboretum,' said Posthumus.

'Do you always do this?'

'Technically, it's up to the undertakers,' said Posthumus. 'But sometimes, if we track down a friend or relative, and they can't be here, they ask us to do it. I suppose it seems more personal. We've become part of the client's life, in a way.'

'One does feel one comes to know them,' said Cornelius. 'Like the dear Mrs Dam.'

They reached the arboretum. A winter's worth of dead foliage still covered the ground, though most of the trees were in delicate, pale green leaf.

'Will Ben Olssen also be one of yours?' asked Cornelius.

Posthumus paused a moment. 'Good point,' he said. 'Even if there is known family, we often deal with repatriations. It depends on the police.'

He led the way into the arboretum. The two men scattered Mrs Dam's ashes in silence, then stood for a moment, side by side among the trees.

'These trashed rooms,' said Cornelius, once they were back in the car. 'Do you really think this Freddie friend of yours had something to do with that?'

'It is just the sort of thing he used to be involved with; which we were *all* involved with, back then,' said Posthumus. 'And it looked very much to me like he had his iPad out, waiting for the news report.'

'And you think he had something to do with Ben Olssen, too?'

Posthumus paused a long time at a junction, missed a gap in the traffic and received a toot-toot from the car behind. He drove on.

'In an odd way, no,' he said. 'Freddie seemed genuinely shocked to hear about that, the attack seemed really to worry him. We had been settling down for a few drinks at Scruff, but after I told him about it he was up and off as soon as could be.'

'To find out what had gone wrong?'

'Or who may have gone too far,' said Posthumus.

'Sorry! Left, just here. It's that building with the glass stair-tower,' said Cornelius. He indicated one of the spine of smart high-rises that had spiked up in recent years at this bend in the Amstel, in jarring contrast to the gentle gables of the city centre. Posthumus turned sharply, and stopped the Smart. Cornelius swung out of the car, and with a farewell tap to his forehead disappeared through the main doors.

Posthumus put the car back in gear, pulled off, and was immediately deflected by a one-way, and a pedestrians-only street. This patch of town had changed completely since he was last here . . . since he was last here . . . He slowed, approaching a street that angled down to the river. Why not? It was his day off, after all. Houseboats still clustered along the banks below the apartment blocks, some of them designer wonders, small floating show-off houses; but others more ramshackle, cosy and pot-plant laden, dinghies tethered at one end, bicycles chained to another, wood smoke seeping from bent metal chimneys. Kees's was still among them, according to the magazine article Posthumus had read. It would be good to see him again, and if anyone could throw some light on the story behind the trashed rooms, it would be Kees.

Posthumus parked the car, and walked along the riverbank. He found Kees's boat again easily. It had barely changed: a few more odd wooden sculptures on the deck, and more battered than before, but familiar to him from many a late night of long conversations. Posthumus wondered how visibly he had aged. He ran his fingers through the greying hair at his temples, crossed the ever precarious gangplank, and gave a couple of tugs to the bell-pull at the door. No answer. Of course. Stupid of him. Kees would probably be at the main Earth 2050 session; Gabi had said he was attending the conference. Posthumus checked his watch. It was nearly half past four. The session could be over by now, but he didn't feel like waiting. Besides, he should get the car back to the office. He turned to leave, then turned back again. There was tonight. It was getting a bit late to go looking for morels at the market now, and he had lost the impetus for cooking, anyway. Perhaps he could meet up with Kees somewhere, instead. He felt in his pocket, found one of his business cards, circled the mobile number, and wrote on the back:

*It's been way too long. A catch-up drink or dinner tonight?*
*Pieter*

Then he slipped the card under Kees's door.

Back at the car, Posthumus took out his phone. If the conference session was over, he had better try to get hold of Gabi, and tell her about Ben. He leaned back against the snubby bonnet of the Smart car, looked out across the river, and tapped 'call'. Three or four rings. Posthumus was expecting the phone to go to voicemail when a woman's voice answered.

'Gabi?' he said.

'It's Christina. That Pieter? Gabi's right here, just finishing off something, she said to hang on. So, how's the most stylish undertaker in town? Who are you giving a touching send-off to today?'

There was a gentle touch of mockery to the questions. Or perhaps just playful teasing. Posthumus shifted uneasily and took a step away from the car. He'd been hoping that Gabi would break the news to Christina. That was cowardly of him, perhaps.

'Christina . . .' he said, but she was in full flow.

'You wouldn't *believe* it here,' she said. 'It's *just* the same as it always is. Everyone very eloquently and enthusiastically agreeing on how far apart their stances really are, creating a hugely positive feeling about absolutely nothing at all.'

And Cornelius said that *she* was all surface? Posthumus began again: 'Christina, sorry to interrupt. I'm afraid I've got bad news. Ben is dead.'

There was a silence on the other end of the line. How he hated doing this over the phone, no matter how often he had to do it at work. He wanted to reach out and put an arm around her.

'Christina? I'm so sorry, perhaps I could . . .'

Posthumus could hear voices on the line, slightly muffled. Christina and Gabi. Christina saying simply, 'Ben's dead.' A scrabbling sound.

'Piet?'

It was Gabi.

'Piet, when? What happened? I thought he was getting better.'

Posthumus told Gabi what he knew, also about Marty, how he was a suspect . . . *had been* a suspect.

'But this is awful,' said Gabi. 'What on earth's going on? *Why?* This isn't Ben; he's so, so *solid.* OK, so people said he sold out when he went to Shell, but they just didn't get it. Look at everything else he's done since, with the UN, and energy in developing countries and everything. All right, I don't always agree with him, but he got things done. Good things done. He was pragmatic.'

Posthumus kept quiet. This was something he did know from work – to let her have her say, a release. It happened often, as if the person who had heard the news were running behind the deceased, and had somehow, in their own way, to catch up with the death. That shift from present to past tense was a good sign.

'It's got to be some sort of mistake. Who is this Marty Jacobs, anyway? You say you know him from De Dolle Hond?' said Gabi.

Posthumus mentioned a little of the sort of world that Marty was involved in.

'No, *no*, that's not Ben,' said Gabi. 'OK, so he was a woman-iser, but in a good way, if you know what I mean . . .'

Posthumus didn't, but he noticed Gabi had dropped her voice.

'Is Christina OK?' he said.

'She's walked off. She'll take this hard, I think. She was closer to Ben than she lets on.'

'She was talking this morning about their time together in Venice. At first she said it was just a fling, but then I got the feeling it really meant something to her.'

'I'd better go and find her,' said Gabi. 'Look, I'll give you a ring later.'

Posthumus realised he had walked quite some way up the Amstel. He turned around and made his way back to the car. The rush hour was beginning to kick in as he drove past the towering office blocks that stood shoulder to shoulder with the Philips headquarters, and joined the traffic towards the bridge back over the river. Perhaps it was because he and Cornelius had just been talking about the man, but as Posthumus crossed the bridge, he could have sworn that out of the corner of his eye he caught Freddie cycling in the opposite direction.

# 10

Flip de Boer walked over the street to where he had parked his car, in one of the local police bureau bays across the way from the hospital. He reached for his cigarettes, and lit up. Computer failure. No wonder the doctors had been reluctant to get into specifics when they first called. A complete shutdown of the ventilator, as well as the alarm system; well, that made sense, he supposed, if it was all computer-controlled. So, no warning beeps, and Olssen had died within minutes. De Boer doubted that would be any consolation to the bereaved. The hospital's IT team were looking into it, but he'd called in the police techies, too. He beeped open the car door as he approached. Something, he wasn't sure what, was buzzing a warning signal in his own system, and de Boer had learned, as a young officer, to trust his instincts.

At the car, he turned and leaned against the bonnet to finish off his cigarette. He took out his phone. The image of that Jacobs woman dogged him: sour, angry, silent. Did she know something about her son's death? Upstairs in the apartment, she had just clammed shut. Hans caught his eye, and de Boer had sensed that Hans might get more out of the woman talking to her alone. There was history there, clearly. De Boer had gone down to the shop for a proper look around, and to wait for forensics. Then he had come up to the hospital. He glanced at the time on his phone: five past four. Nearly two hours since he'd left the butcher's. He'd check the score with Hans. De Boer pressed 'call'. Hans answered immediately.

'You beat me to it,' said Hans. 'I'm just back. The Jacobs woman came with me. She's going to make a formal statement.'

'And?'

'Valuable.'

'Tell me.'

'Dirk Jacobs,' said Hans.

'The father, the one you said was killed,' said de Boer.

'That's the one. Small-time crook, but with big ideas. Ran a few girls, bit of drugs, stolen goods, a little money laundering through the butcher's. I remember him from years back, when I was still on the beat. He used to swagger around De Wallen, liked to give lip. But he had ambitions, tried to edge in on someone else's territory. He was liquidated. Literally. Found in the Amstel back in '85.'

'And the killer?'

'Caught, jailed, died some time in 2000,' said Hans. 'But this is the point. Behind it all, everybody knew, was Henk de Kok.'

Now there was a name de Boer *did* know. Henk de Kok, who had a finger in just about every unsavoury pie in town, but who sat cushioned by fall-guys behind a façade of property companies and small businesses: a nightclub, escort agencies, even the gym down the road from the IJ Tunnel Bureau. No one could ever pin anything on him. The tax office had also tried, de Boer knew.

'And you say de Kok was behind Martin Jacobs's death, too?' said de Boer. 'You think Jacobs was trying some sort of vengeance mission, and got himself spiked?'

'Martin never knew about his father's activities,' said Hans. 'He was only five or six when Dirk Jacobs was killed. I get the feeling the poor shit has been measured up against his father ever since, and fallen short. *Fuck*, I wouldn't have that woman as a mother.'

'Henk de Kok,' prompted de Boer.

'According to Pia Jacobs, Martin started taking up with de Kok about a year ago. Had big ideas about becoming De Wallen's next master criminal, so: like father, like son in one sense, at least. He even got himself beaten up in the process a while back. He thought his mother didn't know all about what he was up to, but she was on to him, used to listen outside his bedroom door and that, and if you ask me she still has her contacts out in the world. And Martin was apparently quite the one for the heavy hint. Anyway, she didn't say anything; watched and waited. I don't know, maybe she was giving him enough rope to hang himself, she seems to get off on humiliating him; maybe she saw Martin as a way back in. Rumour at the time was that she tried to run Dirk Jacobs's show for a while after he was killed, but that de Kok got control of most of it in the end. But, listen to this. Last Tuesday, the night Olssen was attacked, Martin had something big on, according to the mother; he kept dropping hints all day about how things were going to change, talking loudly on his phone about being ready, and keeping in constant contact. Speaking in English, sometimes, too.'

'Hang on,' said de Boer. 'She had no knowledge that we'd made the Olssen connection? She mentioned Tuesday of her own accord?'

'As far as she is concerned, we're solely investigating the death of her son,' said Hans. 'I asked her if she had noticed any odd behaviour in recent weeks.'

'So, he's dropping hints all day, and speaking loudly on the phone . . .'

'And leaves home that afternoon around five o'clock,' said Hans. 'De Kok calls round and picks him up. Jacobs is back around nine, straight up to the bedroom, and the next day is flashing a smart laptop and a mobile phone about.'

161

'Bingo.'

'We've recovered the computer, it was in a bin-bag in the corner of his bedroom,' said Hans. 'I've bagged it up and brought it back. I thought you'd want a look before we sent it off to the techies. It needs a password. Forensics found a flash new phone under the body. Smashed to shit, and no SIM card.'

'That'll be it. His own phone was in his side pocket. We already have that.'

'Shall we pay de Kok a visit?' said Hans.

'Not yet. The man's an eel. I want more than the accusation of a woman with a grudge. But we're well on the way. Let's see what we find on Jacobs's phone. How did you get on with eye-witnesses? With that Irene Kester?'

Hans made a noise somewhere between a laugh and a harrumph. '*Her!* We're going to have to wait till tomorrow till she calms down,' he said. 'There are a couple of others making statements now, nothing special though. All say much the same: two helmeted riders on a motorbike, shooting in through the window. The ground guys lost them, police-copter, too. Not a sign. They probably disappeared into some warehouse north of the tunnel and did a swap over.'

'And Pia Jacobs, you can get her to repeat everything in a sworn statement?' said de Boer.

'So she says, but I don't want her sitting there having second thoughts.'

'Go to it. And Hans . . .'

'Yeah?'

'Great work, thank you. I doubt we would have got much of that without you. And have a good weekend. Pack it in after the Jacobs woman, don't work too late.'

'Look who's talking!'

De Boer laughed. 'I'm already getting the sour-face because I'm on call tomorrow, and said I might come in to the office,' he said. 'But I'm going to be a good boy, and be home before dinner tonight. I tell you what, though. Would you send young Murat up to the Krasnapolsky? I'll meet him there on my way back to the Bureau, and start him off on the room-trashing enquiries. That'll free you up a bit. I've a feeling you and I are going to have our hands full with Olssen and Jacobs.'

Sulung had already gone home by the time Posthumus had spoken to Gabi, and driven back to the office. Posthumus signed the car back in, returned the keys, and went to his desk to see if he had any messages. He'd close up here, then go on up to De Dolle Hond for a drink. He ought to tell Anna about Ben Olssen, in case she bumped into Gabi. And about Marty, of course. *Marty.* What the hell had the stupid boy been up to? Posthumus's mobile rang. Kees, already? He checked the screen.

'Merel!' he said, answering the call.

'Uncle Pieter!'

Posthumus grinned at the teasing tone. Merel only ever used the 'uncle' flippantly, but it still felt good to hear it. Twenty years was a long time.

'I was thinking of you earlier,' said Posthumus. 'I was plan-ning to cook something special tonight and thought you might like to come round, but then my day took an unexpected course.'

'Days have that nasty habit, don't they?' said Merel.

Posthumus's desk phone rang. He hesitated. 'Maybe I should answer that,' he said.

'Hey, don't tell me you're at work!' said Merel. 'I thought this was going to be a day off.'

'That was the unexpected course,' said Posthumus.

'Well, let it ring,' said Merel. 'Nobody expects a council department to pick up at five on a Friday.'

Posthumus let it ring.

'And thanks for the thought,' said Merel, 'but *I* am being wined and dined tonight. At De Compagnon.'

'That little place around the corner from De Dolle Hond, on the water? *Very* romantic.'

'Mmmmm.'

'Does your uncle get to know more?'

'Maybe. We'll see.'

Posthumus could hear the smile in her voice. His desk phone stopped ringing.

'Anyway, the reason I'm calling is that I've just seen Kamil, you know, my friend the set designer, who I said might have some ideas for Anna's party at the Schreierstoren?' said Merel.

'And does he?' said Posthumus.

'Wild ones,' said Merel. 'For inside that room overlooking the water, and for a floating installation. One using the banana from that Andy Warhol album cover. But I thought I'd run them past you. I'm not sure they're quite Anna's thing. Perhaps you could say, you know her best.'

'I'm intrigued to see,' said Posthumus.

'It's just sketches on scraps of A4 at the moment,' said Merel. 'I could drop them round, or we could meet up for a drink before dinner.'

'I was on my way to De Dolle Hond, but we could think of somewhere else, maybe.'

'That'll be fine. De Dolle Hond is perfect, so close to the restaurant. I'm sure we can talk a bit without Anna hearing, it's always busy on a Friday. And if not, I'll leave the sketches with you anyway. Shall we say in half an hour, forty minutes? I'm nearly ready.'

'Perfect,' said Posthumus.

'And you can tell me about your disrupted day,' said Merel.

'It's been eventful, to say the least,' said Posthumus.

He mentioned Ben Olssen. And he told her about Marty, how the police suspected him of involvement in Ben's death, and that he now lay dead himself. Posthumus sensed his niece's journalist ears prick up at the possibility of a story.

'Marty *Jacobs*, from the feature I did on old families in De Wallen?' said Merel. She sounded intrigued, but not particularly surprised. 'Like father, like son.'

'What do you mean?' said Posthumus.

Merel filled him in about Marty's father.

'The mother, Ria, no, Pia I think her name was, mentioned it when I interviewed her,' she said. 'Or at least darkly hinted, and I did a bit more research. It was back in '84, '85, I think. He was found in the Amstel.'

'It would hardly have registered,' said Posthumus. 'I was a wide-eyed village boy, only just arrived in town.'

A callow Catholic youth from Krommenie, about to be launched on the wild seas of the city, with Anna his goad and guide. The Catholicism hadn't lasted long.

'Anyway, we can talk properly later,' said Merel. 'I must finish getting ready. I also want to know all about this celebrity that I hear Gabi's landed.'

Again the journalist. Persistent, tireless. Posthumus smiled. Merel was every inch her father's child. He ended the call. His phone was flashing a missed-call and voicemail alert. He tapped in the number and listened.

'Get off your bloody phone! And nobody's picking up at your office either.'

Posthumus let out a quiet chuckle. Kees was as impatient as ever. The old man's voice was gruff. You could hear the beard in it. And it swept Posthumus back a couple of decades in an instant.

'You could have left your note on something else. I thought they'd come for me at last when I saw a Funeral Team card under my door. Until I saw the name. Pieter Posthumus, you young reprobate! What the hell happened to all your plans to change the world? Bloody city bloody council, you sneaky sell-out!'

Kees's rounded chortle always reminded Posthumus of a department-store Santa Claus.

'Don't think I haven't been keeping track of what you've been up to . . . you old softy. And of course I'd bloody like to see you again. About bloody time! But I can't do tonight. You get your arse over here tomorrow morning, though. Eleven o'clock. Or it won't be worth sitting on.'

Posthumus felt oddly elated as he cycled up the Kloveniersburgwal canal, towards De Dolle Hond.

DI de Boer parked his car behind De Bijenkorf department store, and walked up the stub-end of Warmoesstraat towards the front entrance of the Hotel Krasnapolsky. A poisoning. A shooting. The second victim involved with the attack on the first. Was Jacobs simply a witness? Not walking off with all of Olssen's possessions, he wasn't. But there was at least one other killer involved. The same man? The two murders didn't bear the same mark. And the junkie? De Boer took out his phone, and checked emails as he walked. Yes. One headed 'Frans Kemp'. De Boer scrolled quickly through it. It was as he thought.

On the stairs of the Krasnapolsky someone brushed roughly past him.

'Watch where you're friggin' going!'

De Boer looked up. A scrawny man in his forties, with scraggly hair and a threadbare, motley-coloured jersey pushed past him and down towards the Dam.

'Not quite your Krasnapolsky type!' It was Murat, coming up the stairs.

'Probably one of the Occupy lot, sneaked in for a piss,' said de Boer.

'Better than up against the wall of the Beurs, I guess,' said Murat.

'All set?' said de Boer.

'You bet! I've put together the reports from all four hotels, everything we've got so far,' said Murat. 'I got tired of waiting for Ed Maartens to come up with the goods. Did it myself. Here, I've made you a copy.'

De Boer felt a stab of anger that the so-called liaison officer's antagonism to de Boer's appointment extended to passive-aggressive obstruction of his team. But Murat's eyes were shining. He handed over a thin wallet-file, and stood back to allow de Boer first through the door.

It was barely twenty-four hours since de Boer had last walked into the lobby. It certainly didn't seem like it. The concierge who had taken him up to Ben Olssen's room was again on duty: the one who looked like he drank too much. De Boer's mind flicked back rapidly, as if it were going through a card-index. Koning? No, Keizer. That was it.

The concierge stepped out from behind his desk. 'Good afternoon, sir.'

Keizer clearly remembered who de Boer was. And perhaps recalled his *faux pas* in thinking Hans was de Boer's boss. De Boer introduced Murat, but Keizer seemed somehow offended by Murat's youth, or race, and pointedly addressed only de Boer.

'Something that may be of interest to you, sir,' he said. 'If I may?'

The touchy, tight belligerence of yesterday had been transformed into an unconvincing toadyism. De Boer nodded. He caught a sweet, acrid whiff of alcohol.

'I've been in touch with a colleague, at the Canal City,' said Keizer. De Boer recognised the name of one of the other hotels where a room had been trashed. 'A much smaller establishment. My colleague shares a desk with Reception,' Keizer went on. 'Closer to goings-on in the office,' he added, still keeping his focus only on de Boer.

De Boer held back a 'Get on with it'. The close-knit network of concierges would of course be abuzz with all this.

'My colleague informs me that the Canal City was using agency housekeeping staff. Increased pressure because of the conference, you understand.'

Murat caught de Boer's eye, and looked quickly away, a smile tweaking at his lips.

'It *transpires*,' said Keizer, clearly choosing his word carefully, 'that this was the first time the Canal City was using said agency, and that the room-maid in question upped and left, the day after the guest's room was . . . disrupted.'

Keizer paused for effect, and observing that he had made very little, went on.

'My colleague *further* informs me that the same holds true at the Grand. And I have just this very afternoon had a word with our day manager, and apparently that is the case here, too. The same agency.'

This time Keizer stopped in triumph.

'That's very interesting indeed. Thank you, Mr Keizer,' said de Boer. 'Do you know the name of the agency?'

Keizer handed him a piece of paper. 'Only the website,' he said. 'It no longer works.'

'And your manager?' said de Boer.

'Day manager,' said Keizer, and nodded towards a perfectly groomed young man talking to a receptionist. 'Mr Benois.'

De Boer walked over, and introduced himself and Murat. Benois seemed agitated, and glanced towards the main door.

'We've had a slight disturbance,' he said. 'A not altogether desirable sort, snooping around the staff lifts. But I wonder if I should try to get him back, now that you're the police.'

'Untidy hair, bright jersey?' said de Boer.

'That's the one.'

'I bumped into him on the stairs on the way in. Literally,' said de Boer.

'He was becoming quite rowdy, I nearly had to call security,' said Benois, with another glance at the door. He smiled apologetically. 'With the Dam on one side and the red-light district on the other, we have to deal with this sort of thing from time to time, but he was beginning to get out of hand.'

'I can give the Beurstraat Bureau a quick call, if you like,' said de Boer. 'He may still be out on the square.'

'No, no, it's probably some sort of domestic squabble with one of the housekeeping staff,' said Benois. 'I'd hate to say it happens all the time, but . . . shall we go to my office?' He led the way.

'Do you have an idea when Mr Olssen might be back?' said Benois, indicating to the two detectives to sit down. 'We didn't get the go-ahead from your chaps to clean up the room until well after breakfast. Maintenance is still in there.'

De Boer informed Benois of the lack of any necessity to hurry. Not in regard to Ben Olssen, at least.

Benois looked grim. 'Well, at least it didn't happen in the hotel,' he said.

De Boer made no comment. Perhaps hotel managers, like policemen and doctors, developed a detachment.

'I've been having a word with one of your concierges,' he said instead. 'Apparently the room-maid responsible for Olssen's room hasn't arrived for work, and was agency staff. An agency now apparently uncontactable?'

'Not one of our usual ones,' said Benois. 'But this week it's been impossible. Normally we would have run checks, but we were desperate. They approached us with people available, and were offering extremely competitive rates.'

'The agency approached the hotel? When was this?' said de Boer.

'Early last week, apparently. She started over the weekend. But now we're getting bounce-backs on emails to the agency, the only telephone numbers we have are for mobiles and go unanswered, and even their website's showing a generic "register your domain" message,' said Benois. 'I must emphasise, this *really* is not our normal practice.'

'And the maid is gone?'

'Simply didn't report for work yesterday, no explanation,' said Benois. 'But she wasn't working on Mr Olssen's floor. It was only when Jonas Keizer told me about the other hotels that I began to wonder.'

'Could she have had access to Olssen's room?' said de Boer.

'Pass keys are floor-specific, but I suppose it's not impossible that she swapped with someone, or came up to that floor with the excuse of having to put something in the room. You'd have to speak to the floor housekeeper. We still have the worker's records, of course, though only basic contacts, as it's the agency that employs her.'

De Boer nodded across to Murat. 'We'll check,' he said. 'But it's unlikely she gave her real name.'

'One thing that's a little odd,' Benois went on. 'I've just been speaking to a receptionist who was trying to reset Mr Olssen's room-key code in case someone had got hold of his card, and apparently the room lock is malfunctioning.'

'What make is it?' asked Murat.

'I . . . I'm not sure,' said Benois. His expression reflected de Boer's own surprise.

'No matter, I can find out,' said Murat.

'And Mr Olssen's personal effects?' said de Boer.

'At the moment they're still in the room,' said Benois. 'But they'll probably have been moved about.' He looked concerned. 'Your people who were here earlier said it was in order to do that. And I suppose, now that ... well, now that ...'

'You will be able to clear the room,' said de Boer. 'But first, I would like another look.'

'Why did you ask about the door lock?' de Boer asked Murat, once they were up at Olssen's room. The door was wedged open, but he noticed Murat run his finger under the outside lock as they passed.

'This sort is easy to hack, if you know what you're doing and have the right equipment,' said Murat. 'You plug into the little DC port underneath, fire it up, and presto! You can bypass the card reader and trigger the opening mechanism. It can be a bit touch and go, and it sometimes damages the magnetic reader – enough to affect coded cards, though the master key would probably still work.'

De Boer suddenly felt that he belonged to another generation.

'Impressive,' he said. 'I bet you didn't learn that at the Police Academy.'

Murat grinned. 'You pick things up, here and there,' he said.

De Boer nodded a greeting to the worker who was repainting the wall where the sideways figure eight had been sprayed in red. Dustcovers were draped over much of the furniture, but the room had been neatened up. The bed was made up again, and on it, closed now, was Olssen's suitcase. De Boer walked over and opened it. The catch felt loose in his hand. It had been subtly forced. The clothes that had been scattered on the floor were refolded and replaced. Except those that had been ripped – slashed, rather – which were on the bed, beside the suitcase: a suit jacket, cut up the back seam, and a light windcheater, its lining neatly excised. And the fabric dividing-pocket of the suitcase, which yesterday he thought had been ripped out. That, too, he now saw, had been severed with something sharp. De Boer frowned.

'Has this sort of thing happened in any of the other rooms?' he asked Murat, holding up the jacket.

'Nothing in the reports, I don't think,' said Murat.

De Boer flipped open the file Murat had given him. He skimmed the reports. There was no mention of slashed clothing, or destroyed personal property in any of the others. He glanced at the photos. Ben Olssen's bed had been more thoroughly done over than those in the other rooms, but otherwise all the incidents bore the same stamp: furniture messed about, the infinity symbol sprayed on a wall, shower left running, music on, an Albert Heijn card in the electricity slot.

'Ask about that, will you?' said de Boer. 'And while you're about it, check on your idea with the door locks. See if that could have happened with any of the others.'

A slight movement caught de Boer's attention. The small grey screen of the bedside phone was glowing bright, then dim: 'You have 2 messages'. His mind flicked back over the mental images of the room he had built up when he first saw it. There had been no blinking phone screen. De Boer consulted the laminated instruction card, and accessed the room voicemail. He reached for a hotel ballpoint and notepad as he listened:

Friday, 10.02 a.m.: *'Ben. Greg Robertson. Um . . . what happened with our Skype appointment Wednesday? I've been leaving messages on your mobile.'*

Friday, 12.32 p.m.: *'Greg Robertson again. Last chance. Call me.'*

De Boer made a note of the name and times.

'Two messages in English,' he said to Murat, handing him the slip of paper. 'They might be worth a follow-up. Can you see if the hotel system has recorded the numbers?'

He took out his own phone and googled 'Greg Robertson'. A couple of doctors, an estate agent, twenty-five on Linked-in, a solicitor or two, pages of them. Nothing, at first glance, in Amsterdam. He tried 'Greg Robertson' and 'Amsterdam', and then with 'Ben Olssen'. No direct matches.

'Quite a common name,' he said, flashing the screen at Murat. 'Have a proper look once you're done here, to see if anyone has an Amsterdam connection, but don't waste too much time on that till you've seen what the hotel can come up with.'

De Boer briefed Murat a little further on the room-trashing investigation, but the lad seemed on the ball. More so, perhaps, than Hans would have been: a bright spark, and very welcome. He'd be keeping an eye on young Murat. In the lift, de Boer took out his phone. Five twenty: he was still on track to be home by seven, six thirty even. He hesitated a moment, then began to scroll through his address book.

# I I

As he reached the upper end of the Kloveniersburgwal, Posthumus braced himself. Two streets down from Nieuwmarkt square, it was as if the spirit of Amsterdam – feisty old hag that she must be by now – snapped her fingers and changed the scene. At the rending of a veil, the quiet gables and gentle houseboats of the Kloveniersburgwal became a bellowing, buffeting blast of tourists. The smell of potato *frites* and the acrid saccharine of cheap sweets bit at Posthumus's nostrils. Then a waft of marijuana, as he passed a coffee shop where a group of Earth 2050 delegates, lanyards still around their necks, puffed on ready-rolled joints.

Posthumus dismounted from his bike and began to walk. In the middle of the square, around the medieval weighing-house, market stallholders were packing up for the day. He gave a nod to the mushroom woman as he passed. She did have morels, after all (tomorrow, perhaps), and some evil-looking fungi Posthumus did not know, which looked as if they could lay waste to your entire guest-list at one fell swoop. He pushed on, past the weighing-house. What a day! The image of Ben Olssen lying weakened in bed, surrounded by tubes and computer screens flashed again into his mind. Poison. Why *poison*? The thought that had been tapping in his head ever since dinner at the Conservatorium became more insistent, now that Ben was dead. That had been the intention all along, to kill him. One that almost failed. And then Marty – Marty, who de Boer said was a suspect in the Olssen case. Shot dead. *That* was more the way to do it, if you needed to be rid of somebody, and be sure of it. What had Marty got himself into? He was greedy, and none too bright: not a happy combination.

Posthumus tried to remember more about that exchange with Marty a few months back. Right here, on the Nieuwmarkt. Posthumus paused almost at the exact spot. He let the to-ing and fro-ing around him fall out of focus, into a backdrop against which he reconstructed the scene: February, after the fire at De Dolle Hond, in the midst of that long freeze. Marty swearing at him, confronting him about poking his nose in. Marty, almost shouting, looking more scared than angry, almost in tears. Marty, lurching off back towards the Zeedijk, and turning his head for a parting shot: 'I've got powerful friends, like you don't even know!' And then Marty, a few weeks later, walking past De Dolle Hond, badly beaten up. Powerful friends all right. *Who?* What was behind all this? Something to do with that criminal father Merel had mentioned? Inter-gang warfare? Revenge of some sort? Punishment for something? Somebody trying to silence him? The faintest wisp of familiarity came along with that thought, one that passed from Marty to curl around the bed of Ben Olssen and then blow away, as a voice rang out just behind him.

'Oi! Mate! It doesn't fly! It's called a *bicycle*, mate. You sit on it, and move your legs around. Not stand in the middle of everyone's bleedin' way waiting to be beamed up to bleedin' paradise.'

Posthumus smiled an apology to the market stallholder who was trying to push a full-laden trolley past him, wheeled his bicycle across to where the Zeedijk began, and got back on. The Zeedijk swarmed with tourists, zigzagging all over the street, but with determination and his finger on the bell he could steer a fairly straight course up towards De Dolle Hond. His phone rang as he was about to pedal off. Posthumus muttered a curse, almost ignored it, then checked the screen. DI de Boer. He had better answer.

'Inspector,' he said.

'Mr Posthumus.'

A fraction of a second passed, as Posthumus sensed that de Boer, too, felt oddly uncomfortable with such formality. Yet there was no need for de Boer to be snapping at his heels. Posthumus spoke first, before the detective could say why he had called.

'I was about to ring you,' he said. 'I got through to Gabrielle Lanting and Christina Walraven earlier this afternoon, and I've told them about Ben Olssen.'

De Boer seemed to pick up on the note of irritation. 'That's good of you, thank you, I didn't mean to appear to be checking up,' he said. Posthumus heard what sounded like a lift door ping in the background. 'The main reason I wanted to speak to you is that I've just had the all-clear on Frans Kemp,' de Boer went on. 'It was an overdose, nothing more, certainly no trace of the TTX, so he will be coming back to you next week. I thought you might like to know immediately.'

Posthumus settled back on his bicycle saddle, and propped one leg against the kerb. Not much of an excuse for phoning after five on a Friday, but, still, it was considerate thinking.

'Thank you,' said Posthumus. 'He was scheduled for an afternoon funeral on Monday. I doubt we'll make that, but it is helpful to know.'

'I'll hurry things along this end,' said de Boer. 'The body can be released immediately. Olympia undertakers, wasn't it? I imagine there'll be somebody working over weekends.'

'And the Monday slot may still be free, so you never know,' said Posthumus. He had better alert Cornelius.

'I'll push the right buttons,' said de Boer.

Another split-second silence, as if de Boer was reluctant to hang up.

Posthumus filled the gap. 'I've been thinking about that encounter with Marty Jacobs, a few months back,' he said. 'I'm afraid I really don't recall anything other than his threat that he had powerful friends, and the fact that he seemed upset, frightened even. But I do remember that he was beaten up by someone a few weeks later. And there is something else. Apparently, back in the eighties, Marty's father was involved in some sort of criminal activity. I don't know much more than that, but it may be worth looking into . . .'

That was a little presumptuous of him perhaps. It sounded like he was telling de Boer his job, and besides, the police must know that already. Posthumus faltered. This time de Boer stepped in. Posthumus could hear a touch of amusement in his voice.

'Now *why* doesn't it surprise me that you've already picked up on that, Mr Posthumus,' said de Boer. 'I've only just learned it myself.'

'My journalist niece Merel told me about it,' said Posthumus. 'She wrote a feature a few weeks ago on old De Wallen families, and interviewed Marty and his mother; it came up then.'

'Your niece spoke to Pia Jacobs about her husband?'

'I don't know if she learned much then, but she did some of her own research, too.'

'I'd very much like to speak to her.'

'I'm on my way up to De Dolle Hond to see her now. I can ask her to ring you.'

'De Dolle Hond, you say? Better yet, would you mind an intruder?'

Posthumus did not answer. What was the man on about?

'I'm just coming out of the Krasnapolsky,' de Boer went on. 'I can be there in a few minutes.'

★  ★  ★

De Dolle Hond was not as busy as Posthumus thought it might be, only just gearing up for the Friday evening rush. Through the window, he was glad to see Tina helping Anna out at the bar, both laughing as they shared a joke. That was good: Anna taking to her a little more.

'Hello, girls!' said Posthumus, as he walked in.

'Don't you "girl" me!' said Anna, but she laughed and gave Posthumus a welcoming peck on the cheek. She placed a glass on the bar at his usual spot, against the wall.

'I'll take a table,' said Posthumus. There was one free, near the window.

'Company?'

'Merel is coming, and DI de Boer,' said Posthumus.

'That hunky detective who led the Marloes case, and the fire?'

'Hunky *married* detective, I think,' said Posthumus, with a smile. It was good to hear Anna using words like 'hunky' again. In her way, she was beginning to put the past few months behind her. Posthumus told her about Ben Olssen's death, and about Marty.

'Marty Jacobs, who would have thought?' said Anna.

'*I* would have thought,' said Tina. 'And I ain't sorry neither.'

'No, no, I can imagine, but still . . .' said Posthumus.

Anna was looking over his shoulder, and gave a nod towards the window behind him. Posthumus turned to see DI de Boer was walking up towards the café.

Posthumus greeted the detective as he came in, and offered him a drink.

'A coffee for me, thank you. On duty, driving, and all that,' said de Boer, then caught sight of the bottle of wine Anna had in her hand. 'Though *that* would tempt me badly. No café plonk here, I see.'

'This one's a special I keep for PP here,' said Anna, pouring Posthumus a glass. 'You sure you won't?'

'Hard to say "no", but I have to,' said de Boer.

Anna went back along the bar to the coffee machine. Posthumus picked up his glass, and gestured towards the empty table. He hadn't seen de Boer as a wine man.

'My niece, Merel, should be along in a minute,' said Posthumus. 'Anna might also be able to fill you in on the Jacobs family. Her family, the de Vrieses, have been here for generations, too, though I don't think she had much to do with Pia Jacobs.'

As they sat, he caught a glimpse of Tina, who had retreated to the far end of the bar. The presence of a policeman made her uneasy. Posthumus knew that feeling, yet de Boer somehow didn't fit the mould.

'So, you've been up at the Krasnapolsky?' said Posthumus, filling the gap as they waited for Anna to make the coffee.

'I wanted another look at Ben Olssen's room,' said de Boer.

So that's where Ben had been staying. The news report he'd seen on Freddie's tablet hadn't specified.

'Yes, I heard about the trashed rooms,' said Posthumus. 'I imagine that's landed in your boat now, too. And then Marty Jacobs. It must all be a bit full-on at the moment.'

'Tell me about it!' said de Boer. 'I could do with another good head on board. You're not looking for a career change by any chance?'

Posthumus laughed and shook his head. Finding that he liked a policeman for once in his life was one thing, but that would be going too far . . . and he had a feeling de Boer was only half joking. De Boer got up to fetch the coffee Anna had put on the bar. De Dolle Hond was beginning to fill up. Posthumus closed the fan-spread of beer-mats on the table into a neat pile. One by one he was being dealt more cards about Ben Olssen, but he needed a fuller hand. He laid out a beer-mat for de Boer, one for Merel, when she came, and one for himself.

'I tell you what, though,' he said, when de Boer returned to the table. It was like a thirst, this need he had to make shape of things: insistent, unyielding. 'One way I might be able to help,' he went on. 'There's a strong likelihood, I imagine, that Olssen will end up one of our clients at the department. Repatriation of the body and so on. If it's any use to you, I could start now with tracking down next of kin, take that off your hands at least.'

He hoped he didn't sound too eager. De Boer leaned back in his chair, wiped a palm across the back of his neck, and smiled.

'I'll have to settle for that, then, if you're not going to take me up on the job offer,' he said. His voice had the same amused turn to it that Posthumus had heard earlier on the phone. 'But thank you, Mr Posthumus, yes, that would help.'

'Pieter, please,' said Posthumus.

The detective hesitated only fractionally. 'Flip,' he said. 'As we're colleagues, in a sense.'

Tina came past, gathering empty glasses. She skirted their table, and avoided Posthumus's eye. De Dolle Hond was busy now, and growing noisier.

'I don't suppose there's much to go on, as far as next of kin is concerned,' said Posthumus.

'Nothing in the hotel room. There were no personal documents, nor anything of value there at all. It would seem that he had everything on him when he was attacked,' said de Boer.

'Where was that, by the way?' said Posthumus.

'In the underpass, next to Central Station.'

Posthumus held de Boer's gaze. That he was fishing for, and hooking, more information than was strictly necessary, remained unsaid.

'What would probably be of more use to you is his laptop,' said de Boer. 'We recovered that in Jacobs's bedroom this afternoon, though it is password-protected. We have Olssen's mobile, too, though that is smashed and without a SIM-card. And I can send you the details on that business card you found in Olssen's coat pocket, but we've tried that. The only contact number was Olssen's mobile. Futura Consultants seems to have been a one-man band.'

'Was there anything in the hotel room that might give a lead?' said Posthumus. 'To friends or family, I mean.'

'Apart from toiletries and clothing, nothing personal at all,' said de Boer. 'For the record, when his effects come to you, the damage to them occurred during the room trashing.'

'Damage?'

'Fabric in the suitcase and the lining in two jackets was slit. That wasn't done by police.'

'I know the problem,' said Posthumus, with a smile. Families had a grasping habit of demanding compensation – and the more distant the family, the greedier the demand. 'We always photograph everything the moment we go in to a client's apartment.'

De Boer gave him a nod of sympathy.

'Christina said something about a brother, I think,' said Posthumus, almost to himself. 'Christina Walraven, on the way to the hospital this morning,' he added, to de Boer. 'I'll check whether she or Gabrielle knows anything more.'

Merel was outside, walking up towards the door. She saw Posthumus through the window and gave a wave. For the third time he defended the empty chair he had been saving for her from being snatched away to another table.

'Well, there is a name. Two, possibly,' said de Boer. 'But they're both English, so I don't know how much help as far as family goes. One I may have mentioned this morning: "Humbert", or "Hubbard", one of the words Olssen was trying to say when he was first brought in; and then there were messages left on Olssen's hotel voicemail by a Greg Robertson. Something to do with work, by the sound of it. Google didn't help much, it seems a common name, and he didn't leave a number. One of my men is looking into that now.'

Posthumus hadn't quite caught the name. Merel was coming up to the table.

'Greg Robinson, you say?' he asked de Boer, as he looked up to greet her.

'Robertson,' said de Boer, over the growing hubbub in the bar.

He turned his head to follow Posthumus's gaze. Merel was standing just behind him, slipping off her coat to reveal a tightly fitting 1960s cocktail dress, and wearing a delicate diamond pendant that Posthumus recognised as one his mother had left her; her eye for good vintage clothes Merel had clearly inherited from her uncle.

'My niece Merel Dekkers, DI Flip de Boer,' said Posthumus.

He felt a spring of pride to see de Boer a little flustered by Merel's appearance.

'Oh, I'm sorry, I didn't expect . . .' said de Boer.

'Quite such a creature to have sprung from the same gene pool,' said Anna, who had come up to the table. She ruffled Posthumus's hair. 'This one was quite a looker, too, in his day,' she said.

'Less of the past tense, please,' said Posthumus.

'A drink?' said Anna, giving Merel the customary three pecks on the cheeks.

'Just a mineral water, thanks,' said Merel.

She gave Posthumus an enquiring look, with a quick side-glance at de Boer, as she sat down.

'The DI is investigating Marty's murder,' said Posthumus. 'I was telling him earlier about your interview with Pia Jacobs, and about Marty's father. He wanted to find out if you knew any more.'

De Boer listened to what Merel had to say about Pia and Dirk Jacobs.

'That's pretty much what one of the men on my team was telling me earlier,' said de Boer. He appeared disappointed. 'I was hoping she might have said more to you.'

Merel shook her head. 'Hard as nails, that one,' she said.

'Does the name Henk de Kok mean anything to you?'

It did to Posthumus. Something very faint. In the past but not too long ago. A shadow, moving on the periphery of whatever he had been concentrating on at the time. Merel frowned, and thought for a moment.

'De Kok?' she said to de Boer. 'Property companies, De Wallen, strip clubs, shady deals?'

De Boer nodded.

'I can't remember whether Pia Jacobs actually mentioned his name or not,' said Merel. 'It certainly came up in my research. De Kok was linked with Dirk Jacobs's assassination, Jacobs moving in on his territory, something like that. I'll have to check my notes. And de Kok is still very much around. There's a bad smell follows him, though he somehow manages to keep his companies looking clean: dodgy dealings – money laundering, probably much worse – behind respectable fronts. No one ever manages to pin anything on him. Certainly I couldn't. Why? How does he fit into this?'

'His name has come up,' said de Boer.

'So de Kok is involved with Marty's murder?' said Merel. De Boer did not answer. 'De Kok is your chief suspect? That *is* interesting.'

She looked hard at de Boer. Posthumus again sensed his niece's journalist instincts prickle.

'And a link with Olssen, maybe, that's why you're on both cases?' said Merel. 'What is it? Drugs, perhaps? Dodgy dealing?'

De Boer remained silent.

'Marty was up to something like that, a while back,' said Posthumus. 'He set up some sort of property company, and was trying to buy next door. Anna probably still has the letter. But I don't know if that had anything to do with a Henk de Kok.'

That wasn't where the name had seemed familiar to him from. Posthumus leaned back to allow Tina to clear his glass and de Boer's empty cup. She didn't wait to take a new order.

'I'd be more than happy to check my notes,' said Merel. She smiled at de Boer. 'Though they are quite scattered, if I remember rightly. Can you give me some names, or an indication of what I should be looking for?'

De Boer's look took in both Merel and Posthumus. 'You're quite a pair, you two,' he said. 'I'm not sure I dare meet any more Posthumuses.'

He handed a business card to Merel. 'Phone me, if you come up with anything. I'll be working tomorrow.'

He glanced towards the bar, where both Anna and Tina were busy with customers, and handed another card to Posthumus. 'I'm not sure if Ms de Vries still has my number,' he said. 'But perhaps you could ask her to call me, too, especially if she has that letter you mentioned. I'd like to speak to her about the Jacobs family.'

De Boer got up.

'Thank you for the help,' he said, with a look up to the clock on the far wall. 'I had better put my skates on.'

'What was all that about when I came in?' said Merel, once de Boer had left.

'Someone called Greg Robertson, who left a couple of messages at the hotel for Ben Olssen,' said Posthumus. 'Name mean anything to you?'

Merel shook her head. 'The only Greg Robertson I know is a journalist,' she said.

'No surprise there,' said Posthumus.

She gave him a grin. 'He's *good*. Does a lot of TV: political exposés, that sort of thing. He did a piece on corruption in FIFA a few weeks ago. Brilliant.'

Posthumus shrugged. 'Somebody like that wanting to talk to Ben about fracking, or some environmental issue?' he said. 'Could be. Though it's a common enough name. I'll have to see, I said I'd try to trace Ben's family. Everything helps.'

Merel raised one eyebrow. 'Yes, *sure*,' she said. 'We're not up to our usual tricks at all, are we?'

Posthumus grinned.

'*But* . . . the real reason I'm here,' said Merel. 'I've not got long.' She gave a conspiratorial glance towards Anna at the bar, and slipped out the brown A4 envelope that she'd been keeping hidden under her overcoat. 'The plans!' she said, giving the words a dramatic flourish, and taking out her friend Kamil's sketches for Anna's party.

Posthumus pedalled more lightly as he rounded the corner into the Recht Boomssloot. Gusta, his downstairs neighbour, was letting herself in through their street door. Any faster, and he would end up trapped behind her on the narrow stairs, cricking his neck upwards in interminable conversation, and failing to fend off repeated offers of a glass of wine. 'Yes' was then the only password that would unblock the stairway. Some days he could go along with it, but not tonight. It had been a long day. He waited till Gusta was safely inside, locked his bicycle to the bridge, and walked slowly towards the door, giving her ample time to ascend, in her swathes of second-hand silk and chiffon, to the first floor.

De Dolle Hond had become a crush, and he'd left soon

after Merel, giving Anna the message and business card from Flip de Boer on his way out. She was beaming at the sudden burst in trade, but for himself he couldn't help wishing Earth 2050 over, and De Dolle Hond cosily back to normal. He had brought Kamil's sketches home with him for a closer look. The ideas were zany, among them a giant floating banana rowed by Lou Reed look-alikes and a mobile sculpture of old LPs. Maybe he should run the drawings past Anna first. She might well consider such abuse of vinyl sacrilege. It was, anyway, perhaps not such a good plan to keep the party totally secret, or Anna might start organising something herself, at De Dolle Hond, and part of the idea was to give her a complete break. Posthumus slipped his key gently into the lock of the street door, pushed it open a little and listened. Nothing. Only a waft of face powder and tobacco lingered in the air through which Gusta had passed. He went in and climbed quietly up the stairs, past her apartment, and on again up to his own.

Posthumus closed his front door behind him, and leaned back against it for a moment. A quiet evening in, that's what he wanted. Something simple to eat; to read for a while, perhaps try out one or two of the memory games from the new book he had bought. The ponder-box, maybe. It had been a while since he'd pulled out the black, cloth-covered box in which he kept fetishes and mementos of cases that had perplexed him, from his days working with the unit investigating municipal fraud and, more recently, with the Funeral Team. The box contained an assortment of photographs, documents, handwritten notes and odd objects: a toy Ferrari, a cocktail party invitation, and now also a Namiki pen and a book of poems. Some nights he liked nothing better than sitting with a glass or two of wine, reliving the stories he had managed to make some shape of, or puzzling afresh over those that he hadn't.

Posthumus straightened his back, walked across to the desk behind the spiral staircase that led up to his bedroom, and dropped Kamil's sketches on top of the ponder-box. A simple supper . . . easier said than done. He really ought to have got in some shopping earlier. He wandered to the kitchen at the back of the long apartment, opened the fridge, and stared into it blankly. Some leftover hummus, a lemon, limp parsley and a single cooked beetroot. In the freezer, frozen peas and broad beans, pitta bread in a bag. The cupboard offered more tinned beans and a jar of artichoke hearts. Posthumus felt like the contestant in a TV cookery programme, having to conjure up a menu from wilfully mismatched ingredients. He thought for a moment, and checked the airtight box in which he stored pasta. A small bag of risoni, slightly past its sell-by date. He put it on the work surface. Right. First some wine. Then, to take the edge off his hunger while he cooked, sliced beetroot with hummus spread over it, and grill-thawed pitta. And then a warm salad of the risoni, broad beans and artichoke hearts, with some zest and a squeeze of lemon, and a little lemon thyme, from the pot in the kitchen window. And there was, he remembered, some rather good pecorino he could shave on top. Posthumus set to work.

A little over an hour later, Posthumus was stretched, pleas-antly sated (the beetroot-hummus combination had been especially good), with a half-full bottle of wine beside him, on the sofa up in the front of his apartment. The ponder-box was at his side, and he was holding Kamil's sketches. But he couldn't focus on party décor. Not after all that had happened. He lowered the papers. A friend of Gabi's was murdered. The dead man's coat had ended up on the body of a client of the Funeral Team. And then Marty . . . maybe not a favourite face at De Dolle Hond, but a regular, all the same. Posthumus's mind turned again and again over the odd fragments that the past two days had washed up: pieces, he was sure, of the same story, yet not fitting together at all. Marty had something to do with Ben Olssen's death, or at least according to the police he did. Marty had Ben's computer and his phone. And Marty was dead.

Posthumus topped up his glass, and put Kamil's sketches to one side. Perhaps the clue lay not in how Marty's and Ben's deaths were linked, but in how they were *different*: Marty shot to blazes in broad daylight, and Ben killed by an obscure poison in a railway underpass. Why was Marty not poisoned; or Ben not shot? Posthumus swirled the wine around in his glass, and took a sip. And then Ben wasn't simply poisoned, but injected using a hidden hypodermic, like the dissident Markov had been in London. De Boer had admitted as much in the lift this morning. Posthumus didn't know Marty that well, but well enough to be sure that such a sophisticated attack was way beyond him. Yet he shouldn't forget that the killing of Ben had almost failed. *Almost.* De Boer had said that the problem with Ben's ventilator at the hospital was not entirely straightforward. Had it been tampered with? Perhaps somebody was finishing off the job. A job that Marty had botched in the underpass. That made more sense than Marty as sophisticated poisoner. Or a job that Marty had *seen* botched in the underpass. That made even more sense. Marty was the sort who would not keep his mouth shut.

Posthumus put down his wine, stood up and walked to the window. Marty had somehow been able to make off with Ben's possessions. Except the overcoat. Had the junkie, Frans Kemp, been in the underpass too? De Boer had confirmed that Kemp had simply OD'd, with no trace of the poison that had done for Ben Olssen. Posthumus turned from the window, and began to pace the long room. A scenario: Marty emptying the pockets of Ben's coat, then abandoning it, but missing the hidden inside pocket where Posthumus had found his business card, the sort of pocket where you might keep a wad of emergency cash. Quite possible. Frans Kemp finding or stealing the coat, and striking lucky. Spending his windfall on what eventually killed him. Sudden access to funds was sometimes a reason for OD deaths, Posthumus knew from other clients who had come his way: from using purer stuff than they were accustomed to, or sudden high use after a period of withdrawal. Again, quite possible. Especially as Kemp was being looked after at the Sally Army. But for the moment, not important.

Returning to the window, Posthumus stretched his arms, Samson-like, between the posts on either side. A single star, the first of the evening, flickered over a gable across the canal, then was engulfed by a cloud. Posthumus drummed his fingers lightly on the wooden window frame. More important was the question of why somebody had wanted rid of Ben, what the motive was in killing him. If it was something to do with Ben's work, with fracking, why had only he been attacked, and not the others whose rooms were trashed? Maybe that was still to come . . . or perhaps the room trashing had nothing to do with Ben's death. Again, it wasn't what linked Ben's case with the others, but what made it different. De Boer had said that fabric in his suitcase and the lining of jackets had been slit. 'Slit' is what he'd said, not 'torn'. That sounded as if someone was looking for something, not the work of a vandal; so, two different events. It would be interesting to ask de Boer about whether the same had happened in the other rooms.

Posthumus turned and began to pace again, sweeping up his wine and the bottle as he passed. Somebody looking for something – drugs, hidden money – sounded far more the world of Henk de Kok and Marty than of outraged environmental activists. But, whatever the motive, if they could get

190

into Ben's hotel room, why kill him in the street? Perhaps because a death in the street could be made to look like something else. Robbery gone wrong, maybe, especially if the victim was bereft of belongings. But Posthumus had already dismissed that. Poison was too incongruous a weapon for robbery. Something else, then, that would make Ben Olssen's death appear to be from some other cause, that would disguise the true means. Posthumus ran his mind through the various street deaths that had come his way in the Funeral Department. He walked across to his computer, on the desk beneath the spiral staircase, and googled TTX, the poison de Boer had mentioned at the hospital.

Twenty minutes later, Posthumus got up and again began pacing. He had almost finished the bottle of wine, and the clock was edging towards midnight by the time he finally ascended the spiral staircase to bed.

# SATURDAY

## 21 April

# 12

The lights were still on at the IJ Tunnel Bureau, though it was past ten in the morning. Outside, the sky was a dark, turgid grey. To de Boer it looked bulging, convex: a water-filled canopy about to burst. The office offered a welcoming glow. Certainly after the chill over breakfast about his coming in to work, it did; and after trying to brighten the mood of the sulky child he had dropped off at football club on the way. And he appreciated the relative calm in his part of the building, with most of the non-uniforms happily at home for the weekend. It would give him a chance to pause, to assess and think through what he had so far.

That chance was short-lived. His mobile rang as he was hanging his jacket on the back of his door. The consultant from the hospital. De Boer listened, mostly, questioned insistently (how? who? when? where from?), and rang off frowning. He remembered something one of the techies had said in the canteen one day, about how the fundamental IT systems in a city, such as those governing traffic lights, were often the oldest, the simplest and so the most vulnerable. That any idiot could, if he wanted to, hack the system and turn all the lights to red. Or to green. Hospitals, too, it seemed. Ben Olssen's life support system had not failed. It had been turned off. The hospital techies had beaten his own men to it. Security had been breached, they said. The computers around Olssen's bed had been accessed, and shut down remotely. The alarm

195

signal that should have sounded was also governed by computer.

De Boer walked across to his desk, quietly thumping the wall with his fist as he went. He'd had this case just two days . . . it seemed like a lifetime. The hospital techies were still working on it, but their initial findings placed the system security breach at shortly after noon, with Olssen's computers turned off at twelve forty-seven. That was just minutes before two men on a motorbike had shot Marty Jacobs. De Boer pulled his chair back and sat down. All the elements of this case seemed suddenly to be moving even further apart. Just how many killers were they dealing with here? Where did he find a way in? He glanced at the notes he'd made at home, before going to bed.

*Olssen travel/phone records*
*Business associates/Futura*
*Interpol?*
*De Kok – junkie – Olssen connection?*

De Boer sighed. What with the cutbacks and so many staff tied up with Earth 2050, most of this would have to wait till Monday. A small stack of files lay on his desk, with an FYI Post-it from Hans on the cover of the first. Beside them, photos of Olssen's jackets with the slit lining, which he'd asked Murat to bag, and the forensic report on Olssen's room. Murat had highlighted a phrase here and there, but the report offered nothing much: no traces of drugs anywhere in the room, nor on the suitcase or slit clothing; too many finger prints in general, and none anywhere significant. There was a note from the young detective saying that none of the other room-trashing victims had reported clothing slit, or any damage to their own property, and that Olssen's door was the only one where the lock was malfunctioning afterwards. Interesting. Also the time when the lock corruption occurred: Tuesday, 19.08. Some time *before* Olssen was attacked. Even more interesting. The concierge had said that Olssen left the hotel just after seven.

There was a further line from Murat saying that the hotel would be in touch on Monday to say whether Greg Robertson's number was recorded in their system. De Boer shrugged. That could wait, he had enough to be getting on with. He emailed the hotel authorising the clearing of Olssen's room and the packaging of the remainder of Olssen's effects, to await collection by Pieter Posthumus of the municipal Burials Department. He gave a half-smile. He had been glad of Posthumus's offer to start sorting the repatriation now. And of the man's curiosity. It was good to have brains like that as a back-up.

De Boer flipped through the files Hans had left for him, checking cover titles: Pia Jacobs's statement, one from Irene Kester (so they had managed to calm her down after all), a couple of other witness statements, a thin file on Dirk Jacobs, and a heavier one on Henk de Kok. Well, this little lot seemed as good a place to start as any, but first he took a quick look at his emails. One just in from the Beursstraat Bureau: a motorbike, presumed to be the one used in the Jacobs drive-by, had been found burned out behind warehouses in Noord. There was still no sign of the riders. And another message, which he'd glanced at last night, from the boys downstairs. He read it more closely on the larger screen: the intact phone found in Jacobs's side pocket had been his own, and was easily accessed (a 0000 PIN code). Phone records showed frequent calls over a number of days to a listed landline: Milord, a strip joint in De Wallen. One corner of de Boer's lips twitched upwards. Now why did *that* not surprise him? Milord, he knew, belonged to Henk de Kok. There were also a number of calls, one lengthy, received from a pay-as-you-go number (apparently now inoperative), between 18.07 and 20.23 on 17 April. Tuesday, again. The day Ben Olssen was attacked. De Boer opened an attachment, which listed exact times: some lengthy calls, others a matter of a few seconds only. He scanned it for a moment, then pulled over a pad and noted the times of the calls, labelling the unknown number A.

18.07  First call Jacobs → A (17 seconds)
19.06  A → Jacobs (16 seconds)
19.22  Jacobs → A (34 seconds)
19.35  A → Jacobs (4 seconds)
20.10  A → Jacobs (long call, ending 20.23)

De Boer checked his notes so that he could add the other events they had times for to the list on the pad, and felt a light tingling down the back of his neck.

20.23  CCTV (Piet Heinkade camera) Olssen enters
       underpass

The exact time the call from A to Jacobs's mobile ended. De Boer wrote on:

20.40  CCTV shows Jacobs apparently ditching coat
       behind library

That was five minutes' or so walk from the underpass, so that meant the attack was over by, at the very latest, 20.35 . . . and indeed:

20.42  Passing bus driver calls ambulance, has spotted
       Olssen lying in underpass

De Boer placed his fingertips together and stared at the times on the list for a while. Olssen had left the Krasnapolsky just after seven o'clock, on his way to an appointment at Café 1e Klas at Central Station. A waiter at 1e Klas had said Olssen left the café just after eight. The lock on Olssen's room door had been corrupted at 19.08. De Boer pulled the pad closer to him and began to sketch out a possible scenario.

18.07  First call Jacobs → A (17 seconds)
*Contact established.*

19.06  A → Jacobs (16 seconds)
*A watching Olssen's room.*
*Jacobs in hotel lobby.*
*A phones Jacobs to tell him Olssen has left and give description. Jacobs follows Olssen, while A searches room.*

19.22  Jacobs → A (34 seconds)
*Jacobs notifies A that Olssen is in Café 1e Klas.*
*(Time for Olssen to get computer-repair recommendation from concierge and walk to 1e Klas.) Gives route.*

19.35  A → Jacobs (4 seconds)
*A leaving Krasnapolsky? Arriving at Central Station?*

20.10  A → Jacobs (long call, ending 20.23)

De Boer frowned for a moment, then wrote again:

> *?? Jacobs in café, watching Olssen. A not (wary of CCTV?).*
> *Olssen leaves (after 20.00); rear entrance (unexpected?). A takes over tail and maintains phone contact with Jacobs (giving instructions?).*

De Boer stopped writing, and tapped his pen on the edge of the desk, then he pushed back his chair and stood up in a single movement, and strode out to fetch himself a coffee. Back at the desk, he picked up the files Hans had left him. Pia Jacobs's statement was pretty much what Hans had outlined on the phone: she fingered Henk de Kok for Marty's death, and said that de Kok had picked up Marty shortly after five o'clock on the 17th. She had clammed up tight about her own husband, apart from saying that Marty wasn't half the man that he had been. According to her, Marty had no idea of the de Kok connection. He'd been a child at the time. She had known he was working for de Kok, but had let it go on as she knew it would end badly, and that he would come crawling back to her in the shop. De Boer let out a soft grunt. It had ended a little more badly than she thought. He remembered what Hans had said on the phone, about Pia getting off on humiliating her son, being happy to watch him fail, and constantly measuring him up against his father. And he remembered her sour, hard reaction, with Marty's body still lying in the shop. Sometimes that was a defence, a denial. De Boer had seen that before. Not here. Pia Jacobs seemed to loathe her son because he wasn't his dead father. It was as if she, in a warped way, saw Marty's death as his just desserts simply for being who he was. Or who he was not. For a moment, de Boer found himself feeling sorry for Marty Jacobs.

He exhaled heavily, and turned back to the files. Neither the Kester woman, nor any of the other witnesses had caught the motorbike registration number, and none had much to add to what they already knew. The old Dirk Jacobs file contained an autopsy report – blow to the head, and drowning – a wad of post-mortem photographs, plus a rap sheet listing a couple of minor scams and dirty money charges. Not much that stuck.

And also an investigating officer's summary of the drowning and two witness statements throwing suspicion on Henk de Kok, but not enough evidence to charge him. De Boer put the file to one side, and opened the background file on Henk de Kok. On top were a number of photographs: a passport mugshot, a batch of observation photos, a press clipping showing de Kok beaming alongside the drug dealer Klaas Bruinsma, another of him posing at the Auto RAI show, with a newly acquired, suspiciously expensive sports car. De Kok through various decades and a variety of haircuts.

De Boer spread the photos out in front of him. In each of them, de Kok was wearing a black leather jacket. It was clearly something of a trademark. De Boer went back to his computer and accessed the footage they had of Ben Olssen entering the underpass – the grainy shot, from a camera way up the Piet Heinkade – Olssen, with the figure behind him who had followed him into the tunnel and then left almost immediately. A figure they had not been able to identify: a man in a hoodie, with a bag over one shoulder . . . and not just a hoodie. A hoodie worn under a black leather jacket. OK, so there was nothing uncommon about that, but still. As far as he could make out, the man was broad-shouldered, thickset, a big man. De Boer frowned. De Kok, maybe? Could it be? De Boer paused the video just as Olssen entered the underpass: 20.23. The time the call from the unidentified mobile to Marty Jacobs had ended. He went back a bit, ran it again. It was a bugger that the quality was so bad, and that this was the best resolution the boys downstairs could manage, but de Boer would be willing to bet his last sweaty eurocent that at 20.23, the movement of the hoodie's far arm – down from the head, elbow crooking out behind the line of his back – was him taking a phone from his ear and putting it in his jacket pocket.

★   ★   ★

Not even a quarter past ten, and already all the groceries done. Posthumus turned sideways as he mounted the narrow stairs to his apartment, the hook-on panniers from his bicycle in one hand, two bulging supermarket bags in the other. Perhaps he should try to go to the farmers' market this early more often. Usually, his Saturday mornings were sacrosanct: a slow breakfast at home, mid-morning oysters at the market, a chat with the goat-cheese man. Most of all, he enjoyed the feeling that the reins of the day were in his hands, that he held the control and rhythm of it all. Not today. He'd been up earlier than he'd liked to fit in his weekly shop before the eleven o'clock appointment unilaterally declared by Kees, and had cycled tetchily across to the Noorderkerk . . . to find the market quiet, his list easily ticked off without jostle or delay. Even the supermarket he'd stopped at on the way home was blissfully shopper-free. The bumping as he climbed, and the brushing of bags along the wall, brought Gusta to her door, like some underwater creature looking out from under a rock.

'Can't stop!' said Posthumus, managing to flap both elbows in a form of greeting as he passed.

Up in his apartment, as he separated, categorised and put away his various purchases, Posthumus mentally placed the findings of his late-night internet trawl about TTX in an orderly line. The poison was hard to detect. It did not show up in the standard tox-screening tests that would be conducted on a dead body. When it was ingested from a puffer fish – by far and away the usual reason for TTX poisoning – doctors usually tested the food, rather than the person, to discover the cause. The poison paralyses the nervous system. Ben would have died of 'respiratory paralysis': he would have ceased breathing and his heart would have stopped. *If* the poison had worked. That was the point. Cold provisions safely stowed, Posthumus turned to the fruit and veg. If the poison had worked, if that little pellet that de Boer had mentioned, the one that had got blocked by Ben's fat cells, had done its job properly, Ben would have been found dead in the street. There was no outward sign of violent attack. An examining doctor may well have concluded death by sudden cardiac arrest. That happened. Even to people quite young. With no sign of a criminal act, there would be no detailed autopsy. So Ben's death would have been attributed to natural causes. (There was an ongoing discussion in medical and political circles – it had diverted Posthumus for a good half-hour – on whether examinations currently conducted on the cause of death were sufficient, that there might be cases of poisoning going undetected. That would certainly have been the case with Frans Kemp, if it had turned out that he had been poisoned, too.)

Posthumus paused for a moment. He had reached tins, jars and non-perishables. And he had come to the question of *why*? He could see now why Ben had not been killed in the hotel room. The poison acted within minutes, but not instantly. From a hotel room, Ben would have been able to phone for help. Not so in the street, with his phone taken from him. But the attack couldn't be anywhere too public. The underpass was hardly in open public view. Most pedestrians used the tunnel through Central Station itself. The underpass would have been quieter, darker. So, either Ben had been lured there, or someone had been following him, waiting for an opportunity when there would be no witnesses. If the poison had worked, Ben would have been found either dead, or complaining of breathing difficulties and chest pain, apparently having, or having had, a heart attack. No one would be any the wiser. Was that why all his possessions had been taken? To make Ben appear the victim of a heart attack brought on by a mugging? Or even that a particularly callous thief had robbed the body? Posthumus slowly pushed the door of his larder closed. All this made even more sense of his idea that the attack had nothing to do with the trashed rooms. Whoever trashed the rooms wanted that found out. It was a statement. Ben's murder was just the opposite.

Posthumus crossed the apartment to fetch his coat. One thought jarred. A problem for the killer, anyway, if he was trying to disguise the cause of death. What if Ben spoke? Posthumus slipped on his coat, patting the pockets for his keys. Even if the titanium pellet containing the poison had functioned properly, the murderer ran the risk of Ben being able to say, in whatever time he had left, what had happened. He could identify who had attacked him. Unless, of course, Ben did not know his attacker. Or attackers. Posthumus went out on to the landing, and turned to lock the door behind him. Downstairs, he could hear Gusta singing above the sound of vacuuming. And what was it de Boer had said about Hubert or Humbert? Ben *had* been trying to say something when he arrived at the hospital. That was one for later. He'd have to ask de Boer more about that. Posthumus set off down the stairs. And then there was the question of how Marty fitted in to all this. Posthumus had put together a possible picture of *how*, but still not of *why*; and certainly, he felt no nearer to answering *who*. He heard Gusta's door open as he passed, and quickened his step.

By the time Posthumus was cycling along the banks of the Amstel to Kees's houseboat, he was running a little late. A louring sky was threatening rain, but there was no time to turn back for a cape or umbrella now. The first heavy drops were beginning to explode on the ground around him as he tugged on the bell-rope at Kees's front door, just a few minutes after eleven. Posthumus heard a muffled 'Come!', and ducked his head under the low lintel to step inside.

Kees was sitting at an old wooden office desk, rolling a joint. Books, boxes and ring-binder files were lined on shelves and stacked in teetering piles all round the front part of the boat, which Kees used as a living and working area. Three different easy chairs faced each other around a low table at the far end. Here and there, buckets, rope and cartons containing unidentifiable chunks of metal offered esoteric evidence of life on the water – or maybe they were destined for one of Kees's on-board sculptures; Posthumus had never been able to work that one out. A wave of cosy familiarity washed through him, carrying him back more than twenty years. Apart from a proliferation of the clutter, and the state-of-the-art computer on the desk, the place was just how he remembered it.

'Pieter Posthumus, you cheeky bloody turncoat,' said Kees, rising to greet him and giving him a bear-hug.

Back then, to a twenty-something Posthumus, Kees had seemed old; and he seemed old to Posthumus now, though, curiously, no older. It was as if Kees had remained in bristly white-haired stasis, while Posthumus had been quietly catching him up.

'Coffee?' said Kees. Without waiting for an answer, he walked through to a cooking alcove in the rear part of the boat, and picked up an Italian stove-top espresso-maker, so stained and battered that Posthumus was sure that it was the same one he'd been given coffee from many a time before.

'This is a sudden emergence from the shadows,' said Kees. 'Not unwelcome, I'll say that, but unexpected. I thought you'd done a runner into the land of the respectable.' He gave the pot a shake. 'Just made. Some left,' he said, pouring thick black liquid into a small cup.

'I saw the article about you in the *NRC* magazine,' said Posthumus, 'then I bumped into Bin-Bag, or Freddie as he is now, and by chance I was in the neighbourhood yesterday, so . . .'

Kees was staring hard at him. 'Well, whatever the reason, it's good to see you,' said Kees. 'And I'm glad you could make it this morning. Not much time these days, what with Earth 2050. Bloody madhouse.' He handed Posthumus the cup, picked up his own from the desk, and led the way to sit down.

'Gabi says hello, by the way,' said Posthumus.

'Ah, La Lanting. Bright woman. I was hoping to catch her at a panel session yesterday, but she was pissing about with film stars, I hear.'

'Gabi wanted to tell you about Ben Olssen,' said Posthumus.

'The Young 'Un? He was also bunking off yesterday, didn't get his backside on the bench in time for the discussion on fracking. They're not up to something, those two? The horny bugger!'

Posthumus hesitated, but there wasn't an easy way. 'Ben's dead,' he said.

Kees sat down, suddenly and heavily, in one of the frayed armchairs. Posthumus told him about the attack, and Ben's death in hospital. Kees was silent for a long while, made a move to get up, but sank back into the chair. Again, he looked hard at Posthumus.

'Why are you here, *exactly*, Pieter Posthumus?' said Kees.

Posthumus took a sip of thick, bitter, lukewarm coffee. 'Someone else I know has been killed,' he said. 'And one of the people the Funeral Team is dealing with was found dead wearing Ben Olssen's coat. There seems to be some connection between it all. I'm trying to fit the pieces together.'

Kees's eyes flicked across the room, then back to Posthumus. 'Tell me about this new job of yours, with the council,' he said, giving the word a twist, 'this "Funeral Team". Last I heard you were working with the Fraud Department.'

'Conduct and Integrity Unit,' said Posthumus. 'That meant internal investigations rather than chasing people cheating on benefits. I've been with the Funeral Team well over a year now.'

The way Kees was regarding him was as if he were looking from a distance, and could only just make him out.

'And do you often do this "fitting the pieces together"?' said Kees.

Posthumus told Kees about Amir, the young Moroccan found dead in a canal, and Zig, in a pool of blood at the guesthouse, and how the story he had pieced together for each had been the right one.

'And you think you can do the same for Ben?' said Kees.

'Officially I will probably be seeing to the repatriation, so I'm trying to trace friends and family,' said Posthumus.

'And unofficially?'

Kees got up to walk across to his desk.

'As I said, I'm still trying to fit pieces together,' said Posthumus. 'And as yet not really getting anywhere.'

He noticed that Kees moved with a little difficulty, discreetly holding on to furniture for support as he passed.

'*You* don't know of any friends or family, do you?' said Posthumus. 'I'm not even sure if Ben was ever married.'

Kees emitted a subdued version of one of his Santa Claus laughs. 'Married? The Young 'Un? There'll be plenty of broken hearts, yes. But no grieving wife. He said he only once came close, and he blamed *that* on the air in Venice.' Kees stood for a moment, drumming his fingers on the desktop.

'And friends? Someone called Hubert, or Humbert perhaps?' said Posthumus. 'Or a Greg Robertson. He may be a reporter of some sort.'

Kees stopped drumming, and picked up the joint he'd been rolling when Posthumus arrived. He shook his head. 'So, this wasn't a social call, after all,' he said, coming back to sit down.

'Well, it was primarily,' said Posthumus. 'Most of this is quite new.'

He looked across at Kees, slumped in his chair, seeming suddenly very much older. Best be upfront. The two of them went back too far.

'But there was another reason, yes. I told you that I had bumped into Bin-Bag earlier . . . Freddie,' said Posthumus. 'While we were having a drink together, he was watching a report about those hotel rooms that were trashed around town, where the delegates from the fracking discussion that Ben was supposed to have been part of were staying.'

Posthumus drained the last of the coffee and supressed a grimace.

'I couldn't help but get the feeling Freddie knew something about that,' Posthumus went on. 'When I came round yesterday, part of the reason was to sound you out about Freddie, about whether he may have had something to do with it.'

Kees fumbled about in a pocket, and produced a lighter. 'Maybe he did, maybe he didn't,' he said. 'But that was just a cheeky way of making a point. Pranksters showing people like Ben the error of their ways. But I'd wager what's left of my poor wizened soul that it had nothing to do with anybody killing him.'

Posthumus looked across at him, expecting more. Nothing came. Kees lit up.

'Why do you say that?' said Posthumus.

Kees shrugged, but still said nothing. Posthumus did not push the point. He had come to the same conclusion himself, thinking about it earlier. Instead, he told Kees about Ben's split jacket lining and suitcase fabric. Kees took a long drag on the joint and frowned, holding his breath.

'That doesn't fit, not with the behaviour of someone trashing a room,' Posthumus went on.

Kees offered Posthumus the joint, held neatly between two fingers. Posthumus shook his head.

'It was as if somebody was looking for something,' Posthumus continued. 'But what? Something Ben hadn't delivered, perhaps? As he travelled so much, I wondered whether maybe he'd got caught up in smuggling.'

Kees exhaled and simultaneously let out a snort, and waggled the joint in the air. 'Drugs, you mean? The Young 'Un? He doesn't even do *this* stuff. Never has.'

'And it doesn't really fit with what I know of him,' said Posthumus. 'But it does perhaps with Marty, the other person who's been killed.'

'Marty?'

Posthumus explained the links between Ben's and Marty's deaths. Kees took another draw on the joint. He said nothing.

'But all this seems bigger than Marty,' said Posthumus. 'Even if Ben's death has nothing to do with the room-trashing, it could still have to do with his stance on fracking. He was some sort of consultant in the field, as far as I can work out, quite a high-flyer. He might have tangled with some environmental activist organisation bigger than whoever it was trashed those rooms.'

Kees stubbed out the joint and leaned back in his chair. He closed his eyes, and was silent for so long that Posthumus wondered whether he had gone to sleep.

'Vanilla,' said Kees at last.

Perhaps the old man had been asleep; he wasn't making any sense. Kees opened his eyes, but kept his focus somewhere over Posthumus's shoulder.

'The boy was naïve rather than dangerous,' said Kees. 'Soft. Nothing that would make activists want to kill him . . .' He trailed off, then turned to look at Posthumus. 'Anyone with any bloody sense opposes fracking,' he said. 'And in his heart Ben did too, just needed to be brought to his senses again. But he always thought he could fight people from the inside. He was supposed to be the lone voice of compromise on that panel yesterday. He didn't really belong in the same bag as the others who had their rooms done over.'

Kees's voice shook a little. He cleared his throat, and went on. 'Ben believed that fracking could be a temporary solution, a stopgap that gave countries the time to develop more sustainable sources of energy, so that if you worked with it rather than against it you could avoid catastrophe when oil starts running out.'

He made a move to get up, pushing heavily on the arms of his chair. Posthumus leaned forward to help him and was given a dirty look.

'Remember Hubbard's Peak?' said Kees. 'Or are you so far gone from your old life that you've forgotten what matters?'

Posthumus did not take the bait. 'The high point in oil production, followed by a steep decline in supply,' he said instead.

Kees walked, shuffling a little, to a cupboard at the far end of the boat. 'Four out of ten,' he said. 'Higher marks if you can give me possible effects of that rapid decline.'

'Economic turmoil, and in countries without alternatives, who have not prepared for it, social unrest, financial collapse, famine.'

'Better,' said Kees, returning with a ceramic *jenever* bottle and two small glasses. 'Ben was going on about Hubbard's Peak. He believed that fracking could be used to buy time, a short-term tactic to achieve the long-term solution of developing replacement energy sources, which he could help do by working from the inside, shaping new policies, forming new structures.'

He put the bottle on the low coffee table, and sat down.

'Bloody nonsense,' he said. 'You think governments would magically start getting off their arses? No way. Problem shelved, not problem solved. As I said, the boy was naïve. *He* called it nuanced, taking a holistic approach. But it was all just bullshit, and I told him so. Still . . . the lad managed to make a lot of money telling people what to do about it. Poor sod.'

Kees filled each glass to the brim. 'Good stuff this,' he said. 'For special occasions.'

He leaned over the table to take a sip direct from the glass in the traditional way, nodding to Posthumus to do the same. It was early in the day, but there was no alternative. Posthumus leaned over and sipped the 'camel's hump' meniscus off the top of the drink. Kees straightened up, and raised his glass in a toast.

'To the Young 'Un,' he said. 'His heart was in the right place.'

Good stuff or no, Kees knocked back his *jenever* in a single shot. Posthumus proceeded more cautiously, but Kees was already pushing himself out of his seat again.

'And now I am going to throw you out,' he said to Posthumus. 'There's some work I've got to do before the next conference session.'

De Boer froze the CCTV footage on a still of the figure in a hoodie, and placed a couple of the photographs of Henk de Kok beside the screen. De Kok as the other man who attacked Olssen, as well as nixing Marty Jacobs. De Kok silencing an accomplice. Would that make sense? Possibly. De Boer sat back in his chair and drummed a tattoo on the edge of his desk with his fingers. It was worth following up, anyhow. De Kok had his grubby fingers in this somewhere. He would want de Kok's leather jacket for starters, to send to the lab. And that hoodie, if they could find it. But he didn't want to spook de Kok with a house search if he wasn't sure of his ground. De Kok was a slippery bastard at the best of times. De Boer stopped drumming. He'd need something more on the bastard. He had come close to fucking up on the Zig Zagorodnii case by being in too much of a hurry. That half-smile tweaked at his lip again. It had been Pieter Posthumus who had rescued him then. For a moment he felt like giving the man a call.

Outside, the first few heavy spots of rain kamikazied on to the window pane. De Boer got up and crossed to the far corner of the room, punching one fist into a flat palm. It wasn't only that he needed more, it was that some of what he *did* have didn't entirely fit. Rare poisons and hidden hypodermics struck him as out of de Kok's league. Having Marty Jacobs blasted to bits through a shop window, now that was more de Kok's style. Poison just didn't fit. Plus de Kok didn't strike him as the type to do that sort of dirty work himself. So, were they dealing with two killers here? De Kok ordering the hit on Jacobs, but somebody else helping Jacobs to attack Olssen? De Boer aimed a kick at an imaginary football, then walked, hands in pockets, back to his desk. Jacobs worked for de Kok, and even if the second man attacking Olssen wasn't him, he was implicated somehow. De Boer was sure of it. He had learned to trust his gut, and his gut told him that Jacobs's murder and the attack on Olssen were linked . . . and that the link was Henk de Kok. But how? There were Jacobs's phone calls to Milord, and Pia Jacobs's statement that de Kok had picked up Jacobs just before the attack. And if poison and hypodermics were not de Kok's style, they were even less so that of the butcher's boy. He'd be more of a bulwark, contacted by phone from the other side of the underpass, to stop Olssen in his tracks.

De Boer stood a while at his desk. Another problem . . . motive. Why should de Kok kill Olssen? What was the connection? Olssen had been in town only a couple of days. There was no indication that he even knew de Kok. What could link them? De Boer picked up one of the photographs of Olssen's slit jackets. Whatever it was that had been in these, or whatever somebody had been looking for, that's what. Somebody who had been watching the room phoned Marty Jacobs the moment Olssen left, searched it swiftly and professionally, then with Jacobs's help caught up with Olssen again when he didn't find what he wanted. Something Olssen had not delivered, maybe. But what exactly? Olssen wasn't the type to be a drugs mule. He'd be higher end. And there were no traces of drugs on Olssen's clothing or in the hotel room. Women were slimeball de Kok's main stock-in-trade. There was easier money in that. And Olssen was suave, good-looking. De Boer could see him as a recruiter of some sort. Possible, though not convincing.

An email pinged in. De Boer glanced at the name. Merel Dekkers. For a moment he frowned, then got it. Of course. The Posthumus niece. The hot blonde. And then he got it again, before he had even opened the mail. She had been talking about de Kok's façade companies and dodgy dealings. Money laundering. That could be it. *That* would link Olssen and de Kok. It seemed more Olssen's style. Cash sewn into those jackets. And it could link Olssen and Marty Jacobs: Posthumus had said last night that Jacobs was poking his fingers into some sort of property company. The father, Dirk Jacobs, had form for laundering, too. And that would bring you back to de Kok.

It was raining hard when Posthumus left the houseboat. He helped himself to one of the umbrellas in the basket beside the door. Kees believed umbrellas should be communal property, to be used and abandoned according to need, rather like the shared white bicycles in the 1960s. Posthumus had picked a large green and white one, which he could wield as he cycled, Amsterdam-style, steering with his free hand.

His dismissal had been abrupt, but apart from that, the visit to Kees had unsettled him, created a sense of discomfort, like incipient indigestion. Something wasn't quite right. Posthumus let images of the past hour run through his mind as he pedalled. Kees had known so much about Ben, his stance on fracking, for instance. That had something to do with it. It was as if Kees and Ben had met recently, yet Kees had made no mention of seeing him. The rain was becoming impossible, splashing past the umbrella on to Posthumus's shins and knees. He swung off the saddle and began to walk, pushing the bicycle beside him. Images of Kees, snatches of phrases, kept coming. Posthumus knew himself well enough to allow that to happen, and to pay close attention: Kees with a joint; Kees waggling the joint, talking of Ben, saying, 'he doesn't even do *this* stuff'. That was it. Not so much that Kees used the present tense – people did that all the time with a recent death – but that he spoke with such authority, about *now*. Posthumus took shelter beneath the portico of one of the modern apartment blocks beside the river: Kees putting the *jenever* bottle on the table between them, still talking about Ben and fracking: 'Problem shelved, not problem solved.' Kees filling the tiny glasses to the brim: 'All just bullshit, and I told him so.' Posthumus leaned his bike against a pillar. *And I told him so.* Posthumus turned to shake out the umbrella and close it, and caught sight of the words printed around the edge: Grand Hotel Krasnapolsky.

# 13

The heavy shower didn't last long. After ten minutes or so, Posthumus thought he would risk riding on, and by the time he was back on the riverside bike path the rain had stopped and the occasional sliver of blue was edging the clouds apart. Kees must have spoken to Ben, Posthumus was sure; Ben had probably even visited the boat. So why was Kees acting so strangely, covering things up? Had they fallen out over whatever it was Ben was up to? Posthumus sailed on past the towering Philips headquarters, the Krasnapolsky umbrella now rolled and at an angle, its point jammed tight into the milk crate on the front of his bicycle. Kees had been evasive about Freddie and the room trashing; Posthumus was sure he knew more about that than he was letting on. But, like Freddie, Kees had seemed shocked to hear of Ben's death. And he had summarily dismissed the idea that Ben's death had anything to do with the vandalism, as if he had a better idea as to what might have been behind the attack. But what could that be? Posthumus stopped at the back of a cluster of bicycles waiting for a traffic light. Did Kees know what it was that Ben had in the lining of his jacket? Or at least what somebody had been looking for. Something that also linked Ben to Marty and the world of Henk de Kok. Marty, the would-be property man; de Kok the – what had Merel said about him? – the man followed by a bad smell: strip clubs, dodgy dealings, money laundering.

The light turned green. Two tourists wobbled to a slow start ahead of him, riding abreast. Money laundering. Was that the link? Had Ben been moving cash around? That would fit with the jackets, and with all his travelling. Flip de Boer seemed to be thinking along those lines. And Kees *had* been edgy about Posthumus's job with the Fraud Department. Posthumus rang his bell, and squeezed past a startled wobbler. Or could it be the women? Ben involved with trafficking, an upmarket groomer perhaps. That seemed less likely, despite Kees's remark that Ben was a heartbreaker. Posthumus slowed where the bicycle path crossed the difficult dog leg in the road that led up to the OLVG Hospital. A conversation echoed in the back of his mind. A conversation he had had the last time he was on this street. He stopped against the kerb, his eyes following a black Mercedes that drove past, heading towards the hospital. It wasn't just that he was here again now, it was as if somebody were whispering something, very faintly in one ear, something he couldn't quite hear, something he had to concentrate hard to catch.

*Venice.* When Kees had made that remark about Ben and women, he'd said that Ben had only once nearly got married, and that he blamed the slip on the air in Venice. *Venice.* Yesterday morning. In the taxi. With Christina. She mentioned her affair with Ben had begun in Venice, had joked about that being such a cliché. But she'd said it was a fling, a whirlwind: Venice and a short stay in New York. She'd said nothing about marriage. It was a long shot – Ben the womaniser, in the world's most romantic city. It could very easily not have been Christina he was talking about to Kees. But what if it was? Hadn't Gabi said yesterday that Christina was closer to Ben than she let on? What if Christina knew Ben a good *deal* better than she was letting on? Posthumus was aware of a familiar sensation, as two previously disparate parts of a puzzle moved closer together, and seemed to promise a fit. Not for the first time, he had the feeling that Christina had a clearer idea than she was admitting of what Ben had been trying to warn her about.

Posthumus did not ride on, but pushed his bicycle across the wide street, causing a tram driver to ring angrily as he wandered across the line. Could it be more than that? Did Christina, who Cornelius insisted on dismissing as a little rich girl, also have something to do with whatever Ben was up to? Posthumus had always said to Cornelius that there was more to her than met the eye. She travelled. More than Ben by the sound of things. For her, moving cash around the world would be easy. And hadn't Cornelius said that she had family connections with the Walraven Bank, one of those old, private Amsterdam banks. Not the sort with queues and tellers, but the discreet, plush-carpet sort, with clients by recommendation and no questions asked. Had Christina been helping Ben? That would explain Christina's distress, her insistence on blaming herself for what happened to Ben, saying that she should have been there. Maybe she really *was* supposed to have been there. Possibly, it wasn't cash that was being moved around at all, but something closer to Christina's world. Rare animal parts, perhaps, like he'd suggested to Cornelius at the crematorium; the tiger organs and powdered rhino horn for which the Chinese would pay a fortune. Posthumus stopped at the opposite kerb, and took out his phone. Cornelius answered at the second ring.

Cornelius led the way into the sitting room. Posthumus had accepted the lunch invitation readily, as soon as he heard that Christina wouldn't be there. It seemed unfair, at this point, fully to mention his concerns to Gabi and Cornelius, and he welcomed the opportunity to sound them out a little alone.

But from upstairs, Posthumus could hear voices, and Gabi's laughter cascading from the open study door.

'Is that Christina up there with Gabi?' he said, hesitating and nodding towards the stairs. 'I thought you said she wouldn't be joining us.'

'It is the youth Niels who stirs such merriment,' said Cornelius, with an upward glance that was directed more to the heavens than the room upstairs. 'He will be off, God willing, and Gabrielle down in a moment. We are indeed spared milady's company today, until after lunch.'

Posthumus followed Cornelius on through.

'You don't like her much, do you? Christina, I mean,' said Posthumus, taking a seat in a wing armchair.

They had been here before: Cornelius saying that he found Christina superficial, that she riled him.

'She devours one's energy, and saps the spirit,' said Cornelius. 'But the conference is nearly over, so I dare say we won't see her for another ten years, or until she needs something.'

'That's a bit harsh, don't you think?' said Posthumus.

Cornelius looked at him, over the tops of his glasses. 'You're not still intent on winning the lady's favour, are you?' he said.

'No, no, not in the slightest,' said Posthumus. 'But it seems to me that it's *Christina* who has given Gabi something she needs, rather than the other way around. This star that everyone is making such a fuss about.'

Cornelius didn't answer immediately, but waved his hand towards an already open bottle of wine. 'Drink?' he said. 'Red? White?'

Posthumus could still feel the effects of his hastily downed *jenever*, but, what the hell, it was Saturday.

'White would be good,' he said.

'No doubt I *am* being churlish,' said Cornelius, as he poured. 'Especially now that she has conjured them both tickets to the grandees' gala dinner tonight. But it's the way she does it. Merely to score points, to put Gabrielle down.' He handed the glass to Posthumus and topped up his own.

'Now I think you *are* being unfair,' said Posthumus. 'Besides, Gabi's too sassy to fall for that sort of thing. Or it wouldn't bother her, she'd see through it.'

'She sees it, and doesn't see it. 'Twas ever thus, apparently. Even back when they were children and Christina paraded *her* father as ambassador. She was locked in a competition of her own perceiving with Gabrielle. *My* view is that nowadays this takes the form of Christina relentlessly trying to demonstrate that she, in her flibbertigibbet job, wields more power than Gabrielle as a director. Hence the star, hence the tickets for a dinner for which Gabrielle would otherwise not be eligible. But my dear wife seems inured to it all.'

'And you're not?'

'It is *constant*, from the brand name on her handbag to the names that are dropped over dinner: President Putin at a conference in St Petersburg, Bill Clinton, Bianca Jagger, last night the Chinese ambassador. Ceaseless. As I say, it saps the spirit.'

Posthumus smiled. Christina's first-name terms with the famous hadn't escaped him.

'Forgive me,' said Cornelius, lightly rubbing his temples. 'An inappropriate outburst. These past few days . . . I'm afraid I am worn a little thin by overexposure.'

Posthumus steered talk in a direction Cornelius might find more agreeable. 'And will I be seeing young Lukas today?' he said.

'Indeed,' said Cornelius. 'He's in his room at the moment, editing video and "archiving his childhood photographs". I quote! Can you believe it? The boy is barely twelve!'

Posthumus laughed. 'Lukas was showing me something on a tablet last time I was here,' he said. 'He was all marmoset fingers, and sudden slides and screen changes. I was quite lost.'

'At times I feel my son inhabits a different world,' said Cornelius. 'And next year it will be even more so, when he can join Facebook and Twitter. We shall have to relent. I am trying to instil some sense of privacy in him, and of what it means that these photographs of his might be out there for ever.'

'Or wiped out for ever, if the technology changes, or there's a blip in this Cloud,' said Posthumus. 'And by then we'll have lost our own ability to remember.'

A twinge of sadness deflected him for a moment. When his own father had his memory wiped out, a virus ravaging his brain, Posthumus had sat with him, day after day for months, reading his old diaries, slowly rebuilding the past. That and going to church with him again. Somehow the familiar Catholic rituals had also helped.

'It's more likely that the whole system collapses, over-whelmed by the dross that is fed into it piling ever higher,' said Cornelius.

Posthumus returned to the present. 'I suppose it *is* a chilling thought, all those photographs, those moments, those memories, out there for all time,' he said.

Cornelius stretched back in his chair. 'Memory is all well and good, but there is an art to forgetting, and we are losing it,' he said.

There was a short silence, as both men took that remark in their individual directions.

'That's a phrase I could have used the other day, with Tina,' said Posthumus after a while. He told Cornelius how Tina was struggling with reminders of her difficult past being daily on her doorstep. 'And then it struck me that there I was giving fatherly advice, which I ought to be heeding myself,' he said. 'My brother's death . . .'

Posthumus stopped. He very rarely spoke to anyone apart from Anna, and these days Merel, about how he blamed himself for what happened to Willem, and the subsequent estrangement from Heleen and the girls.

'Merel coming back into my life has gone a long way in helping me to deal with that, but, like you say, there is an art involved in learning how and when to forget the past,' said Posthumus. 'It's the same for Tina, and, I guess, for Anna, in the aftermath of the fire and of Paul. The trick is not so much in forgetting, as in clinching the skill needed to fit the past into the present, and get on with things.'

Cornelius smiled, took a sip of wine, and put his feet up on a kelim-covered ottoman. Out in the hallway, Gabi was saying goodbye to Niels. She came into the room, stretching both arms, fingers interlocked, above her head.

'That's the absolute last of the conference business,' she said. 'No commitments this afternoon, until the dinner. Lovely to see you, Piet.' She turned to Cornelius. 'I'm ravenous, what's for lunch?'

'Salmon quiche from Peperwortel, and I've made a salad of sorts,' said Cornelius. 'There's also a little soup from last night.'

'And I picked up some cheese at the Albert Cuyp market,' said Posthumus, indicating the bag he'd brought with him.

'Well done both. A feast. Just one quiet glass of wine before I summon His Nibs down from upstairs.'

She poured herself a glass, and sat down full length on the sofa.

'You've heard about the banquet tonight at The Grand?' she said to Posthumus.

'With the great and the good? Cornelius was just telling me,' said Posthumus.

'Isn't it marvellous?' said Gabi. 'I can't believe I'm going. You wouldn't *believe* who's going to be there.'

Posthumus caught Cornelius's eye.

'I'll start warming the soup,' said Cornelius, getting up to go to the kitchen.

'I hear Christina has been working her magic again, landing the invitations,' said Posthumus, with a teasing glance to Cornelius as he left.

'It will be really good for her to go, it'll get her out of herself a little,' said Gabi.

'She's OK, is she?' said Posthumus. 'I mean, with the news about Ben.'

'She was shocked at first, of course, weren't we all? Just as we thought Ben was recovering,' said Gabi. 'I'm all for suing the hospital, or at least instigating some enquiry into efficiency, but Chris says she's just had enough of it all. She's stressed out as it is, worrying about her father being ill. Anyway, she's calmer about Ben now than she was in the beginning, when he was in the ICU. Closure, I suppose, a release of sorts.'

'I dropped in on Kees this morning, and told him,' said Posthumus.

Gabi sat up a little straighter on the sofa. 'How *is* the Old Man?' she asked. 'How did he take it? He and Ben were so close.'

'He took it reasonably well,' said Posthumus. He swirled the wine in his glass a little. 'He did say something odd, though. Ben and Christina weren't ever thinking of marriage, were they?'

'Getting married? Christina and Ben? First I've heard of it,' said Gabi. 'Unless it was ages ago. Christina and I had lost touch a bit, until she came back for the conference. As I said yesterday, I think she was closer to Ben than she lets on, but *marriage*? No, she would have said something. Dear old Kees, getting the wrong end of the stick. Or wishing Ben with a good catch, more like. I really *must* get to see him.'

Posthumus took the chance. 'I'm surprised Ben didn't go out and see him, as he was such a protégé,' he said.

'Didn't he? There was no time, I suppose. Ben can't have been in Amsterdam very long when it happened.'

'It looks like I'm going to be dealing with his repatriation,' said Posthumus. 'So I'm trying to trace family. You don't know of anyone, work associates even?'

Gabi shook her head. 'It's been a while since we worked together,' she said. 'I think he may have a brother in Sweden, but I really don't remember him mentioning family. I've a feeling they weren't very close. I'll ask around. Perhaps someone from one of the NGOs he worked with in Africa.'

'The meeting he had planned with Christina, that was purely pleasure? She didn't have any business dealings with him?'

'Not as far as I know,' said Gabi. 'In fact I'm sure not, or she would have been more on the ball about contacting him when we couldn't make it.'

'She wasn't?'

'She let him dangle, didn't answer his texts right away,' said Gabi. 'I got the feeling she was toying with him a bit, playing hard to get. Very Christina. Leaving the poor man sitting in the station café. Even refusing to take a cab back. She can be very naughty, Christina. No wonder she felt guilty afterwards.'

'A response Anna called "self-flagellating crap",' said Posthumus, with a laugh. He remembered Anna's reaction when Gabi had told them that Christina blamed herself for insisting on taking the train to the party on the Vecht that night. The full story made a bit more sense.

'Soup's ready!' called Cornelius from the kitchen.

Gabi swung her legs off the sofa. 'I'll go up and give Lukas a call,' she said. 'See you downstairs.'

★   ★   ★

After a second bottle of wine had been opened over lunch, Posthumus opted for a double espresso then took his leave, feeling that a siesta might not be a bad idea. Cornelius walked with him to the door. Posthumus was on the short flight of steps leading down to the street, when Christina came striding around the corner, carrying a couple of smart-looking shopping bags.

'Don't go in, it's me!' she called to Cornelius at the door. 'You didn't tell me you had such a *darling* little shop so close by!'

She raised her arm, dangling the bags to and fro.

'Some lovely ideas for tonight!' she said, flashing Cornelius a Hollywood smile.

Perhaps Cornelius had a point, about her being all surface, or was she deliberately winding him up? Posthumus could see she was succeeding.

'And how is my knight in shining armour?' she said, turning to greet him.

Was the smile she gave him more genuine? It seemed so.

'Well, hardly, I mean . . . I've hardly been much help, have I?'

What was it about her that reduced him to a bashful schoolboy? Posthumus pulled himself together. Perhaps he should ask her straight off about Ben. He tried to picture her doing some sort of shady deal with him. He couldn't.

'I'm so sorry, about Ben, I mean,' he said.

The smile dropped. For a moment Christina said nothing. Then she spoke, very softly. 'Yes.'

'I . . . I was wanting to ask something,' said Posthumus.

Christina held his gaze. Her eyes seemed incredibly sad.

'Not now, hey. Brave face and all that,' she said. 'Let's have a good evening first.'

With her free hand, she gave him a light slap on the cheek,

then ran up the stairs to where Cornelius had left the door standing ajar.

Posthumus walked slowly towards his bicycle. He was unlocking it when his phone rang: a Dutch number, no name. He answered cautiously.

'Yes?'

'Pieter. It's Kees. I need to talk to you.'

There was none of the usual ho-ho-ho gloss to Kees's voice.

'What about?'

Posthumus was aware that his own tone was none too friendly. Kees's evasiveness earlier had made him wary.

'Where are you?' said Kees.

'Zuid. On my way home.'

'Can I meet you there, at home I mean?' said Kees.

Posthumus did not answer immediately. He wanted to tackle the old guy, but not now, some time when he felt more alert.

'I . . . I haven't been quite honest with you,' said Kees. 'I owe you an apology.'

Posthumus held back from saying 'I should think so'.

'Can't this wait?' he said instead.

'No,' said Kees. 'No, not now.'

Curiosity perked Posthumus up a notch or two. He gave the old man his address.

Kees was already waiting on the bridge when Posthumus got home.

'That was quick,' said Posthumus.

'Taxi,' said Kees. He was holding a large brown envelope. 'Can we go inside?'

Upstairs in the apartment, Posthumus made some more coffee, to give himself a second wind. Kees hung about at the edge of the kitchen.

'Ben came to see me, on Tuesday,' said Kees. 'It must have been shortly before . . .'

'Yes,' said Posthumus. 'I had worked out as much.' He didn't offer Kees an explanation.

'He came to leave me this,' said Kees.

Posthumus glanced at the brown envelope with a frown.

'It was sealed, and I didn't really know what was in it,' said Kees. 'This morning, when you gave me the news, I wanted to check for myself, first. And for the past couple of hours I've been doing a little research.'

Posthumus handed Kees his coffee, and led the way to the front of the apartment to sit down.

'Ben arrived unannounced, wanting advice,' Kees went on. 'I was on the point of leaving and didn't give him as much time as I should have, so I didn't really get a full picture. I'm still not sure that I do.'

'What *is* in the envelope?' said Posthumus.

'Papers. Something Ben picked up by mistake at a fracking advisory meeting in Brussels, or rather was given by mistake among some other files, by one of the older participants who was losing his grip a bit, according to Ben. I remember being pissed off by his presumption.'

A little of Kees's normal sparkle returned for a moment. He shrugged.

'To tell the truth, I didn't really take him seriously,' he said. 'It was good to see the errant bugger again, but I was in a hurry, and he was going on about his computer being hacked, having stuff wiped off it, about emails disappearing and not wanting to leave the papers at the hotel. I thought it was just the Young 'Un being imaginative and excitable, especially when he started on about what sounded like some big-time politico pocket-lining. You know me, I don't mind the odd dose of conspiracy theory from time to time, but not when

I'm already late for an appointment. I thought there were more important things to be getting on with.'

The sober tone suddenly reappeared.

'I was wrong,' said Kees.

'And these papers?' said Posthumus.

Kees slid a thin sheaf of A4s out of the envelope. 'Ben said he couldn't quite make them out at first, and, I have to say, me neither, when I looked at them this morning. Well, not completely.'

Kees put the sheaf on to the coffee table between them.

'You didn't think to look at them before?' said Posthumus.

'As I said, they were sealed. Ben said he was only leaving them for safekeeping, and that he'd be in touch for a proper talk. But then the conference took over, I figured he was also busy, didn't think about it really. I had no idea that this . . .'

Kees's voice faltered; not just his shoulders but his whole body appeared to slump. He seemed ancient, tired. Posthumus reached over and put a hand on the old man's forearm. For a moment it was his own father there, once so strong, at the centre of things, suddenly reduced, in an unwelcomed reversal of roles.

'And the advice Ben wanted?' said Posthumus.

Kees sighed. 'Something about responsibility and loyalty, he said. He didn't go into it,' said Kees. 'I got the feeling that by the time he'd come out to see me he had already made up his mind, that he just wanted reassurance he was right. We all do that. Anyway, he said he was going to be speaking to a journalist the next day.'

'Journalist?' said Posthumus. He recalled what Merel had said in De Dolle Hond. 'I think I might know who that was.'

Kees patted the hand Posthumus had placed on his arm, and straightened up in his chair.

'Sorry, Piet,' he said. 'It came as a shock, the news this morning, and I hadn't seen you for so long. I needed to think. I almost said something then, but after all these years I didn't really know where you were at. I wanted to suss you out a bit more. Sorry. That's my real apology, when I said I wanted to apologise. That.'

Posthumus smiled. 'Come on, let's look at these papers,' he said.

Kees leaned over and separated the top sheet – a page of scribbles and doodles – from the others, which contained lists of initials, dates and figures. Posthumus picked up the page of doodles: across the top of the page was a series of parallel arrows, pointing diagonally upwards. Below that a criss-cross of lines and boxes. At the bottom right-hand corner of the sheet was an odd little sketch of flames, with below it the word PhoeniX, in English and ending with a capital letter.

'And Ben finds this among his papers when he gets back from a meeting, and immediately starts jumping to conclusions about shady dealings?' said Posthumus.

'All Ben said, was that what was on the papers fitted in with something he had been wondering about for a while. He said he couldn't be sure, but he thought that this was evidence of payments, bribes possibly, linked to clients – that means big corporations and governments in Ben's case – suddenly shifting policies when it came to energy issues. Fracking in this instance, but also denying climate change, upping oil production, that sort of thing.'

'Does that make sense?' said Posthumus. 'It sounds all very conspiratorial to me.'

Kees raised his hands. 'That's when it began to sound like the Young 'Un was in fairyland, and anyway I had to go,' he said. 'But since I saw you, I've been having a bit of a root about of my own. Speaking to people I know. Looking around online. Forums you wouldn't really know about, Dark Web stuff.'

Posthumus nodded. Even in the old days Kees's network had been extensive, and one that didn't always bear looking into too closely.

'There's something out there that fits what Ben was talking about,' said Kees. 'There are a couple of powerful lobbyists and corporations – Russian mainly – that seem to see how the big money can be made once the oil runs out.'

'But *why*, for goodness' sake?'

'Because they're negotiating deals, forming alliances, buying shares, companies, interests that will give them the edge in the meltdown that will occur when that happens. Power, in other words.'

Kees spread the other sheets out on the coffee table.

'And money,' he said. 'It's always about power and money.'

Posthumus looked down at the sheets of names and figures. Most of the sheets were headed 'PhoeniX', as if that were the name given to whatever this was about. Or the person dealing with it, maybe? He considered the doodle of the flames. Doodle was the wrong word. It looked accomplished, almost like a signature: a fan of four flames, with a three-pronged squiggle above it. PhoeniX. The squiggle could well be wings and a beak. He sat back in his chair, and tried to pull all this together with Ben's murder. A few days ago, he had felt as if he had opened a box of playing cards to find most missing. Now, it was as if he had two incomplete packs mixed together. He cursed quietly as his landline phone rang.

'That's as far as I got,' said Kees. 'Now you know as much as I do.'

'Let me just see who this is,' said Posthumus, getting up to answer it.

'Charon, you dark horse!'

'Cornelius?'

'You never told me you were a habitué of the Krasnapolsky,' said Cornelius.

'Oh, the umbrella,' said Posthumus. 'I realised just a moment ago that I'd left it behind. No matter.'

'Are you all right? You sound curious, distracted.'

'Just . . . thinking, about Ben Olssen,' said Posthumus. 'You don't know what associations a phoenix might have, apart from the usual rising from the ashes?'

'A *phoenix*? Good heavens, Charon. What on earth does a phoenix have to do with Ben Olssen? Whither does your mind wander, on a gloomy Saturday afternoon?' said Cornelius. 'The phoenix. Associated with the sun, with rebirth, death by fire, with royalty because of its supposed purple hue. I can't think of anything else offhand . . .'

Cornelius paused as if interrupted. Posthumus could hear voices in the background.

'Gabrielle wants to speak to you,' Cornelius resumed.

Posthumus heard the phone being handed over, amid more conversation.

'Pieter! I was just telling Christina, about you seeing to Ben's repatriation and trying to trace family and that, and she says she doesn't know anyone. What?'

Voices again. Gabi resumed.

'And that she hasn't worked with Ben since Greenpeace. Hang on a sec . . .'

Posthumus sighed, and shrugged apologetically to Kees. He wished he had simply let the phone ring.

Gabi was back on the line. 'Sorry about that, it's a madhouse here. That Marie, who goes to De Dolle Hond and has a boutique in De Wallen. She was saying the other day that she has beautiful genuine pashminas. Where is the shop exactly? Christina's developed an urgent need for an evening pashmina.'

'On an alley off the Warmoesstraat. The last on the right before you get to the Dolle Hond end,' said Posthumus.

'Wonderful,' said Gabi. 'I think we still have time. What now?'

Posthumus sighed, as the other end of the line again dissolved into mumbles.

'Christina says we can drop off the umbrella,' said Gabi, speaking again to Posthumus. 'Will you be at home?'

'I really don't want it, it's not even mine, it was part of the communal Kees collection,' said Posthumus. 'So keep it and pass it on, or if you're going to be at Marie's, then drop it back at the hotel. Or leave it at De Dolle Hond, I'll be going up there in an hour or two, and I'll take it to the hotel when I pick up the rest of Ben's stuff.'

Posthumus rang off, and crossed back to Kees.

'An umbrella from the Krasnapolsky,' he explained. 'It was one of the reasons I thought Ben might have been around to your place. By the way, do you know who it was that Ben said he nearly married, that time in Venice?'

Kees shook his head. 'I don't remember,' he said. 'I don't think Ben ever said, just that he got carried away by the romance of it all.'

Posthumus sat back down. 'What next?' he said. 'None of this really gets us any closer to who killed Ben.'

'Well, clearly somebody who didn't like it that Ben knew what he knew,' said Kees.

Posthumus leaned far back in his chair, and closed his eyes. Too many pieces. They were too disparate, too disordered. He opened his eyes, leaned forward and gathered the loose papers into a pile.

'The police?' he said. 'I know the detective in charge of Ben's case. I can take these to him on Monday.' He checked the time. 'He might even be at the Bureau now, he said he would be working today.'

'I guess so,' said Kees. 'Though it's not really going to tell them that much, and there's not much explanation we can give.'

Posthumus upended the pile, patting the edges of the sheets flush.

'Tell you what, let me hang on to these. Tomorrow I'll be able to have a clearer think about it all. If I still don't come up with anything, I'll take it all down to the police Bureau on Monday anyway.'

'And there's always that journalist Ben said he was going to speak to. You said you might know who he was?' said Kees.

'I'll have to speak to my niece. Somebody left messages for Ben at the hotel, Merel said she recognised the name.'

'It would be better for me if explanations came from somewhere other than yours truly,' said Kees. 'I wouldn't want to be going into too much detail about how I found out what I've been telling you. Not unless I have to, anyway.'

He pushed himself up out of his chair, and looked across the apartment to the clock on the kitchen wall. 'Meantime, there's one last session at the conference I'd like to be at. A talk, really, on the failure of macroeconomics. I might still just make it.'

Posthumus rose, going through the motions of seeing Kees out, but with his mind already sifting through fragments, sorting out pieces that seemed to match, prodding at gaps.

'Phone you tomorrow?' said Kees.

Posthumus gave a nod as the old man disappeared down the stairs.

Picking up the sheaf of papers from the coffee table as he went, Posthumus crossed to his workspace under the stairs. He placed the papers neatly on the lid of his ponder-box, switched on the computer, thought for a moment, then googled 'end of oil'. He scrolled down, scanning the two or three lines below each heading. Books for sale, of course, lots of crazy bloggers and conspiracy websites. Quite a bit about Hubbert's Peak. Posthumus's brow furrowed a little and he leaned back. Earlier, on the boat, Kees had said that conversation turned to Hubbert's Peak when Ben came to visit him. And not just then. Posthumus pushed his chair back from the desk. Yesterday morning, in the hospital. The hiss and click of the ventilator, peeps and pings from the machines. Ben's muffled voice from behind the ventilator mask. The words had been pulsing persistently at the back of Posthumus's brain ever since. *That's* what Ben had been trying to say, surely, not Hubbard, or Humbert, or whatever English names he thought he had been mumbling, but Hubbert. Why on earth, when he had hardly the energy to utter a word at all, would Ben be trying to talk about Hubbert's Peak, if it were not to say something about who had killed him? Hubbert and *fada*, no, *fara* . . . the Swedish word for 'danger', de Boer had said. Well, that made sense. Posthumus closed his eyes and tried to reconstruct the scene. There had been something else. When Ben first started trying to speak. He'd made just a hissing fff sound. And then a name. Posthumus honed his focus. Felix, that was it. Of course! Not Felix, but Phoenix: the name that headed most of the sheets of figures. Ben had been trying to talk about whatever was going on here.

Posthumus picked up the ponder-box with Ben's papers on top, and went to sit on the sofa. He paged through the sheets of initials, dates and figures. The figures, Kees had suggested, were payments. There was no indication of currency, but if the numbers were in dollars or euros, the amounts were substantial. Very substantial. Again Posthumus tried to pull together disparate pieces, to examine them for a possible match. Money. Henk de Kok. Last night, while he was cooking, Posthumus had remembered why the name was familiar.

It had come up a few months back, when Posthumus was looking into Zig's death at the guest-house: de Kok as one of the 'powerful friends' of a man Posthumus was asking too much about. A young man at de Kok's gym had used the phrase, warning Posthumus against crossing his boss. And it was what Marty had said, threatening Posthumus on the Nieuwmarkt. OK, 'powerful friends' was a common enough term, but still. And then there was Marty's dabbling in property deals . . .

Posthumus picked up his phone, rang Merel, and explained what he was up to.

'I was wondering if you'd had a chance to have a look at your research notes, from when you did that piece on De Wallen families,' he said. 'If there was anything on Marty's father's or Henk de Kok's financial wheelings and dealings.'

'Not a lot,' said Merel. 'De Kok's companies get lost in a tangle of subsidiaries and shell companies. The main one is something called Amsterdam Real Estate Management, ARM for short, but there seems to be something bigger behind that, some sort of holding company or investment brokers. I haven't really had much chance to look into it, I was out all morning.' Merel gave a little giggle. 'Dinner last night was quite fun. But I'm home now, I'll have another dig.'

'I look forward to meeting the reason for your distraction,' said Posthumus, with a smile. 'He has, of course, to meet my very strict requirements for approval.'

Merel laughed. '*This* one will, for sure,' she said.

'Meanwhile . . .' said Posthumus.

'Of course.'

'And while you're at it, do you think you could dig out a contact number for that Greg Robertson you were talking about, the journalist you mentioned yesterday?'

# 14

De Boer was quicker about lunch in the canteen than he might have been. Ed Maartens, the unofficial ringleader of the band of older officers who begrudged him his promotion, was there, in a foul temper at having to do Saturday duty, and de Boer was in no mood for fencing off snide comments for half an hour. Back in his office, he sat down at the computer. So, dirty money as the gum that stuck Olssen to de Kok and Marty Jacobs. It made sense. He'd want Olssen's bank statements seized, and his assets investigated. That would take time. Olssen was based in New York. That was something for Monday. De Boer skimmed again through the email from Merel Dekkers that had triggered his train of thought. Not too much there that he didn't already know: it was more the hard-nosed journalist pushing him for leads. She had chutzpah, that one. There was a knock on his door. De Boer winced with irritation.

'Yeah?'

Murat came in.

'They said downstairs you were here,' said Murat.

'And what are *you* doing, working on a Saturday afternoon?' said de Boer.

'I thought of something in the middle of the night, and wanted to follow it up,' said Murat. 'I needed access to a database or two.'

Murat was keen, give him that. De Boer hoped his irritation at being disturbed didn't show.

'And?' said de Boer.

'That agency *is* a fake, the one that hired out temp staff to the hotels. There's no trace of it in the Chamber of Commerce records. So it must have been set up to infiltrate the hotels and trash the rooms. But there's more.'

De Boer smiled. Murat was almost literally shining. He looked as if he were about to break into a dance.

'You remember Benois the hotel manager said that he got a generic "register your domain" message when he tried to access the website?' Murat went on. 'I checked it. It's a local website company. I've got friends in the business.'

A thought appeared to ambush him.

'Do I have to go into this?' he asked.

'Tell me the result,' said de Boer. 'A detective should always have a good network, it helps speed things up.' Sometimes, though, it was better not to know all the details.

'Amateurs!' said Murat. 'With no idea how to cover their tracks. For a website to be registered, the administrator requires a physical address and contact. I have that. This "agency" didn't try to disguise it, or to hide their IP address, which is harder to do, but not impossible. The physical address is on Spuistraat. I came in today to do some cross-referencing. I had an address, I didn't have suspects.'

Murat gave a showman's flourish, and put a handwritten list on de Boer's desk.

'Recent arrests at that address. It's a squat. Some of that lot brought in yesterday after the fracking demo at *Het Lieverdje* are staying there, and there's a string of other cases: public order offences, trespass, that sort of thing. And a couple of names that come up more than once: a Gino Antoldi, and one Frederick Harders, also known as Bin-Bag.'

Murat flashed de Boer a wide grin.

'Fine work, Murat!' said de Boer. 'I think we can go and pay them a visit, Harders, Antoldi, and that lot from yesterday.'

De Boer leaned back in his chair and looked across at the young detective.

'Why don't you get yourself a team of uniforms from downstairs, and go and bring them in.'

De Boer smiled after Murat as he left. The arrest at the squat would, he imagined, more likely be a highpoint of the lad's weekend than whatever he had lined up to do tonight. Turning back to his computer, de Boer stared at Merel Dekkers's email without taking it in, his mind back in the trashed room at the Krasnapolsky. He reached over to the photo lying on his desk, of Olssen's jacket. Of all the victims, only Olssen had had his clothing slit; his was the only door left with a malfunctioning lock. De Boer gave a push on the floor with the ball of his foot, swivelling in his chair as it rolled backwards. Outside, it was now bucketing down. De Boer stood up, and crossed to the window.

So: *two* raids on Olssen's room. One amateur, using a housekeeping key for access, and echoing the other three across town. The other more professional, done almost invisibly, hacking the electronic door lock, to search for something. An altogether more sophisticated operation. Like the poisoning. The trashings a cover-up for the more sophisticated raid? No. The first raid was too slick. Only Olssen would have noticed, and the raider knew Olssen wouldn't be returning to the room, or certainly wouldn't complain about what might be missing. The only link was Olssen himself: his connections with fracking tying him in to a series of anarchic raids across town, and the reason for the room search tied up with whatever else he had been getting up to.

★   ★   ★

237

Posthumus locked his apartment door and began to walk slowly down the stairs. What Kees had been saying still cut through him, phrase by phrase. Posthumus paused at the street door, and rested his forehead against the cool glass of its small window. For the past hour, he had sat working with one of the memory exercises he had learned in helping his father: focusing his mind on single points and building scenes around them, reconstructing, as best he could, every moment of the past few days, with Kees, with Gabi, with Christina, at the hospital, in De Dolle Hond: what people had said, what they had done, and what they had said about each other. Posthumus opened the door, and stepped out into the street. He turned to walk up the canal towards De Dolle Hond. He needed an old friend. He wanted to talk this through with Anna.

Two doors down, as he was passing the bookseller's house and coming up to the club where old Chinese folk gathered to share home-food and play mah-jong, Posthumus heard the sound of a car engine. He turned slightly, and saw a delivery van approaching, too close to the narrow pavement. Posthumus moved nearer to the wall and carried on walking, his body at an angle to allow the van to pass. The van – macho black with panelled sides and mirrored glass – pulled up a few metres on, hard up against the long stretch of curtained windows of the Chinese club, blocking the way.

'Typical!' said Posthumus to himself, crossing behind it to squeeze past on the canal side of the road.

It happened in an instant. Like the jaws of a barnacle, the back doors of the van snapped open, Posthumus felt himself wrenched off his feet, flying almost, heard the doors crunch shut behind him. Darkness. A sharp pain as his head hit the metal floor. Hands grabbing at his jacket, pulling him upright, thrusting him against the side of the van. The engine growling, a lurch as the van pulled off, another as it turned right, bouncing him again against the side-panel.

'What the fuck?' said Posthumus, hitting out with his fore-arm at one of the hands grasping on to his jacket. He felt another hand, large and strong, move up around his throat and tighten its grip. He could smell a musty, acrid mix of sweat, tobacco and pine-scented aftershave.

'You speak when we tell you to.'

The voice was gruff, with a harsh, Amsterdammer's crow-caw to the vowels. Posthumus's eyes began to adjust to the dark. Two figures. Big men. Wearing black balacla-vas, pulled down over their faces like some thugs in a movie. Or police storming a terrorist cell. Who the hell *were* they? He drew breath to speak. The hand at his throat tightened.

'When we *tell* you.'

'You sure it's the right one?'

The voice came from the driver, up front in a screened-off cab. Posthumus glanced quickly sideways, but all he could see through a small sliding panel was a glimpse of a pulled-up hoodie. A fist connected with the side of his face in a savage backhand.

'Eyes down!'

'Tall, sandy hair, dresses like a poof,' came another voice, soft, with an edge of mockery.

The blue glow of a mobile phone momentarily lit the back of the van. The man holding it angled it towards the one grip-ping his throat. Both glanced at the screen, and looked at Posthumus.

'That's the one.'

What was that? A photograph? Who were these people?

'Eyes fucking *down*!'

'Who . . .' began Posthumus.

He felt himself yanked forward, turned and thrust face down on the floor. His arms were pulled back behind him, and he felt handcuffs click around his wrists.

'Slow learner, aren't we?' said the soft voice. 'Up!'

Hands jerked him back into a sitting position.

'Want to see the pretty pictures, do we?'

It was soft-voice again. The phone screen was thrust in front of his face. Too close. Posthumus tried to focus. A photo. Him. At De Dolle Hond.

'It *is* you, isn't it, sunshine?'

In a plum-coloured shirt, standing in front of the big De Dolle Hond fireplace, beneath the Delft vases . . .

'Look, I don't know—' said Posthumus.

The blow came with no warning. No tensing of the muscles, no aim, just an arm shooting out like the tongue of a tree-frog, to hit him in the gut. Posthumus bent forward. His body had suddenly stopped working. The impact slammed the air from his lungs, and he twitched and jerked, pulling, pulling, trying to draw air back in. His joints weakened, the balaclava heads began to spin around him.

'Lesson One.'

His ribs flipped back into action, heaving, wrenching in air. Posthumus sucked and gasped. A woollen hat, damp and doggy-smelling, was pulled on to his head and down over his eyes. All the pieces of the puzzle that he had been trying so carefully to arrange, scattered and lay shattered. Ben. Christina. Money. Kees. PhoeniX. Henk de Kok. Marty. He had to think clearly. Who *were* these people? What were they about to do to him?

Another right turn of the van threw him at an angle back against the wall. The hands gripping him let go. Posthumus struggled to sit more comfortably, bracing himself for a kick or further blow. Nothing.

'What now?' It was the gruff voice.

'Boss wants him out of the way.' Soft-voice.

'*Out of the way*, out of the way?'

'Just out of the way.'

The two men laughed at their own joke.

'We're to drive around a bit.'

The van felt as if it were speeding up. The engine now had an echoing sound, and there was a faint whiff of exhaust fumes. The tunnel . . . they were probably in the IJ Tunnel.

'We'll hear.' It was soft-voice again. 'Someone is going to have a nice little chat.'

There was a knowing chuckle. 'Soften him up a bit, first?' said the gruff voice.

'Boss didn't say. No harm in it though.'

Posthumus heard a movement.

The soft voice again: 'Lesson Two.'

Posthumus tensed, waiting for the blow.

For the past twenty minutes, de Boer had been sitting quite still, the only movement his fingers, drumming their customary tattoo on the edge of his desk. Murat was back, buoyed by the arrests. The suspects were making statements: one, the clown known as Bin-Bag, had fessed up to most of it already, but denied having anything to do with the attack on Olssen; had been panicked by the thought they may be blamed, it seemed. It had been him causing the rumpus at the Krasnapolsky yesterday, snooping about, trying to find out if staff had identified the maid. Top marks to young Murat. But de Boer had more on his mind. Someone other than those activists had been in Olssen's room, a more sophisticated operator, in the room and looking for something. Dirty money was behind this, somewhere, de Boer was certain. And Henk de Kok made a link between Olssen,

Marty Jacobs and anything that stank. What de Boer really wanted was not just the leather jacket and hoodie, but de Kok's computer and phone. Computers were sure to throw up a lot more. A couple of barbs still snagged at de Boer, holding him back. A Markov-style poison attack just didn't sound like de Kok; and Pia Jacobs had said her son had been speaking loudly in English, as he would to a foreigner, over his phone on the day of the attack. But these could both mean the same thing: that de Kok had hired someone in to do the dirty work. That was very much his style. If they could find a call from de Kok's phone to the prepaid number that Jacobs had been speaking to just before the attack on Olssen, they'd have him in the bag.

De Boer stopped drumming. Enough. Decision time. There was only one way to find out. Yes, de Kok was a slippery customer, but that was all the more reason for acting quickly. Search the place, and bring de Kok in right away, before he could start covering his tracks. De Kok had his nose every-where, he'd quickly get a hint something was going on, once they started asking questions. They shouldn't kid themselves that they could keep much quiet. That boat had already sailed with the Jacobs woman making a statement. And who knows what chain of whispers would be set off once they started making enquiries into Olssen's finances. No, the scales had already tipped. It was time to move.

De Boer put a quick call through to the prosecutor to request an immediate warrant, to search Milord and de Kok's residence. He resumed his desk tattoo. He would have to gamble on the search coming up with what he wanted. It would be such a raised finger to Ed Maartens and the other old shits who were constantly trying to trip him: to be the man who finally nailed Henk de Kok.

★   ★   ★

Posthumus could hear speeding traffic, a truck hooting. They must be on the ring road. The doggy-smelling woollen hat that the men had pulled over his head and eyes was making him itch. The handcuffs bit at his wrists. The pain in his face, his gut, and everywhere the men had kicked him seemed to fuse into a jagged, single ache. He sensed one of the men coming towards him again, and pulled his legs up, trying to curl into a protective foetal position. A tinny burst of pop music trilled through the van. Then again, louder. A ring tone. Whoever was coming towards him stopped.

'Yes?'

It was soft-voice. Silence. He spoke again.

'Will do.' Then louder, probably to the driver. 'We've got to go back. De Wallen.'

'*Shit*, I'm just at a slip road. Hold on!'

The van lurched to the right, throwing Posthumus harder against the side. He could hear hooting, and a thunk, as one of the men in the back fell.

'Jesus! Watch out!'

'Sorry!'

'We don't want the fucking cops.'

'Where to? Milord?' It was the driver.

'No. Leidekkersteeg, but round the back.'

Posthumus wriggled into a tighter ball. Leidekkersteeg? He could picture the street sign. Wasn't it one of those passage-like alleys in the really rank part of De Wallen? Soft-voice spoke again, this time to the other thug.

'Our friend here is going to the Bad Girls' Room.'

He gave a grunt. It sounded like he was pushing himself off the floor, then sitting down at the other end of the van.

The driver's voice again. 'Probably quicker back along the ring road, than on the 117.'

'Whatever. Just step on it, but don't get caught on any fuck-ing cameras.'

Posthumus heard a click and almost immediately caught a sharp whiff of tobacco.

Soft-voice spoke. 'Henk says to ease up on him for now.'

Posthumus felt a wave of relief that this meant he might be left alone. At least for the moment. But *Henk*? That had to be de Kok. Posthumus remained curled for a while, still taut, then gradually allowed himself to relax. At the other end of the van, the two men had begun talking about football.

Posthumus cut out the talk of the last Ajax match, let the voices meld with the sound of the engine, and tried to concentrate on something other than pain. He moved so that the woollen hat they had pulled over his eyes made a cushion against the side of the van, at a place where his skull did not hurt. In the darkness, he began to arrange the scat-tered pieces of the picture that had been beginning to form when he left his apartment. Order. He needed to create some sort of order so that he could begin to see the connections.

He was being taken somewhere in De Wallen, by thugs working for de Kok. Men who somehow had a photograph of him, working for a man who had his fingers in petty crime, but who also had connections to a deeper, darker world of dodgy finance.

'Hey, sunshine! What do you think? Did Suárez dive, or was it a foul?'

The voice was raised, mocking. Posthumus realised the question was directed at him.

'Not answering? In a little sulk? No matter, there'll be *plenty* of time to talk later. Like a little canary.'

Gruff-voice laughed. The van was slowing, then speeding up, turning. A slip road again. They'd be leaving the ring road and heading back to the tunnel. The two men resumed their argument.

Posthumus retreated into darkness. Order. He needed to put the pieces into order. What did he know? The basics: Ben and Christina were in Amsterdam for the Earth 2050 conference. Christina had decided to come at the last minute: both Cornelius and Gabi had mentioned that. Ben and Christina knew each other from before, perhaps better than Christina was letting on. Ben had been worried about something. Either he'd been trying to warn Christina about it, or they were complicit in it. Either way, again, she knew or at least suspected more than she was letting on. Ben had found, or been given by mistake, a sheaf of papers: papers that belonged to an old man, who had been at a fracking meeting in Brussels. Papers that could be a list of dates, names and payments, that had something to do with a phoenix, or an operation called Phoenix. Papers Ben thought had to do with large-scale bribery related to oil. As he lay in intensive care, Ben had, of all things in the world, been trying to say Phoenix, and the name of Hubbert, the Peak Oil theorist. At a time when he hardly had the energy to speak at all. Hubbert, and the Swedish word for danger, *fara*. Or 'fada', Posthumus had thought at first. The van jolted, and Posthumus winced as a shaft of pain zigzagged through him.

*Fara.* Posthumus winced again. It hurt even to frown. Why would Ben be trying to speak Swedish to him and de Boer? Why not Dutch or English? Ben lived in New York. From what Christina had said, he spoke English when he was working at Greenpeace in Amsterdam. English would be almost a first language to him. As it was now to Christina. As it was between Ben and Christina. Posthumus shifted his position. The argument about football was getting louder. Something about new rules and yellow cards. He focused harder. Christina had only just left the hospital room when Ben spoke. What if Ben had been trying to speak to *her*? In English. Posthumus repeated 'fara' and 'fada' a few times, let the words slide into rhythmical repetition, lose any meaning he had assigned them, imagined them moulded into an English word. Slowly, he extended one leg, rotating his foot as cramp began to grip at his calf. *Father?* Could it be?

Posthumus relaxed his foot and lay dead still. Fragments previously scattered in his mind shot together in an instant, as if suddenly magnetised. Christina's tirade at the taxi driver outside the hospital, when the man had said something insulting about dementia. Gabi saying Christina was worried about her father, who was ill: her father Sybrand, a big-time lobbyist in Brussels. It was like matching two pieces of a jigsaw puzzle that triggers a quick succession of other pieces fitting together to form a small patch of the picture. Sybrand Walraven, working in Brussels, where an old man had inadvertently given papers to Ben. Papers that could well contain incriminating evidence of payments; payments Ben thought were bribes, linked to corporations who wanted to have the monopoly on distribution in the future.

Posthumus stiffened, and felt the leg cramp return. The van was back in the tunnel: echoing traffic, exhaust fumes. A scenario began to shape itself: a plan, a project, call it Phoenix, put in place by a big-time lobbyist acting for an oil company, with the goal of influencing government policy, to (what was it Kees had said?) to keep governments hooked on oil while making alliances and buying shares to give them the edge as it ran out. It sounded mad. But Kees believed it. And so did Ben, and that's what mattered. Ben who had stumbled on evidence of what could be substantial payments, quite possibly bribes: a document that implicated Sybrand Walraven. Ben, not entirely sure of what he had found, contacting the investigative reporter

Greg Robertson: he had told Kees he was going to a journalist about it all. Ben, who had come to Kees for advice, about loyalty, he had said. Ben, who had been wanting to meet Christina urgently. To warn her. Not about any danger, but that he was about to blow the gaff on her father.

They were out of the tunnel now, stopping and starting, making their way through traffic lights to De Wallen. Not far to go.

But what had happened? What had gone wrong? Ben had handed over the evidence to Kees. He had complained to Kees of his computer being hacked, of documents and emails disappearing. So, Phoenix, whoever or whatever they were, were on to him. Someone had searched his room, looking for the papers, or a memory stick, maybe. That made sense of the slit jackets and suitcase lining. And then someone had tried to kill him. At a time when Christina was supposed to have been with him. Was that why Christina made such a fuss about missing the appointment, about feeling guilty that she could have prevented the attack? Could she have? Posthumus located a piece of the puzzle, and slid it into position: a piece that had been lying waiting on one side, a position he had been resisting. Unless the delay at the cocktail party that night was simply Christina giving herself an alibi.

'Wakey wakey, sunshine, we're here.'

The van slowed, almost to a stop.

'I can't go as far as the yard,' said the driver. 'The way's blocked, there's a delivery going on next door. You'll have to walk it.'

Gruff-voice cursed.

'No matter,' said soft-voice. 'It's only a couple of metres. They're all Henk's girls along here anyway.'

Hands pulled Posthumus to his feet. He felt the handcuffs being taken off, then both his arms gripped firmly, one pushed up painfully behind his back. The two thugs came up close, one on either side. Something blunt and hard pushed at the flesh below his ribs.

'Right, sunshine, know what this is? It will blow your guts all over the pavement. But it's not going to do that, because you're going to listen. In a moment your pretty hat is going to come off, and you're going to step out of the van. A little drunk perhaps, with your two good friends supporting you on either side. You're going to look down. Not around, not back, just down. And you're going to walk. Got it?'

Posthumus did not answer. He felt an arm across his back, and the palm of a hand on his neck. A strong thumb and forefinger pressed at the rounded bones beneath his ears, holding his head forward. The woollen hat was whipped from his head, the van doors opened, and he was half pushed, half lifted out on to the pavement. The hands on either side and on his neck steered him, blinded, blinking, stumbling, cramp stabbing at his calves, past a truck, into a dank inner yard, and through a door, before he could even think of crying out. A hand reached out and opened the door. Before him rose a narrow, almost vertical staircase, wide enough for only one person. The hand remained on Posthumus's neck, the gun moved to the small of his back. The man who smelled of pine and sweat came up close behind him.

'Walk!'

Posthumus climbed, pain cutting and stabbing in unexpected places. One flight, then another; a narrow corridor, others branching off along the way; a step up into an adjoining building, two more flights, then a third, a shorter one, off at an angle. Sloping roofs. A door. They must be up in the attic in one of those clusters of ancient buildings in De Wallen. Houses that had sprouted in fits and starts over the centuries, which leaned this way and that in mutual support, with one or two disappearing entirely in the thicket.

'Open it!'

Posthumus was propelled into a room of utter darkness, and pushed face-first against a wall. Hands frisked him, and took his phone from a pocket. Someone pawed at his ankles; he felt something hard and uncomfortable, and heard a mechanical click. Jesus! Leg irons.

'You've got a little wait now. Somebody's coming to talk to you. You needn't waste your breath yelling. No one's going to hear you in here, and any who might, won't care.'

The hands let go of him. Posthumus turned to see a shaft of light disappear as the door closed. He heard the key turn in the lock.

# 15

As soon as the prosecutor faxed the warrants through, de Boer called up two teams from downstairs. Obs reports in Henk de Kok's file said he spent Saturdays at home in Zuid, watching sport. De Boer would take the villa, and bring de Kok in himself. Murat leapt at the chance of leading the search on Milord. De Boer told the young detective to wait around the block from the nightclub for the go-ahead. He wanted to synchronise the operations, so that there was no chance of some underling phoning from Milord to warn de Kok.

De Boer pulled on to the kerb, a door or two down from de Kok's house. De Kok lived in one of those freestanding villas off the Apollolaan, popular among criminal bosses and business magnates. It had huge wrought-iron gates that looked as if they came from a country palace (they probably *did* come from a country palace) with ugly gilding on the gates, and plaster lions on the pillars. But at least the wall was low enough to scale if they had to. The wall was higher around the sides and back of the house. Good. De Boer glanced at his watch: five fifty-eight.

He put a call through to Murat. 'Give us five minutes, then go for it.'

He nodded to the men as they joined him from the other cars, stepped up to the gate and pushed the button on the intercom.

'Yes?'

It was a woman's voice.

'Police.'

For a moment nothing happened. Then the gates buzzed open. A woman came to the front door as they approached: tarty, in her thirties probably, though it was hard to tell. Pneumatic lips, and there was no *way* those tits were real. She clearly kept a team of surgeons in the top 500 rich list.

'Henk's not here,' she said.

Shit. Though maybe not true.

'Mrs de Kok? We're coming in anyway.'

'You got a warrant?'

She seemed unruffled.

De Boer flashed the warrant, and his ID. He turned to the men.

'Two round the back. The rest, work your way up through the house. Make sure he's not here; if there's anyone else, I want one of you with them at all times. No calls. I want all phones and computers – tablets, laptops, everything – bagged and brought in. Also any hoodies and leather jackets, and check out anything that could conceal a hypodermic needle. Top to bottom. I want dirty laundry, bin-bags, the lot. You know the drill.'

From the corner of his eye, de Boer caught a movement.

'I said no phones!'

De Boer nodded to one of the woman officers. 'Stay with her.'

His own phone rang. Murat. De Boer answered. He could hear yelling, a revving car engine, a woman scream.

'He's here, he's *here*!' Murat was shouting. He sounded panicked. 'We were about to go in, and we saw him pulling up near the Oude Kerk. But he's doing a runner!'

'Don't lose him!'

'It's a fucking *Maserati*!'

★   ★   ★

The silence that enveloped Posthumus was dull, deadened. The wall beside him gave slightly if he pushed at it. Rubber? Cork? Some sort of soundproofing. The room wasn't completely dark, not like he'd thought at first. A patch of grey-ish light leaked through what must be a fanlight or air vent, to one side above his head. It was hard to tell how far away it was. The light didn't get anywhere, just a pale glow. Posthumus edged along the wall. He could almost reach the spot, but not quite. The chain pulled at his ankles. In the other direction, he could touch the side where the door must be, but get no further. Back again. Posthumus slid a foot forward, then withdrew it and pressed back against the wall. He couldn't step out into that darkness.

Calm – a cool, crisp-edged calm – overwhelmed him. With it came a piercing clarity, and a sense that he had broken free, was moving away from himself. So this was what it felt like, fear. For the first time in his life: pure, deep fear. He pushed his back against the wall, palms flat. Despite the dark, he closed his eyes. Somehow that was empowering. He felt a contraction inside his head, almost a physical sensation, concentrating his thoughts to a fine point. He held them there a moment, and then allowed his mind to move backwards, and expand. The photograph. The image the thugs had shown him in the van: the plum-coloured shirt, standing in front of De Dolle Hond fireplace. Christina must have taken it. The first time he met her, on Tuesday, at De Dolle Hond. He hardly ever wore that shirt, the Zegna; she had just remarked on it, and was taking photos all over the place. *Christina* . . . that morning in the hotel, when he had stopped by to take her to the hospital. There was a taxi already waiting. Christina had snapped at him for being early. She had been intending to leave without him. And that taxi . . . a private limo from a hire company, where Christina said she had an account. Why not the limo on the night of the cocktail party? What made Christina suddenly so keen on being a 'green girl', as she'd put it to Gabi, and going by train to the cocktail party, if it were not to provide an excuse for their being delayed out there; delayed while (Gabi had said) Christina 'toyed' with Ben, kept him dangling, waiting at the station café, his texts and calls unanswered.

Posthumus took his mind through the scenes he had so carefully reconstructed after Kees had left his apartment, through each moment he had spent with Christina. Her shock at the Conservatorium Hotel on hearing about the attack on Ben. Her demanding to go and see Ben right away. Or had it been shock that he was still alive, a concern to see just what state he was in? Shock, too, maybe, that he, Posthumus, had anything to do with the case at all . . . that he was interfering. Posthumus lowered himself to sit on the floor. Pain still jabbed and stabbed at him all over. Was that who he was here to talk to? Not Henk de Kok, but Christina? Christina and de Kok, linked by . . . what? An Amsterdam connection? Dodgy financial dealings? Both? Something to do with Christina's family bank?

Christina who had engineered staying too long at the cock-tail party with Gabi. Christina who knew already what Ben was about to do. How? From her father himself? An old man, in the early stages of dementia, perhaps, realising where he had lost incriminating papers? Posthumus remembered the fierce sense of protection his own father's disease had awoken in him. Christina was incredibly close to her father, Posthumus knew that from Cornelius and Gabi, and yet she wouldn't tell even Gabi what was wrong with him. Posthumus could understand that. And, God, yes, that doodle. A scribble that appeared practised, like a signature, of a bird surrounded by flames. Christina's father called her 'my little firebird'. She had said so, that time she'd lost her temper in the taxi on the way to the hospital. Firebird, phoenix. PhoeniX, with a capital X: a common symbol for Christ. Or for Christina. A cog from Posthumus's own Catholic childhood locked into gear: those detentions meted out at school, learning lists of saints and their attributes. St Christina, who had survived burning in a fiery furnace, sometimes symbolised by a phoenix. And hadn't Christina, more than once, called herself 'a good Catholic girl'? Christina, not just devoted to her father, but possibly even working with him – in a project that was named after her, was probably to her benefit, even *for* her. Christina, therefore, determined to stop Ben talking.

Posthumus pulled his knees up to his chest, and hugged them. Stopping Ben talking was one thing, killing him something quite different. Unless the stakes were high. Very high. Unless it were true, what Kees was saying, that this involved huge sums of money, powerful international players, bribes . . . Why, at the end of a long and respectable career, was Sybrand Walraven involved in that sort of thing, and on such a large scale? Money, of course. As Kees said, it was always money. But there had to be more to it than sheer avarice. Posthumus shifted a little, to find a position that did not hurt. That evening, back in De Dolle Hond with Cornelius, when Posthumus had first realised Christina's Walraven Bank connection, Cornelius had said the family fortunes had taken a tumble during the financial crisis.

Posthumus's mind moved into a place where it so often operated when he was at work composing an elegy, gathering strands – from a bookshelf, an ornament, music in the CD player, a letter, a handful of photos in a bedside drawer – and tying them carefully together into a coherent story. So, Sybrand, propelled into taking desperate measures to save his family fortune? That might fit. And Christina killing Ben to protect her father's reputation? Possibly. She was devoted to Sybrand. She wouldn't want to see his life destroyed in his final years. Though if she really did love Ben, or even had once, that would be unimaginable. Unless . . . Posthumus's mind took a side step. Why was Christina so secretive about her father's Alzheimer's? Why try to hide it? From whom? From the paymasters, those big corporations? From *their* paymasters? The strands began to twine together. Christina was in this as well. It was her inheritance after all . . . and then all those sheets headed PhoeniX. *Her* transactions. Christina certainly had influential connections, even in her PR job. Hadn't she just been to a big tiger conference in St Petersburg, with Putin? Maybe all that name-dropping was for real.

Posthumus began to turn each element of what he knew, to examine it from a different angle. Then he froze. A noise. Scratching. It was hard to tell where it was coming from. The fanlight perhaps? Posthumus looked up at it. The dim grey glow turned black. A voice. Just a whisper.

'Mr P?'

De Boer covered an ear to block out the voices of the search team.

'Are you driving?' he asked Murat.

'No, Boonsaaier.'

Good. Boonsaaier was one of the best. Murat was still yelling.

'Jesus, *Jesus*, de Kok's just mowing people down!'

He sounded like he was losing it. De Boer could hear people screaming. A car racing through the narrow, tourist-crowded streets of De Wallen, on a Saturday, didn't bear thinking about.

'Radio the choppers and get back-up from Beursstraat,' said de Boer, trying to sound calm.

'Done that,' said Murat.

Good lad. Boonsaaier was ace, but he wouldn't be risking civilian life and if de Kok got a head start, he'd be clean away before Murat could emerge from the tangle.

'Where are you?' said de Boer.

No answer. Screeching car tyres, sirens and yelling. De Boer pictured the place, from his days on the beat at the Beursstraat Bureau. Murat said he'd first seen de Kok pulling up at the Oude Kerk. Where would he be? Not the Warmoesstraat side of the old church, that was mostly restricted for traffic. The canal side, then. Pretty much a dead-end in both directions.

'Murat, you there?'

'Christ! Christ!'

De Kok would try to get out of De Wallen. Via the Dam, or across the canal and up to the tunnel. Probably that.

'Murat?'

De Boer had heard the crash.

'Murat, you OK?'

'Christ!' Murat's voice again. 'He's shot the bridge! He's in the water!'

'You're OK? Where are you?' said de Boer. He didn't try to disguise his relief that the crash hadn't been Murat.

'End of the canal, behind the university.'

De Boer heard another voice in the background.

'Grimburgwal,' said Murat.

'I'll be there. Ten minutes max. Go get him.'

De Boer left one of the uniforms in charge of the search, and ran to his car, plugging his phone in for hands-free as he jumped in. He was crossing the Amstel when it rang again. He flipped the switch to speak.

'Murat?' he said.

'DI de Boer? It's Anna de Vries, from De Dolle Hond.'

'Not a good time, I'm afraid. I'll call you back.'

'Pieter Posthumus has been kidnapped. By someone called Henk de Kok.'

De Boer took a sharp left, up towards the Grimburgwal. What the *hell* was going on now?

'Has there been a threat, or some sort of ransom demand?' he said. 'Is he in immediate danger?'

'Apparently he's locked in a room in De Wallen, a sort of cell.'

'Who's been in touch? What are they asking?' said de Boer.

'Tina, an employee of mine, spoke to him. Friends of hers saw it happen. But no one's been in touch, and no one's answering his phone.'

'Give me a few minutes,' said de Boer. 'We're in pursuit of de Kok. I'll ring back.'

He parked the car on the bridge over the small Grimburgwal canal. A couple of pleasure boats waited down to his left, no longer allowed through; up to the right he could see a partially submerged car; uniformed officers had already taped off the alley alongside. De Boer flashed his card and ran through. Murat was standing beside the water. The ambulance crew had just arrived.

'He's still in there,' said Murat. 'Fire Department are on their way.'

Sirens were converging from every direction. De Boer glanced back up the main canal, towards the Oude Kerk. Officers were still clearing the road of onlookers, as far as the church itself. Four, maybe five, people lay injured. That would all be sorted by the Beursstraat uniforms. He looked back at the car. De Kok wasn't moving. The Fire Department's canal rescue van was pushing its way towards them, down the alley. De Boer took out his phone and tapped call-back. Anna de Vries answered immediately, but seemed to be speaking to someone else. De Boer could hear the voice: high, urgent.

'Sorry,' said Anna. 'Tina is convinced Henk de Kok is going to kill PP . . . Pieter Posthumus.'

'Tell her that we are about to take Henk de Kok into custody,' said de Boer.

Anna passed on the message. This time de Boer could hear the reply.

'Then the others will kill me!'

A young voice, it could even be a girl.

'Best tell me where Mr Posthumus is, and what has happened to him,' said de Boer.

'It will be better if you talk directly to Tina,' said Anna.

De Boer could hear her talking to the girl, trying to persuade her to speak. Eventually a small voice came on to the line. Tina sounded wary, frightened.

'Hello.'

'Hello, Tina,' said de Boer. He hoped his tone was reassuring. 'Can you tell me what has happened to Pieter, where he is?'

'He's in the Bad Girls' Room.'

'And what is the Bad Girls' Room?'

'It's where *he* used to put . . . us. When we'd done bad, kept money or something.'

'De Kok, you mean?' said de Boer. He heard a soft, high-pitched affirmative.

'And also new girls, what had just arrived, if they gave too much lip, to show them a thing or two, teach them who was boss,' said Tina.

De Boer could hear the echo of de Kok's own phrases. The Fire Department divers were already in the water.

'And you're sure Pieter's there?'

'Maria and Kitty seen him, didn't they? They seen Johnnie and Bert take him out of the van and upstairs, and they knew Mr P 'cos they'd seen me and him in the Stadhuis yesterday,

259

and they phoned me, 'cos they knew he'd been kind, and I went, and I talked to him . . .'

Now that she'd started, Tina was racing, breathless.

'You talked to him?' said de Boer.

'There's this flap, see, what you can open from the outside, if you go on the roof from next door. *They* don't know about it. But us girls used to go and talk to whoever was in there, when no one was looking. It helps, you see, if you feel you aren't all alone. Sometimes, if who's in there is tall enough, you can even reach through and touch fingertips.'

De Boer felt a surge of loathing for the figure that was being dragged out of the wrecked Maserati.

'And I talked with Mr P and held his fingers, and it is him, and they will *kill* him, and they'll kill me if they know, *and* Kitty and Maria . . .'

'Hang on, hang on, that's not going to happen. Where is this room? Is it in de Kok's nightclub?' said de Boer.

'Milord? No, but near, round the corner. You've got to go in the back, and then there's lots of passages and stairs and stuff. It's hard to find,' said Tina.

'Tina, you've done brilliantly,' said de Boer. 'But now you're going to have to help me, and show me where.'

'I'm not going in, I'm not, I'm *not*; they'll kill me if they see me!'

De Kok was out of the water now, and on a stretcher. Murat had been speaking to the medics, and was coming towards him.

'Can you wait just a moment, Tina?' said de Boer, his eyes asking Murat the question.

'Alive,' said Murat.

'Arrest him,' said de Boer. 'Have a guard put on him at the hospital, and have his rights read to him as soon as he's conscious. Then get back to Milord and the search. And can you send three men to meet me, up at the church. Call in support from Beurstraat if you need to.'

De Boer put the telephone back to his ear.

'Tina, are you still there? We've just caught Henk de Kok. Now I *really* need you to help me, and to be brave. We can protect you, and Kitty and Maria. But we need you to show us where to go. Will you meet me, not there, but up at the Oude Kerk?'

Tina hesitated only a moment. 'If Anna comes too.'

'Good,' said de Boer.

He glanced up the canal towards the church. Groups of medics were attending to the people hit by de Kok's car.

'I'll meet you on the Warmoesstraat side, not on the canal. You're at De Dolle Hond? Come straight down, I'll see you in five minutes.'

Posthumus felt his way along the wall towards the patch of grey light. Had he imagined it? Tina's voice whispering in the dark, a warm hand gripping his fingers. It was, what, fifteen, twenty minutes since she had run off to call Anna? He had lost track of time in this blackness. He worked his way back to where a set of manacles dangled loose from the wall. Thank God they hadn't used those on him, too. There had been sirens a while ago, lots of them, loud enough to penetrate whatever it was that deadened sound in this hole. For a moment, he'd hoped. But no.

Since Tina, or the wraith of Tina, had gone, Posthumus had carefully been putting pieces together, until he had a picture, not complete, but whole enough. That last phone call, when he had asked Cornelius about the associations of 'phoenix': she must have cottoned on then that he had somehow seen Ben's papers. She was in the room. Cornelius had repeated what he was saying. It was Christina who had made all that fuss about returning the umbrella, working out where he would be. And it had been an hour before he'd left home. Quite enough time for Christina to call de Kok and set up the grab. The thugs hadn't asked him for any papers, or questioned him. But then Christina would probably not even have told de Kok what this was about.

Posthumus pressed himself up against the wall. There were sounds coming from outside: muffled, but loud enough. A shot? Shouting. The door was flung open. Two figures stood silhouetted against a blinding light.

'Mr P!'

More light, as fluorescent tubes flicked on overhead.

'Mr Posthumus, Pieter?'

It was de Boer.

'Are you all right?' he said.

'Hurting all over, but no bleeding, and as far as I can work out nothing broken,' said Posthumus. 'Just very, *very* glad to see you.'

De Boer was in the room. Tina, a blanket over her head, hovered at the door. Two uniformed police officers stood behind her. Posthumus wanted to give her a hug.

'Tina, Tina, *thank you.*'

The little figure stayed at the threshold. She looked terrified.

'Can't come in,' she said, so softly Posthumus could barely hear.

'Manacles!' said de Boer. 'Jesus. This time we're going to make the charges stick, and send the scumbag down for decades.'

'De Kok, sure,' said Posthumus, still blinking in the bright light. 'But it's Christina Walraven you need to get your hands on.'

Posthumus saw de Boer's expression cloud. But the look he gave was enquiring, not one of disbelief. Posthumus began to tell him about Ben and the papers.

'Wait a moment,' said de Boer. 'We've got to get you free first, and to hospital.'

He turned to the officers at the door. 'One of you go and see if either of those goons we're holding downstairs has got the key to this, otherwise get something to cut him out. The canal rescue van might still be down the road, on Grimburgwal.'

He turned back to Posthumus. 'A nice irony there,' he said. 'It will be the same men who have just cut de Kok out of his car.'

Posthumus managed a smile. 'Put a hold on the hospital for the moment,' he said. 'This is more important, especially if you've already arrested Henk de Kok.'

He told de Boer about Christina, the phoenix, the photo of him at De Dolle Hond, and the connection Christina must have with de Kok and the thugs who had abducted him. Carefully, Posthumus laid out the story he had pieced together.

'I think Christina used her international networks to hire a professional assassin. From Russia possibly, someone who could carry off a sophisticated Markov-like attack with TTX. It was probably supposed to look as if Ben had had a heart attack. And I think Henk de Kok was simply her man on the ground, here in Amsterdam. Maybe there's a connection there, in the world of dodgy finance.'

'So, different killers, you mean, for Olssen and Marty Jacobs,' said de Boer. 'That had been bothering me, I admit.'

'I think Marty was meant to wait for the assassin to find the right opportunity, and then to distract or hinder Ben,' said Posthumus.

'His phone records bear that out,' said de Boer.

Posthumus began to sink, sliding down the wall to sit on the floor. Exhaustion suddenly overwhelmed him.

De Boer moved quickly to his side. 'Pieter! Are you sure you're OK?'

'I'm fine, I'm fine; and I'm not concussed, if that's what you're thinking. I've been there before. I'm reasoning quite clearly.'

'I don't doubt that for a moment,' said de Boer. 'If I'm questioning any logic, it's my own. Previous hasty mistakes and all that; you have form, Mr Posthumus, as far as this sort of thing goes.'

Posthumus returned his grin, if a little weakly.

'Someone highly professional had already searched Olssen's hotel room before the attack,' de Boer went on. 'That could well be your assassin. If Olssen had left the papers with your friend by then, it's likely nothing was found in the room. So Jacobs was probably on the scene to destroy whatever Olssen might have had on him. Certainly to carry it off, so the killer could make a quick getaway. We have evidence of that.'

'And Marty saw too much,' said Posthumus. 'Or at least became a danger, when the poisoning went wrong.'

'And then to make matters worse, a certain municipal official produced an overcoat and began asking inconvenient questions,' said de Boer. 'That must have come as quite a shock to Ms Walraven.'

Posthumus pictured Christina's expression that night at the Conservatorium, and remembered Gabi's remark about her seeming calmer after Ben had died.

'I think she went to the hospital that morning to assess what sort of state Ben was in,' Posthumus said.

'And stood there, urging him not to speak,' said de Boer. He was looking at Posthumus intently. 'Or warning him not to speak. A very cold-blooded woman, by this account.'

'I don't know,' said Posthumus. 'Maybe she'd got herself into something beyond her depth. She seemed genuinely upset.'

'From what I know of de Kok, scumbag though he is, he would certainly be out of his depth in something like this,' said de Boer.

He straightened up, and walked across the room.

'She would certainly have had *your* number, though,' he said, turning to face Posthumus again. 'After you started on about poisons in the lift, jumping to conclusions.'

There were noises coming from somewhere outside, a woman raising her voice. Posthumus glanced towards the door. Tina had gone.

'She probably contacted the hackers while she was still at the hospital, when she went off to the Ladies after leaving Ben's room,' said de Boer, as if he were speaking to himself. 'Maybe it was the same person who hacked in to Olssen's computer.'

'You mean someone got into the hospital computer network and turned off Ben's machines?' said Posthumus.

'Someone in Bangalore apparently,' said de Boer. 'Though it would have had to be someone who understood Dutch, to access patient information on ward computers. It's not all to do with codes, apparently.'

Posthumus flinched: it still hurt to frown. He had felt something slip into place in the further recesses of his mind, something he didn't quite want to be there. The noise outside was louder now. Anna came bursting in through the door.

'Sorry, sir, I couldn't stop her,' said the officer running up behind.

Anna flew into the room, and reached down to throw her arms around Posthumus.

'Ouch, ouch! Careful!'

'Sorry! Oh my God, chains!'

'He'll be free in a minute,' said de Boer.

'Haven't you called an ambulance?' said Anna to de Boer. 'Somebody should be seeing to him!'

'I'm OK,' said Posthumus, pushing himself up to stand. 'Just a bit battered, nothing broken. No need for hospital just yet.'

'But *look* at you!' said Anna, helping him.

'That's going to be quite a shiner in the morning,' said de Boer, supporting Posthumus from the other side. He gave a little chuckle of sympathy.

'There's nothing to laugh about,' said Anna. 'If you won't get him to hospital, I will.' She took out her phone.

'Hold it just a moment,' said Posthumus.

Tina had come back up the stairs with a second officer, but she still wouldn't come through the door.

'I have the key here, sir,' said the new policeman, coming into the room.

The key fitted. Posthumus gently shook himself free of Anna and de Boer's support, and limped over to Tina.

'Tina, you have been most incredibly brave,' he said, his eyes leaving hers for a moment, to look back into the room.

Tina gave him a little smile, but said nothing.

'Hospital, now!' said Anna, from behind him.

Posthumus turned to her. 'I promise I'll go and have them check me over,' he said. 'But first we've got to go to The Grand. What's the time?'

Now both Anna and de Boer looked perplexed.

'Going on for half past seven, why?' said Anna.

'Christina's at the Earth 2050 gala dinner. Gabi said it was at The Grand,' said Posthumus. He looked at Anna. 'Christina's behind all this, but I'll have to explain later. We need to move quickly, before she gets wind of what's happened here, or of Henk de Kok's arrest.'

'*You* don't have to move *anywhere*, except to hospital,' said Anna.

'I want to see her face to face,' said Posthumus.

'I have to say, Ms de Vries, it will be helpful to have Pieter with us,' said de Boer. 'I'd like to observe Walraven's reaction when she sees him walking free.'

'But he can hardly walk!' said Anna.

'Anna, I need to do this,' said Posthumus.

Anna held his gaze a long time. 'Oh, PP,' she said, and sighed. Then she slipped a hand under his good arm, to support him. 'Come on. But don't think you're going without me.'

She looked challengingly at de Boer, who nodded to the officers at the door.

'We'll keep this low-key,' he said to them. 'It's unlikely the suspect will be armed, but we'll need to be aware of Mr Posthumus's safety.'

'Should we go and fetch the papers, to confront her with?' said Posthumus.

'I'll need them eventually, but for now I think it will be more effective to call her bluff, let her think we know more than we do.'

He addressed the officers. 'Wait here with Mr Posthumus and Ms de Vries, while I fetch my car,' he said. Then he turned to Tina. 'Now, let's get you safely away from here.'

The Grand was only a few minutes' drive away. De Boer pulled into the courtyard, skirted a small fountain, and parked just beyond the main door. The two uniformed officers drew up behind, forestalling the intervention of a doorman about to move de Boer on. Anna helped Posthumus out of the car and they walked with de Boer into the hotel, the two officers a short distance behind.

Couples in evening dress criss-crossed the gleaming marble floor of the vast lobby. Strains of Mozart floated by, as faint as a scent.

'We look like refugees washed up on a very foreign shore,' said Posthumus, glancing down at his dirty, bedraggled clothing, and for the first time noting a rip in his jacket.

'*Bonsoir*, may I be of any help?'

The young man who approached them, smiling, addressed them quite as if they, too, were in white tie and designer finery.

De Boer showed his ID. 'Police,' he said. 'We need to speak to a guest at the gala dinner.'

'I'm sure we can call whoever it is out, sir,' said the young man.

'No. We need to go in there. I don't want to give her any warning.'

Consternation flickered for the briefest moment in the young man's expression, and he glanced to the corner of the lobby. A broad-shouldered man in a black suit walked over.

'Our head of security,' said the young man.

De Boer explained his business.

'I'll come with you,' said the security officer. 'A number of guests have their own protection in tonight. We don't want to spark anything off.'

He led the way up a broad staircase to the next floor, speaking into the mini microphone that extended from his earpiece as he went. Posthumus and Anna lagged a little. Stairs weren't easy. Posthumus stopped for a moment beside de Boer on the landing. They were in the part of the hotel that had been built as Amsterdam's City Hall in the 1920s. Through double doors, in the wood-panelled Council Chamber, crystal and silver glinted in candlelight, as guests came in to take their seats at large round tables. People were making their way from what must have been pre-dinner cocktails, across the landing and into the banqueting room. Posthumus touched de Boer's elbow, and nodded to the double doors. Gabi and Christina had just gone through. Posthumus stared after them. Christina was wearing a backless gown; the diamonds dangling between her shoulder blades glittered 'Chopard' or 'Cartier'. Certainly not 'save-the-tiger' PR.

'Ms Walraven!'

De Boer's voice rang out hard and clear.

It was Gabi who saw Posthumus first. She had turned the moment de Boer called out. Her expression crumpled, first in confusion, then concern. Christina was more cool. She paused, then pivoted slowly to face them. But she assessed the situation in an instant. De Boer strode directly across to her, Posthumus limped behind.

'Ms Walraven, I would like to speak to you about the death of Ben Olssen.'

Silence.

'We have arrested Henk de Kok,' said de Boer.

Posthumus heard a snap. Champagne in the glass Christina was carrying slopped to the floor. Blood began to seep from between her fingers.

'I would also like to ask you some questions about Phoenix, about your involvement, and your father's . . . and about certain payments made to officials.'

Posthumus shot a glance at the back of de Boer's head: he was taking quite a chance. His eyes moved again to Christina. The look she was giving him made him shudder.

'You interfering little creep,' she said. She spoke slowly, her voice low, a snarl. 'And you, of all people, so sanctimonious about your own father, you should understand. Do you think I *wanted* to kill Ben? Do you think it was easy, having to choose between saving one or the other? That I didn't try to make it as painless as possible for him?'

'Chris, you shouldn't . . .' Gabi put a hand on Christina's arm.

'Oh, shut up, you smug bitch!' said Christina, pulling her arm away. 'Little miss ambassador's daughter, always the best, always in charge. With poor Christina always in your shadow. Well, *you're* in for a surprise.'

De Boer stepped forward. 'Christina Walraven—'

Christina lashed out, and de Boer's hand shot to his cheek as the stem of her champagne glass dropped to the floor. She darted past him, swiped at Posthumus, and ran at the two officers standing in the doorway, thrashing about as they grabbed her.

De Boer walked over, stemming the flow of blood from his cheek with a handkerchief. He began again.

'Christina Walraven, you are under arrest . . .'

Christina stopped struggling. She drew herself up, chin out. Her lips were set straight and hard. She said nothing. The two officers handcuffed her, and led her down the stairs.

De Boer turned to Posthumus. 'Thank you, Pieter,' he said.

'Your cheek OK?' said Posthumus.

'It was just a nick. The blood's already stopping, but I'll go down and see if Reception has anything I can put on it. And you get yourself looked over.'

'Anna will see to it that I do.'

De Boer smiled from beneath his cupped hand and handkerchief.

The gala guests, who had pulled back when the scene with Christina began, as if the participants had been on fire, began to go in to dinner again. Conversation returned to a murmur, as if nothing had happened. In the banqueting room and down the stairs, Posthumus noted more men in black suits, speaking into their collars.

'I won't shake your hand, it looks as if it might hurt,' said de Boer. 'But, again, thank you.' He made his way towards the stairs. 'I'll be in touch, and I'll be sending someone over for those papers.'

Posthumus looked around for Gabi. She was standing to one side with Anna, close to tears. He walked over.

'Gabi, I'm so sorry,' he said. 'Now's not the time, but I'll come round and explain it all tomorrow.'

Gabi simply shook her head, then reached out towards his face. 'But your eye, what happened to you?'

'It's all part of the same story,' said Posthumus.

'I've called Gabi a cab,' said Anna. 'I'll go down with her now. You can manage the stairs?'

Posthumus nodded.

Outside in the courtyard, de Boer was standing beside the police car, talking on his phone. Christina was in the back. She appeared to be ranting again to the officer sitting beside her. Anna was seeing Gabi into a cab. Posthumus stood under the portico. He felt a tug at his sleeve. Tina had come out of the shadows from behind a pot plant.

'Tina! What are you doing here?'

'I had to come and see you was all OK, didn't I? But I wasn't walking into a place like that.'

Anna shut the cab door, and walked over to join them under the portico. The police car pulled out, light flashing, with de Boer driving behind it. Gabi turned her head away as they passed, and her cab followed them out. Posthumus leaned on Anna for support.

'Oh, PP,' she said. 'You!' She sighed and dropped her head against his chest.

Posthumus looked down. Anna had her hand on Tina's shoulder. She drew Tina a little closer towards them.

# EPILOGUE

## *Monday Evening, a week later*

Posthumus covered the quails he'd prepared for grilling and put them to one side. Well, he had been right about Christina's father. The scandal had broken a few days after Christina's arrest: old man Sybrand taken in on extensive bribery charges, his lawyer claiming he was unfit to stand trial due to rapidly progressing Alzheimer's. Christina, apparently, denied that her father had any knowledge of the murder.

Posthumus dried his hands on a clean kitchen towel. Was that true? He folded the towel carefully. Quite likely. He felt a brief pang of pity for the old man, despite it all. But did he feel in any way sorry for Christina? Could he? The last words she'd yelled at him beat out again and again, somewhere deep inside him: 'You, of all people, you should understand!' But *murder*? To have gone that far, that he could not fathom. Christina still had some feeling for Ben. Clearly. She'd said she tried to make his death painless. *Painless?* Posthumus wouldn't call it that. And it didn't excuse murder.

Like a recurring sour flavour, Christina's appeal for sympathy also came back to him. Her saying how impossible it was to choose between saving either Ben or her father. Posthumus knew this was a vulnerable point with him: pity. But, no. Not in this instance. This was about pride, and greed: Christina's terror at the smirching of her family name, and her stony determination to protect her own interests and inheritance. Mixed in

273

with some long-standing hang-up about her worshipped father never really being top dog, something that went all the way back to how she treated Gabi in their childhood. No. He'd been wrong about her. Flattered by her attention, but very wrong.

Posthumus sighed. Enough. This evening was all about moving on. The usual Monday meal he made for Anna on her day off had been transformed – with her go-ahead, of course, he'd been burned once in that regard – into a little dinner party: the two of them, Gabi and Cornelius, and Merel with her mystery guest. By an odd coincidence, this had also been the first day available for the junkie Frans Kemp's funeral, once the body had been released for a second time. So they were getting together on the day that Posthumus had buried the man with whom, for them at least, the whole story had begun. Posthumus looked about the kitchen. He was done: quails with a sweet rose-petal and cinnamon sauce, Texel dune lamb with sea aster and early green asparagus, then the lime and black pepper ice cream he'd made earlier. Perfect for a fine spring evening.

He wondered who Merel was bringing. The man she had been out with the other night? He was intrigued. Posthumus had also asked Flip de Boer along. Now *that* was an odd departure. He gave a half-smile. Pieter Posthumus buddies with a policeman, who would have thought? But he liked the man. De Boer couldn't come, but had dropped in earlier for a drink, bounding up the stairs to the apartment faster than Posthumus had known anyone do before. The conversation with the detective had been interesting, to say the least. Posthumus spooned some fat, black olives over a twig of fresh rosemary in a bowl. *Quite a woman!* de Boer had said. *She got de Kok off the hook for the actual murder, but even then did it with a nasty stab – said he was just an oaf out of his depth, but that she needed someone with local knowledge as back-up. She hired a professional hit-man from Russia.* So, Posthumus had been right about that, too: Christina's international network had some very dark corners. *And you're happy that's true?* Posthumus had asked. *De Kok had an alibi for the time of the murder,* said de Boer. *Of course. And his statement tallied with what she said. My God, Piet, you should have heard her! Talk about high friggin' horse. Said she'd spent her life surrounded by idiots.* Christina had been high-handed and arrogant with the police, it seemed, flaunting her prowess. *She laughed at me, Piet! Boasted that she'd been able to commission the OLVG computer-hacking right under my nose, while we were still at the hospital, the moment she realised that Ben was going to survive the attack and might speak at any moment.* De Boer said that Christina's statement to the police had pretty much amounted to a confession – if 'confession' was the right word for anything delivered with such hauteur.

Even so, Christina must have been in some conflict about what she was doing. Posthumus's mind ran back to the moment in the Conservatorium, when he told Gabi and Christina about Ben surviving the attack; and to the taxi trip to the OLVG to see him, when Christina had been so sad, distracted and explosive. Perhaps it had not only been de Kok who was out of his depth.

Posthumus set out the snack of cherry tomatoes he'd stuffed with herbs, olives and anchovies on a plate. A single shadow had flitted through the conversation with Flip. The detective had revealed that Ben's laptop and the hospital system had been hacked from the same source. In Bangalore. Yet the hacker would have needed to speak Dutch. For once, Posthumus had allowed the shadow to pass. Interpol was on to it, Flip said, and already had a lead on the hit-man. The search of the villa in Zuid had yielded enough to prove de Kok's involvement. That and his property companies' links with the Walraven Bank, which were leading to further fraud and tax evasion charges. And de Kok would be nailed for Marty's murder, as well as Posthumus's abduction. All of which had made DI de Boer quite the star back at the IJ Tunnel Bureau. To top it all, Tina, brave little Tina, had agreed to testify against de Kok on charges of torture and human trafficking, with three or four other women following in her wake to do the same. Anna had let Tina know she had her backing, all the way.

Posthumus carried the tomatoes and olives to the front of the apartment. The doorbell rang. He poked his head out on to the landing, and heard a hubbub of voices.

'We've all arrived at once!' Merel called up the stairwell.

Posthumus smiled, and stepped back into his apartment, opening the door wide to let them all in.

# ACKNOWLEDGEMENTS

Huge thanks to our editor Ruth Tross for her care, astute comments and imaginative solutions, and to Morag Lyall for her eagle eye and attention to detail that continues to astound us, and has saved us from many a mishap. Thanks, also, to Ton and Jos for help with hospital life, and to Hans for coming up with odd toxins.

Read the first Pieter Posthumus mystery

# LONELY GRAVES

'An atmospheric and glorious Amsterdam crime story.' *JAN*

A suicide. A drowned man. A sudden death.
For some people, it's just another day's work.

In Amsterdam, there's a council department known
affectionately as the Lonely Funerals team. It exists to
arrange burials for the abandoned or unknown dead,
with the care and dignity that every life deserves.

Pieter Posthumus hasn't been doing the job long, but
he's determined to do it well. He finds that he cares
deeply about the people whose files land on his desk.

So when something doesn't seem quite right
about a Moroccan immigrant's 'accidental'
drowning, Posthumus starts digging.

His quest for justice will lead him down some dangerous
paths, and into conflict with some very dangerous men...

Out now in paperback and ebook.